TREASURE

MOST

DEADLY

BOOKS BY TERRY AMBROSE

Seaside Cove Bed & Breakfast Mysteries
A Treasure to Die For
Clues in the Sand
The Killer Christmas Sweater Club
Secrets of the Treasure King
Treasure Most Deadly

McKenna Mysteries
Photo Finish
Kauai Temptations
Big Island Blues
Mystery of the Lei Palaoa
Honolulu Hottie
North Shore Nanny
A Damsel for Santa
Maui Magic
The Scent of Waikiki
On the Take in Waikiki

License to Lie Series
License to Lie
Con Game
Shadows from the Past

Anthologies with Stories
Paradise, Passion, Murder: 10 Tales of Mystery from Hawai'i
Happy Homicides 3: Summertime Crimes
Happy Homicides 4: Fall into Crime
Happy Homicides 5: The Purr-fect Crime

TREASURE MOST DEADLY

Seaside Cove

Bed & Breakfast Mystery #5

Terry Ambrose

COPYRIGHT

ABOUT THE AUTHOR

Once upon a time, in a life he'd rather forget, Terry Ambrose tracked down deadbeats for a living. He also hired big guys with tow trucks to steal cars—but only when negotiations failed. Those years of chasing deadbeats taught him many valuable life lessons such as—always keep your car in the garage.

Terry has written more than a dozen books, several of which have been award finalists. In 2014, his thriller, "Con Game," won the San Diego Book Awards for Best Action-Thriller. His series include the Trouble in Paradise McKenna Mysteries, the Seaside Cove Bed & Breakfast Mysteries, and the License to Lie thriller series.

You can learn more about Terry and his writing at terryambrose.com.

1

ALEX

APRIL 17

Hey Journal,

We got out of school early today, so I get to have lunch with Daddy and Marquetta. I'm gonna talk to them again about Miss Barone. Ever since she checked into the B&B a few days ago, she's been super secretive. Most of our guests are friendly and like to ask questions about the town, but all she's asked about is the San Mañuel. It's like she's super obsessed with where the shipwreck is and how much the treasure's worth.

And while I was serving her breakfast this morning, she started in on it again. When I asked why she was so interested in a sunken treasure ship, she said she's a reporter from the East Coast. She's working on a story about it. That totally made sense, so I told her I'm personal friends with the archaeologist in charge of the treasure recovery and that I could get her an interview. I was sure she'd want to do it, but she said she'd have to think about it. For real? I might only be eleven, but I can't believe any real journalist would turn that down!

Marquetta said Miss Barone dresses like a fashion model. She wears flowery dresses and has some awesome hats. When my dad was a reporter in New York he always tried to blend in when he was working on a story. Now I'm wondering why she's trying to stand out so much. I so want to figure out what she's up to, so Operation Reporter Watch is on!

    By the way, I also saw Grandma Madeline this morning. She wants to have a powwow about our plans to get Daddy and Marquetta married. I don't know what a powwow is, but if Grandma Madeline thinks it will help make the wedding happen sooner, I'm totally down with it.

    Xoxo

    Alex

2

RICK

THOUGH HE WAS ONLY THIRTY-two, Rick Atwood felt it had taken far too many years for him to find the love of his life. Marquetta Weiss was that woman and, now that he'd found her, he never wanted to let her go. Her gray eyes had captivated him from their first meeting. And, even now, she made his pulse quicken just standing here next to him at the kitchen sink.

Though it had been over a year since their first meeting, the memory of Marquetta standing just inside the front entrance of the B&B, looking anxious at the thought of meeting her new boss, was one he'd never forget. He and Alex had walked through the door, she'd introduced herself as the B&B's cook and maid, and he'd found himself at a loss for words. For him, it had been love at first sight and, ever since that day, he'd found himself constantly wanting to hear her laugh and see those dimples he'd grown to love so much.

"What are you smiling about, Mr. Atwood?"

He took Marquetta's hand in his and stroked her fingers. "Just thinking about how we got here. How I fell head-over-heels in love with you the moment I saw you. And how it took my daughter playing matchmaker for almost a year before we got together."

Marquetta's mouth curled into a crooked smile. "If it hadn't have been for her, I don't know if you ever would have made the first move."

"She's quite the little matchmaker, isn't she?" Rick took in a slow breath and looked into Marquetta's eyes. "In all seriousness, are you sure you want to postpone the wedding?"

Marquetta removed her hand from Rick's and looked away. She rotated her family's heirloom engagement ring in circles as she spoke. "There's just so much going on. That's all I'm saying."

There were few things in life Rick wanted more than to marry this woman, and if he were completely honest, there was really only one. He wanted his daughter to grow up safely into a strong, confident woman. Actually, a strong confident woman like Marquetta. And that made this particular discussion even more difficult. Rick held back saying it, but this conversation had to be difficult for Marquetta, too.

"Go on. I'm listening." Rick noted she was still fiddling with the ring as he waited for her to continue.

"Well, the way business has been lately, we've barely had time to think. And you haven't been able to spend time with Alex. And what about my mom? She's become obsessed with the wedding."

"You're right about that. It seems like your mom offers me her services as a wedding planner three or four times a day."

"Only three or four? She must be getting tired of asking." Marquetta rolled her eyes and stifled a smile. Her tone shifted from flip to serious. "Mom is definitely not a wedding planner. But between her and Alex, it's just getting to be too much. Sometimes I think they have eyes and ears everywhere."

"They're both spies and plotters. No doubt about that. It's probably why they get along so well. Speaking of which, I don't think either of them would be happy with a delay. They've been hatching some grand plan to make this happen sooner rather than later."

"I know. I'm feeling less like this is my wedding than it is theirs."

"I hope you don't mean to each other," Rick quipped. "Alex is only eleven. I refuse to let her tie the knot with anyone until she's at least...twelve. Or twenty. Maybe thirty."

"Very funny, Rick. But I'm being serious. They're out of control. And it's making me very nervous."

"Sorry. Making light of it is the only way I've been able to cope." It had taken so long to get to the point where they'd both let their pasts go. Now that they were looking forward to a future together, it would feel like a disaster to see it all evaporate. Did he dare ask whether this change of heart was just about the wedding, or if it might truly be uncertainty about their relationship? He bit back the question, desperately wanting to ask, but afraid of what the answer might be.

"Why don't we try talking to them both tonight? We could order a pizza and dive into the whole subject. They need to understand we can't be rushed into this, right?"

It was as though a dark cloud moved into the room. Marquetta's dimples faded, her brow furrowed, and their joint uncertainty felt stronger than ever.

"Are you...never mind," Marquetta said.

"What?"

"It's...silly. That's all. Nothing."

But, the hesitancy in her voice was clear. This wasn't about nothing. Rick reached out, took her hand, and rubbed her palm with his thumb. "It's okay. We'll get through this. Just tell me what's bothering you."

"Between the B&B, my mom, all the things the mayor is asking you to do, and the guests, you barely have time to spend with Alex. What are you going to do when the wedding gets closer? Maybe it's too soon."

"What do you mean, too soon?"

"Maybe you're not ready. You know, so soon after your divorce."

True, it hadn't even been a full year since his divorce, but he and Giselle hadn't been 'man and wife' for many years. Her pursuit of her acting career at the expense of her relationship with him and Alex had extinguished any flame that had once existed. "That's not the problem. It's...well...there is a lot going on. But I don't want to push you into marriage, either. I come with a lot of baggage—and a daughter. I'm not exactly the world's greatest catch."

"It's not that. I love you, but I keep wondering if you might have been attracted to me because you were on the rebound."

Rick squeezed her hand firmly. The last thing he wanted was to make their wedding an event that might tear them apart. "No, this is not a case of me being on the rebound or anything like that. I think what's happened is we're being forced into a compressed timeline neither of us expected. But, you know what? I'm looking forward to marrying you more than anything. Let's talk to both of them tonight at dinner."

"Okay. Alex is going to be down for lunch any minute. We don't need her getting ideas and trying to outflank us."

"She's eleven," Rick chuckled. "How's she going to do that?"

Marquetta raised her eyebrows and held his gaze. "Rick, this is Alex we're talking about."

"You're right. Things were so much easier when she was five."

The butler door to the kitchen burst open and Alex entered, a smile on her face. With reddish-blonde hair and blue eyes, she was looking more and more like her mother each day. She now stood just under five-feet tall. Her willowy frame was a reflection of both genetics and being an active eleven-year-old.

"There's my chief maker of gray hairs," Rick said with a smile.

Alex scrunched up her cheeks and frowned at him. "What?"

"Your dad's trying to be funny, Sweetie. And not doing a good job of it, I might add. How about some soup? It's kind of a chilly day."

"Soup's good." Alex stood at the island with her hands resting on the countertop. "Daddy? Marquetta? What do you guys think of Miss Barone?"

Rick wished he could use mental telepathy to ask Marquetta what she thought Alex might be up to. Instead of sending back her own message, she went to the refrigerator and removed two containers, one with leftover tomato soup, the other of rice. Rick's shoulders slumped—so much for mental telepathy.

"I think she's an interesting young woman," Marquetta said as she transferred the soup into a saucepan. "She does seem awfully young to be a reporter working on such a big story. Would one of you grab the French bread?"

"Sure," Rick said. "Did she take you up on your offer to hook her up with Flynn, kiddo?"

Alex shook her head. "I totally don't get that. If she's writing a story about the *San Mañuel*, why wouldn't she want to interview the person in charge? She like blew me off without even thinking about it."

Rick retrieved three mugs from the cabinet, then opened the bread box to pull out the remainder of a French bread loaf he'd bought the day before. He let out a long sigh as he studied the empty box. Not again. He turned back to face Alex and said, "Reporters have different ways of handling interviews. What exactly did she say?"

"She said she'd let me know if she needed any help."

"Well, during my days as a reporter, I never would have treated a source that way. If the day ever came when I needed that person's help again, I didn't want to have burned the bridge. Then again, Miss Barone is from a different generation. Who knows, maybe she's already got something lined up. If she did her homework before she came here, she might have it covered."

"Nuh uh. I asked Flynn and she said she'd never heard of her. Weird. Right?"

"That is strange," Rick said. "What's also strange is we're out of French bread. Again."

Alex groaned and looked up at the ceiling. "I think maybe Grandma Madeline took it."

"Really?" Rick sighed. "Do you have any idea what she's doing with all these loaves of bread? This is the third one she's... borrowed."

"I think she might be taking them someplace. I saw her leaving with a big bag and it kinda looked like bread sticking out the top."

Rick turned back to the breadbox and closed the lid. If only he could dismiss his worries about Adela Barone so easily. If Miss Barone wasn't a reporter, then why was she really here? And why was Alex taking such an interest in her?

"I'll talk to Mom," Marquetta said. "I'm sorry, I had no idea my mother had turned into a food kleptomaniac."

3

RICK

SITTING NEAR THE FIREPLACE ON one of the living room couches, Rick felt a warm glow that came, not so much from the flames of the gas log, as it did from the B&B. Everywhere he looked there were reminders of his grandfather, a man Rick had only known as Captain Jack. Their one 'official' meeting had taken place when Rick was not even Alex's age. As his grandfather's only heir, Rick had inherited the B&B, along with it's massive debt and a slew of questions he might never be able to answer.

Rick checked the time. It was after nine and their last guest was due to arrive any minute. All of the others were already upstairs and settled in their rooms. Alex was hopefully finished with her homework and ready for bed, so he had little to do except sit here, wait, and soak up the ambience.

The gas log, one of the many changes his grandfather had made during 'the grand remodel' many years ago, made the room feel warm and cozy without the hassles of wood. A hard man with old-school ideas, Rick was still amazed that Captain Jack had switched from chopping logs to flipping a lever to start a fire.

The sound of the front door opening and closing interrupted Ricks' thoughts. He craned his neck to see who had come in. It was a woman he'd never seen before. She gripped her blue trench coat tightly around herself and shivered. She'd dressed for travel in comfortable shoes and had pulled her dark brown hair back into a ponytail. It was all very sensible attire for traveling.

Rick closed the lid on his laptop and placed it on the couch, then waved to the woman as he approached. Keeping his voice low, he said, "Ms. Kama?"

"Yes. I'm sorry it's so late," she whispered. "I never expected my plane to be delayed out of LA. I appreciate you accommodating my late arrival."

"There's no need to whisper. We won't disturb anyone. Perhaps you'd like to stand by the fire for a minute? It's a chilly night for Seaside Cove."

"I'll be fine. I'm exhausted and just want to get to bed. I never realized how tiring waiting in an airport could be."

"Well, then. Let's get you checked in. You're staying with us for a week. Is that correct?"

"Yes," she said cautiously.

Her voice, which bordered on husky, seemed incongruous with her delicate facial features—fine cheekbones, straight nose, and a wide mouth. Not a lot of makeup either—she was definitely a sensible woman. Rick went behind the front desk and pulled out the key to the Mainsail Room.

"Let me know if there's anything we can do to make your stay more comfortable. Is this a special occasion? Or just a typical vacation for you?"

"I'm actually thinking about moving here. I've been living in LA for too long and need a break. Quiet is what I need."

"Of course. Well, we have plenty of that. You'll find Seaside Cove a very relaxing place to visit—or live." Rick gestured at the single carry-on she'd set down next to her sensible shoes. "Is that your only bag?"

Using both hands, she picked it up and clutched it to her chest. "Yes."

"I'll show you where your room is. I can take that for you if you'd like."

Rick reached out, but she shrunk back as though she were shielding herself with the bag. It seemed an odd reaction in a way. Most guests were happy to let someone else schlep their luggage. Clearing his throat, Rick explained the layout of the B&B as he led the way upstairs. All guest rooms were on the second floor, they served a full breakfast with a limited menu in the dining room between six-thirty and eight, and the lobby was available at all hours.

At the top of the stairs, Rick turned left. "You're the second door on the right."

After he'd let Ms. Kama into her room, Rick hurried down the hall to check on Alex. Her light was still on, so he knocked and eased the door open. As he'd expected, she was sitting up in bed, her jammies on, with her phone in front of her.

"Hey, kiddo. Time for lights out."

Alex laid the phone next to her on top of the bedspread. "I know. School tomorrow." She hesitated, then asked, "Have you and Marquetta set a date yet?"

"Alex, we just went over this at dinner. We need time to plan everything. Our first step is to get a timeline together, then we have to arrange for the services."

"I know, Daddy, but me and Grandma Madeline were talking and we could do all that stuff for you. You have like a built-in wedding planning team ready to go."

A planning team? Right now what they needed was time to sort out what they really wanted. It wasn't like remodeling a room. If only things were that easy. When Marquetta had decorated Alex's room with the furniture she'd had as a girl, it had been a simple decision. It was one that could have easily been fixed. But, he had a business to run and a daughter to raise, not to mention a thousand other things that came up each day. And with many of those daily tasks, the consequences were far greater than having a child disappointed by a choice of furniture or paint color.

"Alex, you know how I've always told you to believe in yourself? Well, this is the time when you need to let Marquetta and me do the same. We need to sort out everything so we can decide when we'll be ready. Our timeline won't necessarily coincide with the one you two came up with, but I need you to be patient and let us work through this. Are you okay with that?"

Alex's chin puckered and she wrinkled her nose. "I guess. That's so not romantic at all. You need to lighten up. You're like all business all the time."

Rick winced at the harsh reality. Alex was right. He'd been letting outside forces rule his life. It was time to take control.

"You're pretty smart for an eleven-year-old, kiddo. You know that? You're right. I've been letting life run me, not the other way around. The good news is our last guest has checked in and I'm going to take care of some paperwork." He gently pressed his finger against Alex's nose and winked at her. "Your job is to get a good night's sleep so you can have a good day in school tomorrow."

"Okay," Alex said, but quickly asked, "Daddy? What about Flynn? Is she gonna be okay?"

"Alex, you should know Flynn is quite capable of dealing with her detractors. Why do you ask?"

"She hasn't been able to do her job right ever since she found the *San Mañuel.*"

"You're right. I think Flynn's feeling the same pressures as the town. It's like we've been overrun by reporters, TV crews, and tourists wanting a glimpse of the dive site or the recovery efforts. But, you know what? She's dealt with this type of situation before. I'm sure she'll be fine."

"What if she's not?"

Rick frowned and shook his head. "What are you talking about?"

"Miss Barone thinks Flynn's stealing artifacts and she wants to write a story about it. Flynn's not dishonest. She's totally committed to doing the right thing,"

"I know, Alex. Flynn will get through it. And as for Miss Barone, if she's a decent reporter, she'll figure out that the allegations are unfounded. Now, you need to get some sleep." Rick pulled up the covers and kissed Alex on the forehead.

"Do you think she'll get the facts right?"

Rick sighed. This was one of those times when Alex's laser focus was going to require him to intervene. There was only one way to nip this in the bud. "I want you to keep a little distance from Miss Barone. Don't be bugging her a lot or trying to help. It's not like it was when I was reporting in New York and you were little. She needs to be able to do her work in peace and quiet, not to be fending off questions from an eleven-year-old."

"But Daddy, if she gets the wrong idea about Flynn, she could write a bad story about her."

"The more you interfere, the more it's going to look like we're trying to hide something. Besides, it's exactly what I said a minute ago. Flynn can handle herself."

Alex shifted in bed and eyed Rick. She didn't look happy, but at least she wasn't arguing. He had to trust she'd do what he recommended.

"Now, I'm serious. Turn off your brain and get some sleep. It's getting late. Good night."

As Rick closed Alex's door and headed to his office, he thought back to the days when he'd been a reporter himself. How he'd worked many late nights with his little girl sitting on his lap while he researched or wrote up a story. Although Alex had usually fallen asleep before he'd finished, those long nights must have instilled in his daughter the type of curiosity and determination he was seeing now. He didn't regret that part of his early parenting at all, but he did wish he'd done more to teach Alex how dangerous real crime could be. Her fearlessness worried him. A lot.

4

ALEX

Hey Journal,

I hardly slept at all last night. I am sooo tired, but I have to leave for school in a minute. Today, I'm gonna find out more about Miss Barone and what she's really doing here! All right, gotta go!

Alex

When the bell rings at the end of the school day, Miss Redmond excuses everyone else, but asks me to stay after class. That kinda worries me. I really like Miss Redmond and I don't want to do anything to make her mad at me. I'm also worried that if she keeps me too long I won't get to Howie's Collectibles so I can talk to Grandma Madeline.

Miss Redmond's got long, blonde hair. She wears it down a lot, and it kinda reminds me of those hair styles you see in old movies. She's really pretty and super friendly. In fact, she's the most favorite teacher I've ever had.

"Hey, Miss Redmond. What's up?"

"Alex, you seemed very distracted today. Is there something going on?"

"My Grandma Madeline said we should have a powwow to help my dad and Marquetta get married sooner."

Miss Redmond laughs and shakes her head. "A powwow? Do you even know what a powwow is?"

"I had to look it up. It's like a meeting. Right?"

"Exactly, But Alex, don't you know you can't rush love? I'm surprised your grandmother doesn't understand that. Let your dad and Marquetta work out everything on their own. It will all happen when it's time."

"But I want a baby brother. And Grandma Madeline wants a grand baby. Don't you see, we gotta get them married soon."

She folds her hands on her desk and sighs. "Love's not that easy, Alex. Believe me, I have a mother who badgers me constantly about when I'm getting married and, quite honestly, it gets annoying. Sometimes I don't even want to talk to her because I know what will be coming."

"Really?"

"Yes. Really. Are you sure there's nothing else going on?"

"No, that's it," I lie. I'm not gonna tell her about the article in the *San Ladron Times* my dad and Marquetta were talking about this morning. I didn't see it, but they said it claims Flynn O'Connor is stealing artifacts from the *San Mañuel* and selling them on the black market. It makes me super mad 'cause Flynn's fighting to bring up the treasure safely for a museum and she doesn't need some guy from a different town making bogus claims.

Miss Redmond keeps looking at me. Oh, man. She totally knows I'm lying.

"Are you sure there's nothing else?"

"No. Everything's cool."

"All right, then. You're free to go, but think about what I said. Okay?"

"For sure."

I grab my backpack and rush out the door. It only takes me a couple minutes to ride my bike downtown. I lock it at the rack that's about a block from Howie's Collectibles. As I walk to the store, I have to dodge a couple of tourists who aren't paying attention to where they're going.

Across the street is Mayor Carter. She's sweeping the sidewalk in front of her shop. Or, at least she's pretending to sweep, but I know she's keeping an eye on everything that's going on. My dad says Mayor Carter is a total busybody, but at least she works hard for the town. I wave to her and she waves back, then she hurries inside.

Howie's Collectibles is busier than I've seen in a long time. There's three couples looking around, and Grandma Madeline is standing behind the counter talking to Mr. Dockham. They're collecting money from a man who bought an old nautical lamp. Mr. Dockham carries a ton of awesome stuff. Some of it costs a lot of money, and I wonder how much he got for the lamp.

When Grandma Madeline sees me, she smiles and waves, then excuses herself. She comes around the counter and puts her hand on my shoulder. What's kinda funny is that I'm almost as tall as she is, but she still acts like I'm really little. It's okay. I guess if it makes her feel good, it's cool.

"Hey, Grandma, how's it going?"

"Well, dear, I've almost got Howie convinced he needs to hire me. That's not why I asked you to come here, though. We have a conundrum."

Oh, I hate conunderums. Whenever Daddy has one of them, it's usually about me. "What's up?"

"Our plan to get your father and my daughter married is taking far too long. We need to find a way to speed up the preparations."

"I totally agree." Even though Miss Redmond said they'd get married when they were ready, I so want it to happen sooner. "Do you have any ideas?"

"I was thinking maybe a romantic dinner. We get them to loosen up. Good food. Good wine. Romantic music."

"Awesome. When do you want to do this?"

"Well, it depends. How much money do you have?"

Me? Money? "I'm eleven, Grandma. Daddy gives me an allowance, but I can't afford a fancy dinner. I have like twenty dollars saved up."

"Don't worry, dear. That's part of the reason I want to work here. I want to be able to splurge once in a while. I do suppose this dinner could be the first splurge. I just thought that with you working at the B&B, you might have a larger savings account. Save your money. We'll need to start planning."

"What can I do to help?"

"I'd like to make a reservation at the Crooked Mast. I think the table in the back Ken Grayson keeps for special guests would be perfect—do you suppose you could make the arrangements?"

"I'm on it! I'll talk to Mr. Grayson and see when he can get us a reservation. He'll totally want to help!"

"I'm sure he will, dear. Now, we'll need to work out the logistics to make sure there are no surprises. We want this evening to go off smoothly."

"Awesome! I'll have Marquetta as my mom, and you'll have a new grand baby before you know it!"

I couldn't stop thinking about the talk with Grandma Madeline on the ride home. I have to admit, it does feel a little like we're rushing things. But if Daddy and Marquetta won't do it on their own, we need to help them out. Right?

I walk my bike along the path that goes around the house to the back yard. There's some awesome gardens back here that are starting to bloom. There's also a gazebo and fountains and a big tool shed that's kinda like a small garage. Daddy gave me my own key to the shed when I got my bike. He also warned me that it was my responsibility to put it away each day. After I get my bike locked in the shed, I follow the path back toward the house. The gravel crunches as I walk. I totally love it out here, just like a lot of the guests. It's a super peaceful place.

When I get in the house, I want to find that article in the *San Ladron Times* and read it for myself. I'm totally sure I can find it 'cause I'm kinda like following in my dad's footsteps with my job as a junior reporter for the *Cove Talkers Newsletter*. My dad calls our town newsletter a gossip rag, but I mostly like to write about the hard news. Okay, Seaside Cove doesn't have a lot of hard news, but I've become the go-to person when it does happen.

It's kind of a cold day, so I'm surprised by the sound of a woman's voice. It sounds like Miss Barone. She's talking to someone on the phone. Most of the guests don't hang out in our gardens unless it's warm and sunny. I wonder why she's out here.

There's a couple of big hibiscus bushes between us, so I can hear her, but she can't see me. She must not have heard me either 'cause she's still talking. I peek through the bushes, and there she is. She's wearing another one of those pretty dresses, but no coat. It sure looks like she'd be super cold out here.

"Yes, Uncle Ethan, I've gotten settled in...I know, I'll be careful...Nobody will know why I'm here."

So she is here on a secret mission! I knew it!

"No, there won't be any problems. There's a kid who lives here at the B&B. She's nothing but a little busybody."

My jaw drops. I ought to rush around the bushes and tell her she's two-faced, but that would give me away. I'm staying right here and getting the down low on her scam. She's probably not even a real reporter like she said she was.

"No, don't worry. I can handle her, and when I get done with this story that crooked archaeologist won't be able to sell anything anywhere on the black market...okay, bye."

Her footsteps crunch on the gravel path. They're getting louder and then, there she is. Right in front of me. She still doesn't see me 'cause she's not looking this way.

I step toward her and she jumps back. She grabs at the floppy brim of her hat and gawps me with those big, dark eyes of hers.

"How long have you been there, Alex?"

Oh, now she gets all icky sweet. After she called me a little busybody. "Flynn is not crooked."

"You were eavesdropping on me?"

"You were like right there so anybody could hear you. You're trying to frame my friend."

She shakes her head, but her face gets all red. She's like super embarrassed 'cause she totally knows I caught her. Then, she takes a step closer, but I'm not gonna let her scare me. She's the one who's wrong. And I'll bet she's the one who'll chicken out first. I hold my ground, cross my arms over my chest, and stand tall.

"I'm not gonna let you get away with this."

"I don't answer to you." She shakes her head and takes a step back. "You have no right to accuse me of anything."

"My dad was a reporter in New York. I know all about the business." Okay, that's only kinda true 'cause I was always more interested in the story than all the stuff that went with it. But my dad always said he couldn't turn in a story that wasn't true.

"I have the proof, you know." But then her eyebrows go up. "Your dad was a reporter? In New York?"

"That's right. And he covered the crime beat."

She looks around and runs her tongue over her lower lip, then she bats her big, dark lashes a couple times. Her voice gets all icky sweet again. "How much do you know about this *San Mañuel*?"

"Why? When I said something before, you weren't interested."

"That was totally a misunderstanding. So?"

I want to say, I know way more than you, but I hold back. "I can tell you all about it."

"Have you ever been out there? To see it?"

"At Dead Man's Cove? Of course." Well, that's not exactly true, either. But I know where it's at. I've mapped it and Flynn has shown us photos. "Why?"

"I was thinking of going out there. This afternoon. You know, like, now."

"You can't go out on the water. But you can see the dive site from shore." I think. Maybe. Isn't that what Flynn said?

"Would you show me where it's at?"

For real? That's not what I expected her to say. The reason I haven't been out there is because my dad says I have to be with an adult and he's been too busy. So has Marquetta. And Grandma Madeline doesn't drive. "We don't have any way to get out there."

"I can drive."

"My dad says it's dangerous out there. There might be treasure thieves trying to get out to the site from shore."

"What? Are you afraid? I get it now, you're nothing but a big chicken."

"Me? No. But it's just...like..."

Her voice gets high and whiny, like when the mean girls at school try to make you feel bad. "Maybe you should go ask your daddy for permission?"

What? Does she think she's dealing with a little kid? I'll show her. No newbie reporter's gonna make me chicken out. Besides, I don't think she knows anything about the *San Mañuel*. Fine. It's game on. Time to make Miss Barone eat her words.

5

RICK

RICK LOOKED UP FROM HIS desk, stretched, and checked the time. Quarter after three. Alex was probably already downstairs with Marquetta chatting merrily about her day. He was missing out. He closed the lid on the laptop and stood, happy to have a break from the mundane paperwork involved with running a business. After locking his office, Rick checked Alex's room, saw that it was empty, then went downstairs, his spirits buoyed by the idea of spending time with two of his favorite people.

As he passed through the living room, Rick spotted Amy Kama sitting on the couch to the right of the fireplace. She'd removed her shoes, had a pillow propped behind her back, and sat sideways with her feet on the couch as she scrolled up and down the screen of her phone.

"Ms. Kama, it's nice to see you've found a comfortable spot."

She jumped slightly and lowered her phone. "Sorry, you startled me. I hope it's okay that I have my feet on the furniture."

"It's no problem at all. We do appreciate you removing your shoes. Are you checking out our local real estate?"

Her eyes flitted towards her screen and she sighed. "There's not much for rent here."

"Ah, so you're looking for a rental, not a place to buy."

The delicate line of her jaw tightened and she pulled her phone closer to her chest. "Why do you ask?"

The defensive reaction took Rick by surprise. Last night when she'd checked in, she'd had that same sort of reaction when he'd asked to take her bag. Apparently, she was a very private person. Perhaps the best thing was to give her plenty of space. "Sorry, I didn't mean to pry. It's just that this is a small town and, for the most part, everybody knows everybody else."

"It's my fault. I shouldn't have reacted like I did." She winced, then laid her phone down on her lap. "I was a court officer in LA. I've seen a lot of people trying to take advantage of others. I just...I'm sorry."

"Not a problem at all," Rick said casually. "I'll let you get back to your search. Good luck." He gave her a parting smile as he headed toward the kitchen.

Expecting to find Alex and Marquetta chatting at the island, Rick burst through the butler door with a smile on his face. But instead of there being chatter and laughter, the room was empty. No sign of Marquetta. Or Alex.

Daylight streamed through the bank of windows over the sink. At the far end of the room, more daylight came through the French doors. The room should have felt bright and cheery with all the light reflecting off the white granite countertops and pale green walls. But despite the abundance of illumination, the quiet made the otherwise cheerful atmosphere feel lonely and cold.

"Marquetta? Alex?"

"Back here," Marquetta called out.

The loneliness Rick had felt at the sight of an empty room evaporated into nothing. He felt foolish. Of course, Marquetta was doing laundry. And Alex was probably helping her. They'd had two guests check out and two more would be arriving within the next couple of hours.

When he turned the corner into the laundry room, though, Marquetta was all by herself.

"I'm surprised," Rick said. "I thought Alex would be in here with you."

"No. She hasn't come in yet. Since you're here, would you grab that end and help me fold this last sheet?"

"My help doesn't come for free, Ms. Weiss," he said with a wink.

"What's your price, Mr. Atwood?"

Rick approached and kissed her. "That'll do."

Marquetta gave him a playful smile and kissed him again. "Downpayment. In case I need more help. My boss doesn't pay me very well and my best helper is missing. She's probably doing her homework."

"I don't think so. She wasn't in her room."

Marquetta looked in the direction of the backyard and her brow furrowed. "I don't understand. I saw her out back with Miss Barone. She didn't let you know she was here when she came in? She's always so good about that."

"No. I assumed she was down here with you. You saw her? When was that?"

"Forty-five minutes ago. Maybe a little more. You don't suppose they're together right now, do you?"

Rick pulled out his phone. "I'm going to find out. And I'll put a stop to this if that's the case." While the line rang, Rick continued. "When I went up to say goodnight last night, Alex was quizzing me about Miss Barone. I told Alex to keep her distance."

When the call went to voicemail, Rick felt himself tensing up. Alex knew better than to leave without first checking in with him or Marquetta. He opened the app he used to track Alex's phone.

"She didn't answer?"

"No."

"Don't be too hard on her, Rick."

"She'd better have a very good excuse or she's getting grounded...again." The app opened. Normally, Alex's phone would appear right away, but for some reason all he could get was a map showing Seaside Cove. There was no icon indicating her location. He felt the color in his cheeks drain. Cold dread slowly filled his chest. He swallowed hard and looked at Marquetta. "Her phone's not on the map."

"There must be an explanation. Maybe her battery died."

"Impossible. She charges it every night. I hate to say this, but I really don't have a good feeling about Miss Barone."

Marquetta's hand went to her throat. Her eyes brimmed with tears, but she blinked them back. "Miss Barone's number should be listed on her registration."

"Right. I'll call her."

Rick rushed out of the laundry room, through the butler door, and to the front desk. He logged into the registration system and found the number. He dialed, waited, then slumped down in the seat when he got voicemail. He left a message, but had a sick feeling he wouldn't be hearing back anytime soon. What had Alex gotten herself into now?

He looked up. Marquetta stood before him, her eyes again brimming with tears. "You didn't get her, either?"

"Voicemail."

"Call Adam."

Rick took a deep breath and dialed the number for Adam Cunningham, the town's chief of police. "Doing it right now."

The call connected and Adam's voice, sounding cheerful, greeted Rick. "Hey, buddy, what's up?"

"Alex is missing. Marquetta and I are trying not to panic, but the last time she was seen was with one of the guests on the grounds. Alex's phone isn't coming up on my tracker app. I'm worried something serious has happened to her."

"Okay. Let me put on my chief of police hat. How long has she been gone?"

"She must have gotten home about an hour ago. Marquetta saw her and Miss Barone together outside."

"What's your guest's full name?"

Rick gave Adam the information he had, including a description of Adela Barone. Throughout his recitation of the facts, his mind kept drifting back to worry. This couldn't be happening. At one point, he asked, "You don't think she'd kidnap Alex do you?"

"I think you're jumping the gun, Rick. The best thing you can do right now is keep a level head. I'm going to call Deputy Jackman and ask her to keep her eyes peeled. This is a small town, so they can't get far."

"Adam, Alex's phone is either dead or out of range. Either way..."

"Hang tight a sec. Let me call Jackman."

Rick put the call on speaker and looked at Marquetta. She, too, was obviously in full panic mode. If anything happened to Alex, they'd both be devastated.

"She'll be okay. She has to be," Rick said, but the words felt hollow.

They both jumped when Adam came back on the line. "As luck would have it, Jackman saw your guest at about two-forty-five. She cut the traffic light on Main Street a little too close and Jackman said she gave her the evil eye. When I described your guest, she said she thinks that might have been her. She was driving out of town, so Jackman didn't bother pulling her over.

She's not one-hundred percent on this, but there might have been a passenger in the car."

Marquetta put her hand to her heart and almost fell into the chair. "Oh, God," she whispered.

"They were leaving town?" Rick stammered.

"It looked like they were heading to the coast road. That road terminates a few miles out of town."

"Just beyond Dead Man's Cove," Rick muttered. Everything suddenly made sense. Adela Barone and her interest in the shipwreck. Alex and her fierce defense of Flynn O'Connor. Even though he understood why the two had left, he still didn't know what they were up to. Or how a twenty-four-year-old woman could be so irresponsible that she'd take an eleven-year-old girl with her on a potentially dangerous trip.

Alex knew Flynn was dealing with reporters and fending off allegations about stealing artifacts for the black market. With Flynn tied up, her team wasn't diving and there should be nothing happening out at Dead Man's Cove. So why would they go there?

The shoreline in the area was treacherous, filled with rocks, undertows, and riptides. And rogue waves. It was not a place for a child or an inexperienced reporter from the east coast.

"I have to get out there. Right now."

"I'll pick you up in less than five. We'll go with lights and sirens all the way."

6

ALEX

MISS BARONE'S NOT A REAL good driver. She's so busy talking and looking at stuff going on around us that she's ignoring the traffic. And she never saw the light she ran. I think she was watching some guy on the street. When she asked me why I kinda freaked out, I told her about the light. She said she thought she saw someone she knew. Like that's a reason for not watching where you're driving?

The road to Dead Man's Cove is twisty and Miss Barone's all hunched over the wheel and drives super slow. It totally feels like it's taking forever to get there. My dad never wanted to come out here 'cause he says there's no place to park. Even after what happened in town, Miss Barone's so busy looking around that she drives by the path from the road to the bay.

"Park here!"

She yanks the wheel to the right and jams on the brakes. Her face gets all super scrunchy as she looks around. "Where? There's like, nothing here. There's not even a parking lot?"

"Nope. We park on the side of the road and take the path we just passed down to the bay." I think. I hope. Where else could the trail go?

She looks around some more, then down at what she's wearing.

"You're gonna be super cold in that dress, Miss Barone."

The dress is pretty. It's all pink-and-gray flowers with some flecks of red. It's also totally impractical. Her shoulders slump.

"This dress is one of my favorites. I hope I don't ruin it."

Duh. She should've thought of that before we left. And I don't wanna go back now 'cause I may never get out here again. "It is pretty. You'll just have to be careful."

"I can always make another if I have to."

"Wow. You made it? Yourself? That's awesome."

"Thanks. I'll have to deal with it. I don't want to have to drive that stupid road again. And call me Adela. I hated it when I was your age and I had to call everyone Mister and Miss."

I don't really hate using the guests' last names. It's kind of our thing at the B&B. It's like the way we show respect for them, but if that's what she wants, I'm cool with it. "Okay...Adela. Let's go. And you better leave your hat in the car 'cause somebody might see it."

She wrinkles her nose at me. "Really? You should never go anywhere without a hat."

What is she, like, the fashion police? "We totally need to blend in." I open the door and get out of the car.

Adela hugs herself when she locks the doors. "You're totally right. It's freezing out here." She shivers, hugs herself again, and says, "Lead the way."

Even though I'm wearing jeans and a jacket, the wind coming through the trees makes me want to go back to the B&B and sit by the fire. But I'm not gonna chicken out now. If Adela can do this in that dress, I can totally do it.

Flynn told me it wasn't a long walk from the road to the bay. I just wish I knew for sure how far that was. Adela stays right behind me. Our footsteps crunch on the dirt path as we walk. Around us, the wind whistles through the trees, kinda like all the leaves are talking to each other.

We're like the only people out here, and that's making me kinda nervous. My stomach's in a knot 'cause I should have asked permission to do this. My dad's gonna be so freaked out. He'll ground me for sure if I don't call. I pull out my phone and the knot in my stomach turns into a huge lump.

"There's no service," Adela says. "I just checked."

I look around. There are mountains behind us and Dead Man's Cove opens to the ocean. This is one huge dead spot. "My dad's gonna kill me," I mumble as I put my phone back in my pocket.

"How much further is it?"

Really? We've been on this path for like ten seconds. I stop and turn around. She's got her arms wrapped around her and she's shivering. Her dress must have brushed up against something 'cause it's got a dirty spot on it. And her super cute boots are all dusty.

I turn around and start to walk. "Not far. I can hear the waves now." The path turns and goes between the trees and a couple steps later there's water ahead. "There it is. Dead Man's Cove."

There's a boat bobbing up and down in the bay. Kind of like where I'd expect the *San Mañuel* to be. Flynn's told me stories about how the four-hundred-year-old Spanish treasure ship might have gone down. I can almost see her crew jumping into the water to save themselves. A noise next to me makes me jump. It's only Adela. Not a ghost. Not a treasure thief.

"Is that her boat?" Adela sounds excited, like she's won a game or something.

"There's not supposed to be anyone out here. And that's not Flynn's boat. I don't know who it is." A second later I duck back into the trees, pull Adela with me, and hiss, "Get down."

She doesn't kneel so I have to pull on her hand. That makes her mad. She snaps, "What's with you?"

I point toward the shore where a man is climbing around on the rocks. There's a green mesh bag laying next to him. It looks like he's moving some small rocks so he can make room to hide the bag. "I think that guy's a pirate."

Her eyes get all wide. "We caught her in the act? This is awesome!" Adela gets out her phone and starts to video what's happening.

Then I realize what she said—her? She thinks this guy's working for Flynn. But Flynn's tied up in meetings for a couple days and she'd never tolerate anyone stealing artifacts. I start to tell Adela she's wrong, but stop. Why should I tell her? Let her find out on her own. "That guy's totally a treasure thief."

"You think maybe he found the skeletons? Maybe he stole jewelry off of one of them."

What? Skeletons? Where did she come up with that one? I am so not getting it with her. "We need to report this so Chief Cunningham can call out the Coast Guard."

"But there's no cell service. I wish my uncle was here. He'd know what to do."

"Well, there's nobody but you and me. One of us has to go back to where we can make a call." Just to make sure she doesn't tell me to go, I add, "And I don't know how to drive."

Adela takes another look at her phone and sighs.

"Besides, I can get closer than you. I'm wearing jeans so I can crawl in and stay out of sight."

"Take video," Adela says as she stands and hurries back into the trees.

Holy crap. I'm all alone. A gust of wind comes off the bay and cuts through my jacket. It sends a chill all the way down my back and makes me wonder if it's really the cold or if I'm just afraid. I didn't expect anyone to be out here. Especially a treasure thief. If this guy's not working for Flynn, that means he's a total bad guy. I have to get the video, but I need to stay low. When I peek out at the shore, the guy isn't looking my direction.

I scramble forward on my hands and knees. The rocks are super hard and some of them are sharp. One of them bites into my knee when I stop. I totally wanna cry out, but if I do the thief will know he's being watched. From my spot behind the rocks, I can see all his equipment. His tank and fins and mask aren't that far from where I am. I'll have to be super quiet.

The boat is getting bounced around and the waves are way bigger than I thought they'd be. I can only see one guy on deck. I take a picture and duck behind the rocks again. My heart is pounding so loud the treasure thief could hear it if the waves weren't crashing onshore. I crane my neck so I can see the treasure thief around the rock. He's kneeling down. He's got something in his hands. I take a picture, then turn on the video.

He's wearing a wetsuit, so it's like watching a ninja at work. He moves a small rock, then puts whatever he's got in his hands in the open spot. Why's he hiding something on shore when he's got a boat to go to? Unless it's a double-cross! Holy moley. Is he stealing from whoever's on that boat?

I need to get closer for a better look. While he's moving the rock back into place, I crawl forward. This is super close. Maybe too close, 'cause if he sees me, I don't know if I can run fast enough to get away. He's not super big, but he looks like he's in good shape. I wonder if wearing a wetsuit would slow him down. I so don't want to find out.

A wave comes rushing in toward my hiding place and I get splashed by freezing cold water. I taste the salt when I bite my lip to keep from crying out. Everything around me is wet, but my phone is okay, so I keep the video going.

The man crab-walks back to where he left his tank. Oh, he is totally stealing from whoever's on that boat. He's getting closer, but still doesn't see me. I shift my position so I can get a better picture. If I can get his face, that would be awesome.

He picks up his tank and starts to put it on. If I don't get this picture before he puts his mask on, the cops won't be able to identify him. I lean forward a little more. Half stand. I snap a picture...

The man jerks and looks right at me. "Hey, you!"

I do the only thing I can.

Run.

7

RICK

THE SIREN ON THE POLICE 4x4 wailed, drowning out any hope of conversation. Not that Rick wanted to talk. All he wanted was to find Alex. How they would do that, he had no idea. This was a huge coastline. Between the rocks along the shore, the treacherous currents, and the unpredictable conditions, this was a dangerous place all the time. If Alex fell in the water, Rick wasn't sure she'd have the presence of mind to find her way out. And with the water temperature in the fifties, would she even have the time before she succumbed to the effects of hypothermia?

"Stop those dark thoughts."

Rick shot a sideways glance at Adam, surprised he'd even heard the words over the siren's wail. "I can't. There's just so many ways she could..."

"Don't go there, buddy. We'll be at the bay in less than five minutes. Jackman will be right behind us. She's wrapping up a complaint from Mary Ellen Herbert."

Rick forced his thoughts away from Alex, hoping to make the time go faster. "What happened? Is Mary Ellen okay?"

"Clive, again. He just can't let her go." Adam sighed and looked at Rick. "The guy can be a real..."

"Car!" Rick yelled.

Adam slammed on the brakes. The 4x4 skidded to a stop diagonally across the road. Rick mentally prepared himself for the impact as a white Honda careened toward them. When the front end dipped and the Honda slowed to a stop, Adam killed the siren.

Rick pulled in a breath and held it as he stared through the windshield of the other vehicle. There was only one person in that car. Adela Barone. He threw open his door and charged forward.

"Rick! Stop!" Adam yelled.

Looking back, Rick shook his head. "No. I'm getting the truth out of her. I want to know what she did with my daughter." When he whirled back to face Adela, she'd gotten out of her car and was standing behind the open driver's door.

She waved frantically in the direction she'd come from. "Help! Alex could be in trouble!"

"Where is she?" Rick demanded.

Adam grabbed Rick's arm. Rick tried to jerk away, but couldn't shake the vice-like grip. "Back off, Rick. Let me handle this." Adam marched forward, his voice commanding authority. "Miss Barone, where is Alexandra Atwood?"

She pointed to the bend in the road behind her. "She's back there. We saw that archaeologist's boat out in the bay and there was a diver onshore. They're totally stealing the treasure. We wanted to call, but there's no cell service out there. Alex stayed behind to get video."

What? Did this girl have any reasoning skills at all? Who in their right mind left an eleven-year-old out here on their own? Especially if there were treasure thieves in the area.

"You're taking us there, right now," Adam said. "Rick, pull her car over to the side. Miss Barone, come with me."

While Rick moved the Honda off the road, Adam took Adela Barone's arm and guided her to the back of the cruiser. She protested all the way, but by the time Rick was out of the Honda, Adam was already rolling toward him with the 4x4. Rick got in and Adam hit the gas and turned on the siren simultaneously.

"Where exactly did you leave her?" Adam asked.

"I think it's around the next bend. There was a trail..." The siren drowned out the rest of her words.

It was actually three turns, and with each one Rick's confidence in Adela Barone's navigating capabilities diminished. When she finally called out that they were at the spot, he was tempted to ask if she was sure or just guessing. As Adam pulled to a stop, he again turned off the siren.

"Down this path?" Adam asked.

"I'm...I'm sure of it."

Rick rolled his eyes. "We don't have time for games. Do you know for sure or not?"

The young woman looked around, then nodded vigorously. "This is totally the place. I recognize that tree. The one laying on its side."

"Let's go, Rick. Miss Barone, you're staying here for your own protection."

Adam locked the 4x4 with the girl inside. She pressed her face and hands against the glass as they left her behind. A chill wind blew through the trees, bringing with it Alex's cries for help. Rick ran forward with Adam only steps behind.

"Help! Help!" Alex yelled as she ran toward them.

Rick rushed to her, wrapped his arms around her, and lifted her off the ground. She knotted her legs around his waist as he squeezed her tight. "Oh my God, you're safe. You're safe."

Alex's body trembled, but she pointed back into the trees. "A man was chasing me. He must have stopped when he heard the siren."

"I'll check it out," Adam said. "Jackman should be here shortly. You two stay put." He continued along the path, disappearing at the first bend.

Alex pulled away from Rick's embrace, then checked over her shoulder and shivered. "You should go with him, Daddy."

"Adam can take care of himself. And Deputy Jackman will be here any minute." Another siren, sounding distant and forlorn, grew louder, then faded. When Rick heard it again, it had grown in intensity. "Why did you come out here on your own, Alex?"

"I wasn't alone, Daddy. I was with Adela."

"You know what I meant, Alex. Don't dodge my question."

"You've been too busy. I didn't want to bother you."

Tempting as it was to call her out for exercising poor judgement, Rick held back. She had a point. He had been busy. Torn in ten different directions is what Madeline had called it. He bit his tongue, sure that engaging with Alex on this subject was only going to result in him chewing her out and probably grounding her. He'd deal with that issue later. Right now he was just happy to have her back safe. He stifled a critical response in favor of something he hoped would get Alex to open up. "I can always make time for you, kiddo. If you need to interrupt, do it. Or talk to Marquetta."

Alex slumped into him and wrapped her arms around his neck. She sniffled a couple of times, then said, "I'm sorry. Adela was treating me like I was a little kid and I wanted to prove she was wrong about Flynn stealing artifacts."

Artifacts? Rick recalled the girl's words when he'd first confronted her. "What did she say?"

The siren, which now pierced the air around them, suddenly stopped. They waited on the path for Deputy Jackman, Rick holding Alex close, while he also listened just in case Adam needed help. When the deputy appeared, Rick gestured toward the bay. "The chief went looking for a lone male. Apparently, there's a boat in the bay, too."

Jackman, who Rick had found to be a no-nonsense, all-business kind of deputy, nodded her understanding and continued along the path. As she disappeared, Alex clutched her arms around Rick's neck tighter and shivered again. Rick set her down, pulled off his jacket, and draped it over her shoulders.

"Miss Barone should never have belittled you," he said. "She demonstrated her own immaturity when she did that. The best thing is for you to avoid her. I'll let Adam have a talk with her, but I want to tell him how this started before he does that."

The crunching of footsteps on dirt grew louder along with a pair of voices. Adam and Deputy Jackman appeared on the path.

"He's gone," Adam said.

"What about the boat? It was in the bay," Alex said.

"Boat's gone, too, munchkin. There's no sign of anyone. Your guy probably panicked when he heard the sirens. I'd alert the Coast Guard, but I have no idea what to tell them."

"I have a photo of the boat. I also have one of the man we saw."

"Good enough. You can send them to me when I get your statement. Fortunately, the mayor just authorized us to buy a drone for search-and-rescue operations. Jackman's going to stay here and check the area with the drone while I run you two back to town. I've also radioed the sheriff for help. They can send a helicopter and help with the search. The problem is, this area is heavily wooded. Even if your guy didn't make it back to the boat and he's on foot, he could hide almost anywhere."

"What about the treasure? Did you find what he hid?" Alex asked.

Adam shook his head. "Didn't see anything."

"I can show you where to look."

Adam raised his eyebrows and regarded Rick. "I'll leave that up to you. If you want to get her out of here, I'll understand."

"Please, Daddy? Please? It might help Flynn."

Rick let out a heavy sigh. "I'll never hear the end of it if we don't do this. All right. We'll go down there. You can show us where to look, and then we're getting you home."

"I'll go get the drone from my vehicle," Jackman said.

"Thanks, Deputy," Adam said, then led the way back to the shore.

Without a jacket, the bite of the wind dug especially deep. Despite the chill settling into his bones, Rick wasn't about to take his away from Alex. By the time they'd made it to the shore, Alex had pulled Rick's jacket closer and snuggled down into the warmth. She pointed to a small outcropping of rocks where she said she'd seen the man. It appeared the area had been recently disturbed, but there was no sign of treasure.

"I think we're going to have to be very lucky to find this guy," Adam said.

Rick grabbed Alex's hand and gave it a gentle tug. "Come on, kiddo, let's get you home. Marquetta has to be worried to death."

They made it back to the police 4x4s, where Adela sat sulking in the back seat of Adam's. She had her arms crossed in front of her, her shoulders hunched forward, and her eyes locked onto the back of the front seat as though she might be able to stare through it.

"She totally looks mad," Alex said.

"Let's hope she's mad at herself. I don't think she had any malicious intent, but this whole thing reeks of bad judgment on her part."

"I agree with that," Adam said. "I'll let her go when we get back to her car, but I'm going to bring her in for questioning. The more of an impression this experience makes on her, the better."

"Don't kick her out of the B&B, Daddy. It was partly my fault."

"If she wants to stay, she's perfectly welcome. I don't want you getting friendly with her, though. I'm also not going to ground you for this because I think you've learned your lesson— at least, I hope you have. However, if you do anything like this again, I will not hesitate. Do you understand?"

"Yes, Daddy."

Alex looked so sincere, so contrite, that Rick wondered if maybe this time she really had learned something. Maybe, but he knew from past experience how little effect grounding his daughter actually had. In some ways he thought of her as his little adrenaline junkie, which meant that while Adela Barone was in town, he and Marquetta needed to keep a close eye on Alex.

8

ALEX

Hey Journal,

Well, I didn't get grounded, but Daddy and Marquetta said I should spend some time thinking about the mistakes I made today. I get that they want to keep me safe, but I don't want to spend my whole entire life hiding in my room. I gotta admit, almost getting caught by a treasure thief was totally scary. My heart was racing super fast. What a rush!

Adela was totally bummed out, and I had to sit next to her. She wouldn't talk at all. When Chief Cunningham was letting her out at her car, he said he wanted to talk to her when they finished out at Dead Man's Cove. He agreed to stop by later, so she's stuck here until he shows up. It's like she's the one who got grounded. That's kinda funny. Right?

After I told the chief and my dad what Adela said about the thieves working for Flynn, they said they were gonna straighten her out. Man, she's never gonna talk to me again!

When we got back to the B&B, Marquetta squeezed me so tight I thought she might break me. I never thought about how upset she was gonna get when I disappeared. I totally don't want her to worry too much 'cause I don't wanna mess up the wedding plans. I'd feel awful if she said she couldn't marry Daddy because of me!

Grandma Madeline doesn't know what happened yet 'cause Daddy and Marquetta don't want to tell her. I bet she's totally gonna get on my case if she finds out. The thing is, I think it was worth all the trouble. Right? Now I know there are treasure thieves trying to get to the San Mañuel. I texted Flynn when we got back, but I haven't heard from her yet.

I need a plan, Journal. It's gonna have to be a really good one, too. Otherwise, I won't get off so easy the next time. I'm also worried about what Adela's gonna do next. If she's still convinced Flynn is dishonest, I need to change her mind. So, Operation Reporter Watch is still on and even though she's not gonna want to talk to me, I totally need to find out what she's up to.

Xoxo,

Alex

I close my journal and lay it next to me on the bed. I've got a couple of pillows behind me to prop myself up. Looking around, I think about all the things I love about my room. What's so awesome is that Marquetta had it set up before me and Daddy ever arrived. She'd asked him what my favorite colors were. When Marquetta showed it to me the first time, she said her favorites were the same as mine. I love the way the white furniture fits with the teal walls and the purple accents. I almost always get cheered up when I'm in here, especially after something bad happens like this afternoon.

Dinner's gonna be in about an hour, so Daddy and Marquetta are probably downstairs in the kitchen. I just hope that after my dad talks to Marquetta he doesn't change his mind about grounding me. Since he said he wouldn't, I'm probably in the clear. But with Chief Cunningham coming back and dinner only an hour away, I don't have a lot of time to try and get more information out of Adela. If I'm gonna do it, I gotta do it now.

9

RICK

WITH THE EXCEPTION OF TWO soft-blue placemats and two partially filled mugs of tea, the island countertop was spotless. Marquetta sat next to Rick, fingering her mug. Rick felt terrible because normally she would have already prepared the next day's quick breads. Instead, while he'd gone with Adam to find Alex, she'd stayed behind and worried. He'd already apologized twice for Alex's rash behavior, and each time Marquetta had told him it was just part of growing up.

"Alex has gone too far this time," Rick grumbled. "Leaving town with a total stranger. I don't know who she might go off with next."

"She did it for a reason, Rick. Alex isn't stupid. And she's not naive. She might have acted carelessly, but that was because she didn't think Miss Barone was a serious threat."

"And what if Alex had been wrong? What if they'd met up with someone who actually was a serious threat? My God, what they might have done to her."

"I kept thinking that myself, but everything turned out. Let's just keep our eyes on her and when Miss Barone checks out, things will go back to normal."

Rick rubbed his forehead with his palms. "Keeping an eye on Alex. That's a good trick. I have to make a change. This thing with the mayor is completely out of hand. Whenever she needs a favor for the town council, she summons me for a meeting. It's got to stop. If I can get that off my plate it will free up time for me to do some actual parenting."

Marquetta took a sip from her mug, then sighed as she set it back on the placemat. "You know that's not going to happen."

"I just have to tell her no. That's all there is to it."

"Francine doesn't like taking no for an answer. Besides, I think what she's really doing is grooming you for a seat on the town council. Two of the members are so set in their ways that they can't look to the future. Francine wants someone more forward-looking. She needs you, Rick. The town needs you."

Rick let out a slow, heavy breath. "I know."

They sat in silence, with Marquetta drumming her fingers on the white granite and Rick staring out the windows over the sink. Ever since he'd inherited the B&B, his life had felt more full and complete. There was something satisfying about owning a business like this. Each day was different. Every guest brought with them new stories and perspectives. And while a seat on the town council might benefit him professionally, it would also give him a chance to show Alex the value of civic engagement.

Marquetta broke the silence and reached out to touch Rick's forearm. "Maybe we have another option."

He took her hand in his, pressed his thumb against her palm, and gave it a gentle squeeze. "I'm all ears."

"What about my mom? She's been looking for something to do and the two of them get along so well. Why don't we bring her into this? If we split the Alex watch into three parts, it could make things easier."

"That might work. You think she'll do it?"

"She adores Alex. I don't see why she wouldn't jump at the chance to spend more time with her. She should be here…"

The butler door swung open and Madeline Weiss bustled in. She plopped an empty cloth shopping bag and her purse on the island. With a dramatic huff, she put her hand to her heart. "What a day I've had! You won't believe what happened."

Marquetta smiled at Rick. "Any minute." She looked at her mother and said, "What happened, Mom?"

"Howie Dockham offered me a job! Isn't that wonderful?" Madeline's face glowed with satisfaction as she looked at them.

"A...job? I didn't know you were looking," Marquetta said.

"Well, dear, if I'm going to be living in Seaside Cove I want to keep myself busy. Howie's Collectibles is perfect."

Rick lowered his head to avoid revealing his disappointment. Ever since Madeline had arrived, it felt as though nothing had gone according to any sort of plan. It was almost like dealing with an adult version of Alex. He looked up and gave her a wry smile. "I'm happy for you, Madeline."

"Thank you, Rick. You know how much I love antiques, and Howie and I are becoming such good friends..."

While Madeline prattled on, Rick considered his options. What good would it do to take away Madeline's joy? The only thing he could do was work things out with Marquetta. On the plus side, if Madeline had a job, she might be less inclined to pressure them about planning their wedding.

"Mom, there's something Rick and I need to talk to you about," Marquetta said.

"What's that, dear?"

"We're just happy for you," Rick blurted. He looked at Marquetta with raised eyebrows. "Right?"

"Yes...we're happy for you," she said halfheartedly.

Madeline looked to be so over-the-moon that she must have missed Marquetta's obvious disappointment, thought Rick.

Rather than ruin Madeline's big announcement, Rick asked, "When do you start?"

"I already did. It happened just before I left. Howie and I were...having a little discussion, and he 'popped the question', so to speak." Madeline giggled like a teenage girl. "Naturally I said yes right away. I was also thinking that when you two get married, it solves the problem of what to do with the house."

"Excuse me?" Marquetta asked.

"Well, dear, you're not going to be living with your mother once you get married. I'm sure you'll be moving in here with your new family and I thought I could just take my house back."

Okay, Rick hadn't seen that one coming either. Holy cow. Another game changer.

"But you always said the place reminded you too much of Dad," Marquetta stammered.

"You're father's been dead for many years, dear. Anyway, I'm in a rush. I'm going home to freshen up, but I just had to share the good news first! Did you want to have dinner here again tonight?"

"Yes, Rick and I were talking about..."

"Wonderful! I'll see you both in an hour or so. Ta ta!" Madeline picked up her bags and dashed off so fast that the butler door swished several times in her wake.

Rick rubbed his hand against the back of his neck to release some of the growing tension. "That was...um...unexpected."

"It does explain a few things," Marquetta said.

"Like all the food she's been 'borrowing' from our kitchen?"

"Yes. And where she's been during the day. And why she started talking about remodeling a couple of days ago."

Rick cleared his throat. "She was the original owner...along with your dad."

"I suppose I should be happy she wants to move back to Seaside Cove. I just wasn't prepared for it. That's all."

"Unfortunately, your mother scuttled our grand plan."

"I know," Marquetta said. "I also think we've only heard one part of her plans. If I know Mom, she's gotten tired of waiting for us to set a wedding date and returning to Seaside Cove is one way she thinks she can move things along." Marquetta's eyes widened as she gazed past Rick. A smile spread across her face. "Hi, Flynn. Come on in."

Flynn O'Connor stood in the partially opened butler door. "I'm not interrupting, am I?"

"Rick and I were just discussing ways to keep Alex occupied."

"Amongst other things." Rick gestured at one of the vacant barstools. "Have a seat. What brings you here?"

"Chief Cunningham called me. He told me all about Alex's trip to Dead Man's Cove."

"Then you know about the boat in the bay and the man who was hiding something onshore," Rick said.

"Fortunately, the chief contacted me before I responded to Alex's texts. I've gotten three from her. Before I do anything about them, I want to be sure you're okay with me answering her questions."

"It depends on what kinds of questions she's asking," Rick said.

"How would a treasure thief get rid of his find? Whether the man onshore was from the boat or are we dealing with multiple attempts to plunder the treasure all at once? Those kinds of things."

Rick hung his head and rested it on his open palms.

"I'm sorry, I didn't mean to upset you," Flynn said.

"No. You didn't upset me. I don't know whether I should be happy or sad that my daughter has taken an interest in crime. I guess the good news is that at least we're not dealing with a murder this time."

Flynn shook her head adamantly. "These people can be just as dangerous. I've seen them do some despicable things on more than one occasion. They can be cutthroat."

"I know. We've seen it before. It's like the gold rush all over again, but this time everybody has better technology."

"The big difference is, most of the miners had legal claims." Flynn grimaced, then added, "Unfortunately, we're dealing with the ones who jumped a claim, not those who staked one."

"The criminals, not the good guys," Rick said.

"That's right. And you spent enough years covering the crime beat in New York to know once someone starts breaking the law, it's easier to keep going than it is to stop. So, with all that in mind, what do you want me to do about Alex?"

10
ALEX

ADELA'S STAYING IN THE JIB Room. It's real close to the upstairs coffee station, so I've got an excuse if I need one. If any of the guests come out of their rooms, I'll just pretend to check the supplies like I did when Miss Kama left a few minutes ago. We smiled at each other and I told her to have a good night, but she didn't say anything. She's one of the quiet ones.

Seeing Ms. Kama leave reminded me it's almost dinner time. That's why my stomach is growling. Now that the coast is clear, I can stand by the door again and listen. I can hear Adela's voice, so I know she's in there. She must be on the phone again 'cause I don't hear anyone else. I need an excuse to knock on her door. I also have to make sure she doesn't get suspicious right away.

My heart is pounding like crazy. I don't want anyone to see what I'm doing, especially my dad. He's gonna be super mad if he finds out I'm spying on Adela. Everything's so quiet I can almost hear my heart beat. I stand closer and press my ear against the door.

A loud creak makes me jerk back and suck in a breath. Whoa! I thought it might be Adela coming out, but it must've just been the old house. It happens all the time when the wind is blowing. The hall is still empty, so I put my ear back against the door.

Rats! I still can't hear all the words, but I think she said something about treasure and danger and not letting something happen again. It's all super hard to put together. It's probably her uncle again. When I hear her slam something and say the word 'infuriating,' I figure she's done with the call. I go back to the coffee station, pull my phone from my back pocket, and wait a few seconds.

When Adela doesn't leave and nobody else comes down the hall, I knock on her door. She only opens it a crack and gives me a mean look. "What do you want?"

"To talk. Can I come in?"

"Aren't you going to get in trouble for being here?"

"Nah. My dad's cool."

She shakes her head. "I don't believe you."

"Okay, I'll totally get grounded for being here, but..." I hold up my phone. "Don't you want the photos I took?"

She wrinkles her nose like she did when I told her to leave her hat in the car at Dead Man's Cove, then looks up and down the hall. She grabs my shirtsleeve and drags me into the room. The door slams behind me.

11

RICK

FLYNN'S QUESTION OF WHAT RICK wanted her to do about Alex hadn't come as a big surprise. He'd been expecting her to check in because she tended to be as protective of Alex as he and Marquetta, or even Adam. Come to think of it, almost anyone who knew Alex was concerned about her safety. It was one of the things he liked about Seaside Cove.

After a heavy sigh, a blend of frustration and uncertainty, Rick said, "I don't know what to tell you, Flynn. We all know Alex will find a way to stick her nose where it doesn't belong if she wants to."

"I can try avoiding her. That's what I've been doing so far, but I can tell she's getting tired of me not responding to her texts."

"I appreciate the effort, but we all know that won't work for long. She'll simply escalate to email, phone, or in-person. The best way to deal with her is to face it head on. Be honest, but reassure her you've got things handled."

Marquetta's face lit up and she motioned for someone to enter. "We're going to need a bigger island if this keeps up. Come on in, Adam."

"Mind if I join you?" Adam Cunningham stood holding onto the butler door looking as though he'd just started his day.

"What did you do? Go home and change?" Rick asked. "It doesn't look anything like you've been mucking around in the woods hunting for a missing treasure thief."

Marquetta tsk'd a couple of times, then gestured at the stool next to Flynn. "Ignore him. Have a seat. Want some coffee?"

"Thanks, Markie. You wouldn't happen to have any of your Zucchini-Pineapple Bread left over, would you?"

"As a matter of fact, I do. Coffee and bread coming up. What about you, Flynn?"

"No, but thanks. Hey, Chief. Did you ever find the boat?"

"Coast Guard says there's no sign of it. Which probably means they're hiding along the coast somewhere. There's plenty of little bays they could duck into."

"And my treasure thief? I take it he got away, too?"

"Jackman went over the area with the drone and the sheriff did a few sweeps with their helicopter. We found where he'd left his wetsuit and all his equipment, so he's definitely on land. He's probably headed this way or they had a prearranged meeting place in case they got caught. We're not giving up, but it's going to take some luck."

Rick sipped his tea as Adam talked. He could hardly believe the captain of a boat voluntarily left one of his crew members behind. "So they abandoned him? That just seems so...cold."

"Tough business, being a treasure thief," Flynn said. "They all know going in that if there's trouble, it can turn into every man for himself. If he's without his wetsuit, he should be easy to spot. Look for the guy wearing swim trunks and freezing his butt off."

Adam chuckled. "I agree. Maybe I should pay a visit to the clothing stores in town."

"He has to be headed this way," Rick said.

"Not necessarily," Flynn said. "If they had a contingency plan, he could have gone any direction. What about the artifact Alex thinks she saw? No sign of that, either?"

Adam shook his head. "Nothing. He might have stashed it in a different hiding place somewhere close by. Assuming he's not taking it to..."

"A prearranged meeting place," Flynn, Rick, and Marquetta parroted together.

Adam rolled his eyes and smirked. "Did you three rehearse that or something?"

"We're not telling," Marquetta said as she placed a mug of steaming coffee and a slice of bread in front of Adam. "Did you skip lunch again?"

"This day officially classifies as off-the-charts crazy. The mayor's called me to complain about all the traffic on Main Street. Mrs. Cantwell has called me three times because Tommy Cat's run away again. Mary Ellen Herbert filed another report after her neighbors reported seeing Clive around her house. And, never mind. There's more."

"You said something about that on the way to Dead Man's Cove," Rick said.

"Crazy case, those two. Mary Ellen's done everything she can. Legal separation, divorce, restraining order—and now she's got the neighbors on the lookout. Clive just doesn't seem to get the point. Mary Ellen wants him out of her life."

Flynn chuckled to herself. "Glad I don't have time for men."

Marquetta sat next to Rick and nudged his elbow. "They're not so bad. And Adam, don't be so sure Mary Ellen wants to get rid of Clive completely. The rumor mill has it that the reason he's been hanging around her so much is he says he's changed and Mary Ellen is having second thoughts."

Adam regarded Marquetta for a few seconds, then said, "You have got to be kidding me. Please, tell me you are."

"Sorry, but no. I have it from a reliable source that they were seen together in the park two days ago. It was just a picnic lunch, but it looked amicable."

"Then why did my deputy spend an hour with Mary Ellen taking a complaint from her about Clive? You're saying they're involved again? I'm the Chief of Police and nobody reports this kind of stuff to me."

"Face it, buddy," Rick said. "Nobody wants to talk to a cop, but they're happy to gossip with their neighbor. And since Marquetta knows every single person in town, if you want to know something, just ask her."

Adam shook his head and sighed. "I'm going to have a talk with Mary Ellen. We have far better things to do than help her play hard-to-get."

"Like return Tommy Cat to Mrs. Cantwell," Rick deadpanned.

Adam gave him a mock sneer. "Or save eleven-year-old girls from dangerous treasure thieves."

"Ouch." Rick winced, then added, "You win. I guess my daughter was a big part of the problem today."

"That's actually why I stopped by. I'd like to talk to her and Miss Barone. I need their statements. Can I..." Adam closed his eyes at the sound of a message chime on his phone. "Oh, no. Please, not Mrs. Cantwell again."

His eyes widened as he read the message on the screen. With another shake of his head, he wolfed down the last of Marquetta's quick bread and then finished off his coffee.

"Mrs. Cantwell?" Marquetta asked.

"No. There's been a theft at Ocean Surf. Dennis Malone says a naked man stole everything out of his cash drawer." Adam shook his head and stood. "How do you let a naked man get close to your cash drawer?"

"I guess we know where our treasure thief went," Rick said.

"Yeah. Looks like those statements will have to wait. This shouldn't take too long. I'll be back in about an hour. Rick, would you let Miss Barone and Alex know?"

"Sure. Was this an armed robbery?"

Flynn laughed. "Oooh. I wonder where he hid the gun?"

"Very funny. I'll be back." Adam said a quick goodbye, then made his exit.

"He really needs to get that other deputy position filled," Rick said.

Marquetta shook her head. "The mayor is trying to save money. She's not convinced Seaside Cove needs three police officers. She says it creates a bad image."

Flynn did a double take, then eyed Marquetta. "She told you this?"

"Francine is one of the biggest gossips in town," Rick said. "And Marquetta knows exactly how to get her to talk."

Marquetta's cheeks colored slightly, and she pursed her lips. "It's an art form. Anyway, we still need to figure out what to do about Alex. What do you think, Rick?"

"Avoidance isn't going to work. Flynn, I think the best thing is for you and I to talk to Alex together. Can we do it right now?"

"That's one of the reasons I came here. The other was to introduce myself to Miss Barone. I hate dealing with the media —any kind of public relations for that matter. Unfortunately, this whole thing is spiraling out of control and if I don't take steps to stop it, it's only going to get worse."

"Okay, then. Let's do this." Rick was happy to have Flynn's support in his attempt to keep Alex out of the archaeologist's problems. If Flynn reassured Alex the situation was under control, maybe then she'd believe him. If that didn't work, he'd try something else. Whatever he had to, that's what he had to do to keep his daughter out of danger.

When they reached the second-floor landing, Rick pointed to his left. "Let's go deal with Miss Barone first. She's in the Jib Room. I believe you know where that is."

The corners of Flynn's mouth turned up into a faint smile. "Passed it every day when I was staying here."

At the door to the Jib Room, Rick decided to give Flynn a final chance to opt out. "You sure you want to do this?"

"Like I said, this is the part of my job I hate, so let's get it over with."

"Right." Rick turned to knock on the door, but stopped when he heard voices coming from the other side, one of them sounding suspiciously like Alex. "Watch that door. I'll be right back."

He hurried past the second-floor landing and down the hall to Alex's room. He knocked, got no answer, and checked the doorknob. It was locked. Using his key, he did a quick check. Indeed, Alex was nowhere to be seen.

He retraced his steps to the Jib Room and rapped his knuckles on the door. When there was no immediate answer, he pounded again. "Miss Barone? Alex? Open this door. Now!"

12

ALEX

ADELA'S WEARING DARK BLUE SWEATS and has her hair pulled up like me and Marquetta do when we're working. It's the first time I've seen her in anything other than a dress. The way she looks right now, she could easily pass for a kid in high school.

"Send me the photos and then get out of here." She picks up her phone, unlocks it, then tries to stare me down.

No way. She's not getting them that easy. I've got questions and she's gonna answer before I give up my photos. "Are you really here from a magazine?"

"What? Why would you ask that?"

"Because you don't act like a real reporter. Since you got here you've been all about making sure Flynn is proven guilty of stealing. But we saw the boat. That wasn't hers. It proves you were wrong, but you haven't admitted it yet. It's like you totally don't want her to be innocent. What's up with that?"

"I don't have to answer your questions."

"You will if you want those photos. And the video."

She grits her teeth and puts her arms straight down at her sides. It looks like she's gonna throw a temper tantrum or something. "I am not gonna be intimidated by you. You're... you're eleven."

"I've helped the cops solve a bunch of murders. You haven't even published one story. Have you?"

"Just send me the photos and go."

Why? I've totally got this. She's super scared now 'cause she knows I'm onto her. "No photos until you answer my questions. I can expose you whenever I want. I write for the town newsletter and can make sure everybody knows what you are. And Marquetta knows the whole entire town, so if I tell her you're a fake, you won't get anything from anybody."

Her eyes are getting kinda red and teary. "Why are you being so mean to me?"

Seriously? That's like so sixth grade.

Adela plops down on the edge of the bed. She slumps over and hangs her head. "I have to get this story. I have to."

"Why?"

She swipes at her cheek with the back of her hand. "I can't tell you. I just can't. Please? Give me the photos."

Wow. She's like ready to cry. I sit next to her. "We don't have to be enemies. I can help you."

"You already threatened to ruin my story. Why should I trust you?"

"Because I showed you where Dead Man's Cove is. Because I haven't told anybody what I heard you talking about outside. You're not with a magazine, are you?"

Adela shakes her head. "No. I'm a Journalism major at USC. I've never had anything published."

"How'd you hear about the *San Mañuel?*"

"From my uncle. He's always supported me, even when my dad hasn't. But if I don't get the story here, he might lose faith in me, too. That would make my dad super happy because he doesn't want to pay for school anymore."

"Aren't you like twenty-four?"

"How do you know that?"

"I saw your registration card. Aren't you like close to graduation?"

"I still need some courses. You wouldn't understand, but I've had to change majors a few times."

That sounds kinda bogus to me. I didn't like my last teacher in New York, but my dad told me I had to deal with it. "So what did your uncle tell you?"

"He said the *San Mañuel* was an old Spanish galleon that sank here after it returned from the Far East. It was kind of a cool story, so I did some checking on my own. I decided to write about it and see if I could get it published."

"What's the deal with Flynn O'Connor? Why do you wanna make it look like she's stealing?"

"Where's the story in an archaeologist diving for a bunch of old artifacts? That's like super boring. I need something with some kind of a hook."

Adela sighs and looks up at the ceiling. There's a small chandelier that my great-grandfather installed when he remodeled the B&B. My dad says it's made of some kind of super expensive glass, so him and Marquetta are the only ones allowed to dust it. Not that I like dusting. It's kinda boring. Sort of like sitting here watching Adela feel sorry for herself.

I stand up and she looks at me. Her eyes are all red, like her world's being destroyed. But, it's not. "You've got a hook, Adela. You have to follow the real story, not the one you want."

"What? A stupid treasure thief who got away? We don't even have whatever he stole. I've got like nothing."

A knock on the door stops me from telling her she's wrong. Oh, crap. Chief Cunningham must be here already. Adela gets up to answer the door, but I grab her arm.

"They can't find me here," I hiss.

Adela's eyes get wide. She looks around the room. There's like no place to hide. I'm so dead.

And then I hear the worst thing in the world for when I've done something wrong—my dad's voice.

"Miss Barone? Alex? Open this door. Now!"

Oh crap. My dad's so gonna ground me.

13

RICK

ADELA BARONE OPENED THE DOOR to the Jib Room a crack and peered out at Rick. Her eyes were red and teary, her cheeks, puffy and flushed.

"Hello, Mr. Atwood. I was just watching TV. It's a sad movie. Did I have it on too loud?"

"That wasn't the TV, Miss Barone. You and I both know my daughter's in there." Rick raised his voice. "Alex, come out or I'm coming in." Exercising his right as the proprietor to enter the room wasn't an option he wanted to use, but if all else failed, he'd do it.

There was a small groan from inside, followed by Alex's resigned reply. "It's okay, Adela. Let him in."

The young woman stood to one side so Rick and Flynn could enter. Alex stared at them, a look of shock on her face. "Where's Chief…"

"No," Rick said sharply. "What are you doing here, Alex?"

"I came to give Adela…Miss Barone, the photos from Dead Man's Cove."

"Really? It sounded like you were doing a lot more than sending a couple of photos. You and I are going to have a talk about appropriate friends. Miss Barone is not only a guest, but she's far too old for you to be socializing with."

The young woman looked sideways at Flynn and straightened her back. "We weren't really socializing."

"Then let's call it pestering." Rick held her gaze and she seemed to shrink away. "Alex, I want you to go to your room. I'll come talk to you when Flynn and I are done here."

Alex looked up at Rick with pleading eyes. She wrinkled her nose. "If I promise to be quiet, can I stay? Please?"

"I'd like to have her here. As a witness."

The young woman chewed on her lower lip. She looked both vulnerable and afraid. Rick was tempted to remind her that Alex was still a child, but in many ways, young Miss Barone was acting much like one herself.

"Very well," he said. "Alex, what's the parenting philosophy I've always told you I disagree with?"

Alex screwed up her face and said, "Children should be seen and not heard?"

"Right. This is one time you need to abide by that philosophy, not because you're a child, but because you're here as a witness. And witnesses listen. They don't talk because a witness..."

"Doesn't influence the facts," Alex said dejectedly, then made a motion of zipping her lips shut.

Rick felt terrible about treating her this way, but if Adela Barone was going to try and treat Alex as an adult, he didn't see that he had a choice, especially when his guest had clearly demonstrated her own immaturity. Once she was gone, he could relax the rules again.

"All right, Miss Barone. This is Flynn O'Connor. She's the archaeologist who's in charge of the recovery efforts for the *San Mañuel*."

"I know who she is." Miss Barone sniffled and crossed her arms over her chest.

"I'm not sure you do," Rick countered. "Flynn, why don't you take it from here?"

"Miss Barone, it's nice to meet you. I've never met a member of the press who's so young. Which publication are you with?"

Next to Rick, Alex squirmed. His temperature rose because he was certain Adela Barone had been lying to him. She turned bright red, then confessed she was not really with the press. It only took a couple of minutes, but by the end of the introductions, Rick realized the girl had been lying to everyone. Now he had even more reason to keep her away from Alex.

Flynn seemed to take the confession in stride. "Miss Barone, don't feel too bad. Even the seasoned reporters that are in town don't fully understand what's involved in an underwater recovery operation. Based on some of the things I've heard, I think you may also be under the impression I had something to do with that pirate out at Dead Man's Cove today."

"Who else would be out there? You're the only one who knows the location. Right? You had to send that boat there."

"No, I didn't. As a matter of fact, it wasn't long ago that a different band of treasure hunters came to Seaside Cove for the express purpose of plundering the *San Mañuel*. They weren't successful, thanks in part to Alex and her determination. But the truth is, there are plenty of forums where these people talk. Some are in the open, and some are on the dark web. And then there's the ones on the deep web. For those, you have to know where to look. What I'm saying is, after the location was discovered, it became almost impossible to keep it a secret."

"So the boat we saw wasn't yours?"

Alex mouthed a quiet, "Told you."

"It was not mine," Flynn said. "The name of my boat is the *Blue Phoenix*. I have no idea who sent the one you saw, but because they got away before the Coast Guard arrived, they'll be able to come back whenever they can sneak in. You both should realize that man you saw on the shore could have been quite dangerous. Fortunately for Alex, Chief Cunningham was already on the way."

"So my story's a total loss? That sucks."

Heat flushed through Rick's veins at the girl's selfish view of the world. She'd left a child alone in a dangerous situation and all she could think of was her own failure to get a news story— one she'd had completely wrong in the first place? He took a slow breath to keep from saying something he shouldn't.

"Actually, there is a way that you might still get the story you want," Flynn said. "It would involve doing what reporters do."

"What would that be?" She eyed Flynn suspiciously.

"You could begin by giving Chief Cunningham a thorough and unbiased account of what happened out at Dead Man's Cove. That would include a description of the man you saw."

"I didn't see him up close. Alex got closer than me."

"Whatever you saw might be pertinent," Rick said firmly. "Chief Cunningham still wants your statement."

"That's right," Flynn added. "I'll also be happy to give you an interview during which you can ask any questions you want about the *San Mañuel*."

"You would?"

"Yes."

"What if I want to ask questions about you?"

"Me?" Flynn spread her hands apart. "I have nothing to hide. You'll be able to ask me anything you want."

"How do I know you're telling me the truth?"

"Miss Barone," Rick said. "I used to be a journalist, so let me give you a little bit of advice. True journalism is about finding the truth. If you approach your subject with an open mind, you'll be able to see both sides of the story. If you write based on the facts, and not just on unsubstantiated claims made by others, your work will be much better. And by that I mean more accurate. If you don't... you'll get a reputation—one you may not want."

"He's right." Flynn's voice took on a sharper edge. "And as the person giving you my time, I'll add that if I think you're wasting my time or that you're still intent on railroading me, I will cut you off. There will be no second chances. So, Miss Barone, what would you like to do?"

"What if you don't like what I write?"

Rick's phone pinged with a message. He checked to see who it was from.

"If you need to deal with that, we'll be fine here," Flynn said.

Obviously, Flynn must have seen the surprise on his face. Rick couldn't figure out why Adam would be asking him to call, but there was no reason to stick around here. The conversation with Adela Barone was going in circles. She seemed stuck on the same bias she'd arrived with, and Flynn was, quite likely, wasting her time. That, however, was not his problem.

"Thanks, Flynn. If you'll excuse us, we'll let you two come to some sort of arrangement. Come on, Alex."

"But Daddy..."

Flynn knelt in front of Alex and took hold of her shoulders. "It's fine, Alex. I've got this. You and your dad have things to do. We'll work this out—one way or another."

Alex screwed up her face and looked at Flynn.

"It's okay. Really."

Alex gave Flynn a hug and stood. She took a deep breath, then said, "Okay."

"What about me? What if I want her to stay?"

The more interactions Rick had with Miss Barone, the more she reminded him of a spoiled child. He gently guided Alex toward the door. "Wait for me in the hall. Okay?"

"What are you gonna do, Daddy?"

"I just need a minute with Miss Barone."

Alex's shoulders slumped and she hung her head as she opened the door. When the door closed, Rick looked at his guest. "Miss Barone, you're a guest in my establishment and I want you to feel comfortable here. We'll do everything we can to make your stay a pleasant one. However, in return I'd like your assurance that you'll keep Alex at arm's length. No more escapades. No more investigations."

"Sure. Whatever."

That was the best she could do? Whatever? Well, if she couldn't abide by the rules on her own, he'd have to make sure Alex did.

"Thank you," Rick said as he turned and left, a sense of sadness washing over him. Until today, he'd never had a guest he couldn't trust. He supposed all he could do would be to keep a close eye on Adela Barone for the rest of her stay.

14

RICK

ALEX REMAINED SILENT AS THEY went down the stairs. On their way through the living room, Rick asked how she was doing, but all he got in return was a mumbled, "Okay."

They saw no guests on the way to the kitchen, but that wasn't unusual during early evening when most went to one of the town's two restaurants.

"Hey, Sweetie," Marquetta chirped when they entered the kitchen.

"Hey, Marquetta," Alex said glumly.

Marquetta's smile fell and she came over to give Alex a hug. "Oh, somebody's having a bad afternoon."

"Daddy clipped my wings."

Rick snickered and Marquetta burst into laughter. "Where did you pick up that expression?"

"From Miss Redmond. Class was kinda rowdy one day and she said she was gonna clip our wings if we didn't settle down."

"And you kids knew what she meant?" Marquetta asked.

"Nah. But she explained it." Alex rolled her eyes. "In detail."

Now that they'd actually gotten a tiny smile out of Alex, Rick thought maybe they'd have a better evening—until his phone pinged again.

"Uh oh, I forgot to call Adam back." Rick read the message, which asked him to come to the Main Street alleyway. "I have to go. Adam wants me to meet him."

"Does it have something to do with that theft at Ocean Surf?" Marquetta asked.

Alex immediately perked up. Her eyes widened as she let her gaze flit between Rick and Marquetta. "What happened?"

"Marquetta can tell you. As for why Adam's being so persistent, I have no idea."

Rick said a quick goodbye and ran upstairs to grab a jacket. At a slow pace, it was a ten minute walk to Seaside Cove's downtown. He made it in seven. That included a momentary stop to gape at the size of the crowd near Deputy Jackman's cruiser, which was parked at the head of the alley with the lights flashing.

The crowd consisted of some he recognized as guests, a few locals, and others he assumed were reporters. The difference was easy to see. The locals and tourists watched and jabbered excitedly among themselves while the reporters scribbled notes or recorded video. When Rick made it to the front of the crowd, he stopped at a barrier made of crime scene tape.

Mary Ellen's husband Clive approached. He had blood stains on his shirt and was being followed by Deputy Jackman. On closer inspection, Rick realized Clive was being guided forward by the deputy, who had Clive's hands locked behind his back. It was then that Rick saw the body of a man lying on the asphalt further back in the alley. A large pool of blood coated the asphalt in the immediate area. Obviously, the man was dead, and Clive must be the number one suspect.

"I didn't do it! I didn't do it! Rick, you have to help me," Clive bellowed as they passed, the deputy pushing him steadily forward.

Jackman quirked her head to indicate Rick should cross the yellow crime scene tape. "Chief wants you to join him. He says you know the drill."

The drill? Rick thanked her and slipped under the tape. As he walked toward the body, he kept hoping Clive hadn't actually killed someone this time.

"What've you got, Adam?"

Now firmly in the role of police chief, Adam looked up with green eyes that were filled with determination. He sighed. "Murder victim. Puncture wound to the abdomen. Late twenties, I'd guess. Looks like he hasn't shaved in about a week, but he's wearing brand new clothes and flip-flops. I recognize the brands as ones Dennis carries at Ocean Surf. Check out the bottoms of his feet. This guy's got some serious callouses. He must walk barefoot all the time."

Rick eyed the shirt, unable to fully ignore the blood that had soaked into the lower half. "You're right, the shirt looks like a pattern I've seen in Ocean Surf."

"I've called Dennis. I told him I think I've found the naked man who robbed him. He's not going to be happy when he sees what happened to his stolen merchandise. I also wanted you to see this poor guy before you told me you were too busy to help. That knife wound he took? Whoever did it was either incredibly lucky or knew exactly what he was doing. I'm guessing this guy bled out in no time."

"I saw Deputy Jackman taking Clive away. Do you think he did it?"

"Could be. He was kneeling over the body when Ms. Kama was walking by and saw him. But Clive? He's never been in a knife fight, and he's never had combat training to my knowledge. He looks guilty, but I don't think he's capable of murder."

"Then why'd you arrest him?"

"I'm calling it resisting arrest for now. It's flimsy, but I want to keep him away from the reporters until we can assemble the facts. By the way..."

Adam cocked his head to the other side of the alley. Rick turned and saw Amy Kama standing next to a dumpster under the harsh illumination of the alley's security lighting. She had her back against the adjacent building's wall and had her arms crossed in front of her. A pang of sorrow pierced Rick's gut—the poor woman couldn't seem to take her eyes off the body.

"I have a favor to ask," Adam said. "Can you get her out of here? Maybe see that she gets something to eat? This happened on her way to dinner and I don't think she's up to restaurant dining. I'd like to keep her away from the reporters, too."

"Sure. I'll get her home. Marquetta will whip up something. Do you want me to come back?"

"I'd appreciate it. And when you do, would you bring a copy of the photo Alex took of that guy out at Dead Man's Cove? The only thing in the victim's pockets was a wad of bills."

"He had money on him?"

"Big wad of cash, but no wallet. No ID. No keys. I suspect our treasure thief made his way to town, hit Ocean Surf for some new clothes, raided the register, then got himself killed for some reason."

"Why would Clive kill a perfect stranger?"

"Unless he wasn't a stranger at all. I talked to Jackman about that complaint she took from Mary Ellen. It sounds a lot like Clive's jealousy coming out again. Since Clive was seen kneeling over the body, maybe there's some sort of connection. Anyway, the sooner we can lock down who our victim is and what he did today, the sooner we can put away the killer. Are you willing to help?"

"This is the last thing I need right now, but of course I will. I just have to put the brakes on a couple of other things. I'll get Ms. Kama settled and be back in about fifteen to twenty minutes."

"Great." Adam grinned and reached into his pocket. "I brought you a little present. With all the cases we've worked together, I figured you finally deserved your own official Seaside Cove Police Department notepad."

Rick looked down and smirked at the spiraled pad. It had a plain blue cover, was about three inches by four and about a half inch thick. He'd used the same thing during his days as a reporter and had bought them in any number of places and colors.

"Thanks, Adam. I can see you went all out."

Adam chuckled. "Yeah. I have a huge budget for office supplies and consultant incentives."

"I can see that." Rick pocketed the notepad and walked over to Amy, who didn't take her eyes off the body until Rick inserted himself into her line of vision. She'd come to Seaside Cove seeking serenity and might now be a witness to a murder.

"I guess you're my guardian?" She hugged herself tightly and shivered. "I just never expected..."

"It's okay," Rick said. "Let's get you back to the B&B."

He extended his elbow, which Ms. Kama took, then guided her past the crime scene tape and through the growing crowd of onlookers. A couple of reporters approached, but Rick warned them off with a peremptory 'no comment.' Neither of them said a word until the commotion and reporters were half a block behind.

"Thank you for getting me out of there." Ms. Kama's voice shook as she continued, "When I saw the one man kneeling over the body, my instincts kicked in. I called the police, but once they arrived, I just crashed."

"It's understandable. It was a gruesome sight."

"I'm not really that bothered by blood. It was more about the man I shot in LA." Her cheeks tightened and she looked at Rick. "It was ruled a justified shooting."

Rick's pulse quickened. Hadn't she told him she'd been a court officer? What sort of nightmare had she gone through? "That must have been terrible."

He had no formal training, but he could listen. He'd done plenty of that while chasing stories in New York. Plus, if he was going to help with the investigation, questioning her now certainly fit with the other hat Adam wanted him to don.

"How did it happen?" Rick asked.

She lowered her head and watched the sidewalk as they approached the roundabout. Their footsteps seemed to drift away on the wind gusts coming in off the ocean. At first, Rick thought he might have misread her feelings, but when they reached the other side of the street and turned toward the B&B, she began to talk.

"I'd just gotten off work. There was an altercation on the front steps of the courthouse. I tried to step in and calm things down, but one of the men involved pulled a knife. I don't know where he got it, but I gave him warning. I warned him again when he started toward me, but he kept coming. I shot him." A few steps later, she added, "He died on the way to the ER. That's why I'm here. My therapist says I need more time to process the trauma."

"I'm sorry," Rick said. "What an awful thing to have happen."

She raised her face to the sky and took a deep breath. "God that feels good to not be hiding it. I think that's what bothers me more than anything."

"Talking about it?"

"No...holding it in. Letting it out has helped."

They again fell into silence until they reached the front walkway leading to the B&B. "I hope this incident hasn't dampened your interest in Seaside Cove."

"To be honest, I'm struggling with it. I wanted to leave the violence behind. I thought this would be a sleepy little town with very little crime, someplace where I could heal. Now that I'm a witness to a murder, I don't know how I feel."

"I understand." Rick opened the front door for her and said, "Let's go back to the kitchen. We'll see what Marquetta can put together for you."

"I don't want to be a bother. I'm not very hungry, anyway."

"Then we'll just get you something light. Come with me." He took her elbow and guided her back to the kitchen. Alex and Marquetta were there sitting at the island with Madeline.

Ms. Kama stood awkwardly next to Rick as he introduced her and asked if she could join them for dinner. Marquetta said she had plenty of spaghetti and salad, so why not?

"I have to go back," Rick said. "Would you save me some?"

"Of course." Marquetta kissed Rick, then playfully slapped his thigh. "Now, scoot. Adam probably needs you."

"I almost forgot. Adam wanted me to get the photos Alex took. Send them to me. Would you, kiddo?"

When Rick had the photos on his phone, he looked at the one of the treasure thief. "Alex, I do believe you've just help identify our murder victim."

15

ALEX

AFTER MY DAD LEAVES, Ms. Kama says we should call her Amy since she's intruding on our dinner and she hates formalities. So, now I have another guest I can call by her first name. Having her join us for dinner seems kinda weird 'cause technically we only serve breakfast. We make suggestions about where guests can go for lunch or dinner, but we've never actually had one of them join us.

"So what happened?" I ask after Amy's got a small plate of spaghetti and some salad.

"Alex, dear, you're prying," Grandma Madeline says.

Amy watches her plate and pokes at her spaghetti. It seems like she might be too upset to talk, but when she looks up, she says, "It's okay. I'm just trying to reconcile it all in my head. I was wandering around downtown before dinner when I walked by this alley and saw a movement. It turns out it was a man kneeling over the murder victim."

I can feel my eyes get big as I look at her. "Did you like actually see him kill the guy?"

"No. I came in after. I'm not even sure he was the killer. He could have been walking by and seen the body. Like me."

Marquetta sets a glass of wine in front of Amy. All the adults are having white wine and I've got milk. Marquetta always says

I'm having 'white wine', too. That was funny the first time she said it, but now it seems kinda lame.

"Was this the dead guy?"

I show Amy the photo I took of the treasure thief. She nods absently and gets a little teary. "That's him."

All of a sudden Grandma Madeline's interested and wants to see it, too. We pass my phone around and I have to go through the whole entire story about Dead Man's Cove. Grandma Madeline isn't happy about that, but at least she backs off when Marquetta says something to her.

Amy hasn't really touched her spaghetti. She's mostly moving it around the plate with her fork.

"Is there anything we can do for you?" Marquetta asks.

"Not really." Amy pushes her plate away. "I don't think I'm hungry. I'm sorry. Everything was delicious, but I don't have much of an appetite."

How could she know it was delicious? She didn't hardly touch her food. "Were there any other witnesses? Is the main suspect another treasure thief?"

"Alex!" Marquetta snaps. "Amy's upset. She doesn't need you interrogating her." She turns to Amy. "I'm sorry. Alex gets carried away with criminal investigations."

Amy twirls her wine glass between her fingers, then takes a sip. "It's okay. I...I had a bad experience in LA. I came here to find some tranquility, so I think I'm just in shock over stumbling on a murder." She takes another sip of her wine. "I really don't know if the man they took into custody is a treasure thief or not. He seemed like he knew Rick."

"What was his name?" I ask.

Marquetta huffs, but she doesn't say anything, probably 'cause Amy answers right away.

"I didn't hear his name—no, wait, I did. It was an odd name. Kind of old-fashioned. Clive something-or-other?"

Me and Marquetta stare at Amy. Since I've already gotten a couple of dirty looks for my questions, I'm gonna wait and let Marquetta handle this. She's probably just as curious as I am.

"I've known Clive Crabbe since I was a little girl," Marquetta says. "He's always had a temper, but I can't believe he'd commit murder."

While Grandma Madeline is twirling some of her spaghetti on her fork, she looks up at Marquetta. "I remember him from when he was a little boy. Wasn't he the one who was always sweet on Mary Ellen Herbert?"

"That's him, Mom. They got married right out of high school. They had a baby a few years ago, then separated. They're now divorced and Mary Ellen has taken back her maiden name. There's talk that they might get back together, but one minute Mary Ellen's head-over-heels and the next she says Clive's still too possessive."

"Oh, my. The town has changed so much since I left. I must say, we never had crime like this before all this treasure business." Grandma Madeline stabs a tomato kinda like she thinks it did something bad.

"So is that what your dad does, Alex? Help the police investigate?" Amy picks up her fork and sticks it into a piece of celery.

I look at Marquetta. She makes a face like she's not happy. "Go ahead. I know you're dying to say it."

"He helps Chief Cunningham, but sometimes they need a little extra help to figure things out."

Amy smiles at me. "And that's where you come in?"

"Totally."

16

RICK

BY THE TIME RICK MADE it back to the scene of the murder, most of the bystanders had disappeared. A few, those willing to brave the cold wind gusting off the bay, stood in groups of two or three near the yellow tape. Deputy Jackman was nowhere to be seen. Her vehicle was also gone. Unfortunately, that left nobody to warn the looky-lous to stay behind the tape and away from the crime scene.

When he got closer, Rick recognized the worst of the offenders, a group of three who were guests at the B&B. John and Melody Gardner were staying until the weekend, and Phillip Gibson had come in yesterday and had booked a one-week stay for him and his wife. Judging by the way they were pushing against the tape, none of them appeared the least bit squeamish.

Rick approached the small group and said, "Mr. & Mrs. Gardner, Mr. Gibson, why don't we back up a little? We want to make sure the chief has plenty of room."

When the Gardners both gave Rick a blank look, he told them he also consulted with the police.

"Oh, sorry." Mrs. Gardner, an older, heavyset woman with a pear physique and a penchant for running suits, stumbled when she took a step backwards and landed on her husband's foot.

"Watch out!" Rick called as she tottered and jerked herself forward.

Her husband grabbed one elbow and Rick, the other. Between the two of them, they kept her upright.

"That was a close one, dear," Mr. Gardner said. He then looked at Rick and added, "Her balance isn't the best these days."

"No worries," Rick said as he released the woman's elbow and slipped under the tape. After doing another check on the Gardners, Rick turned to ask Mr. Gibson if his dinner at the Crooked Mast had met his expectations, but he'd already left. Rick wished the Gardners a good evening and continued over to where Adam was taking photos.

"You get Ms. Kama home safe and sound?" Adam asked.

"She's having dinner with Marquetta, Alex, and Madeline. There should be no shortage of talk going on in that kitchen for the foreseeable future."

Adam's eyebrows went up and he gave Rick a crooked smile. "The munchkin will definitely be in prosecutor mode."

"I would hope not, but you're probably right. Where's Deputy Jackman?"

"I had to send her home. She's diabetic and her blood sugar was crashing. She was white as a sheet and looked like she was going to pass out. The last thing I need is a deputy going into a diabetic coma while we're investigating a murder."

"What did she do with Clive?"

"Stashed him in the back of my vehicle. The Coroner showed up and took the body. I don't know how busy they are, so who knows when we'll get the autopsy report. As soon as the forensic team shows up, I'll be done here. While I'm finishing up I'd like you to go to the Crooked Mast and tell Mary Ellen her ex has been taken into custody."

"Sure, no problem. So you're going to press charges against Clive?"

"Right now, I just want to keep him out of the way. I have to decide whether we've got enough to hold him."

"Okay, I'll let Mary Ellen know." Rick started to leave, then stopped. "Uh, Adam, I don't have to go very far. She's at the end of the alley. I'll talk to her." He waved to Mary Ellen, who stood in the circle of illumination cast by a streetlight.

The closer Rick got, the more numb Mary Ellen looked. She stood on the opposite side of another strand of crime scene tape, her eyes glazed over, her hand over her mouth, and her normally bubbly personality distinctly absent.

"Mary Ellen, are you okay?"

Her hand went to her heart and she shuddered. "Maisy came back from break and said a man had been murdered here. She said they took Clive away in handcuffs. Is it true?"

"I'm afraid so. He's in the back of the chief's 4x4. Clive was seen near the body. The chief wants to question him before he decides what to do."

"Clive's not a murderer." She squeezed her eyes shut, then swiped at her cheek with her fingers. "Will he be arrested?"

"It's too soon to tell. Mary Ellen, you should be aware that this doesn't look good. Clive's clothes were covered in blood. When was the last time you saw him?"

"In the Crooked Mast. He'd had a couple of drinks and then one of the customers made a pass at me and Clive went crazy."

"Whoa...whoa..." Rick held up both hands to stop her. He'd expected an answer like 'last Tuesday' or something, but tonight? At dinner? "You're telling me he got into an altercation with one of the customers earlier tonight?"

"Yes. But he didn't do anything. Ken made them both leave."

With each question, Clive looked more guilty. Did Mary Ellen even realize what she was saying? For her sake and Clive's, he desperately wanted to believe her ex was just the victim of circumstance. "What time was this?"

"It was at the beginning of my shift, so a couple of hours ago." She quickly added, "I know what it sounds like, Rick, but Clive's not a killer. He wouldn't do that. He's changed."

"So I've heard," Rick said, already regretting the next question he knew he had to ask. "Does Clive own a knife?"

"Is that how the man died?"

"Yes. Does he?"

"He usually leaves it on the boat."

"Did he have it with him when you saw him at dinner?"

Mary Ellen's expression hardened. "I don't know."

"Is there anything else you can tell me?"

"Clive wouldn't do this."

Right. Clive wasn't a killer. He got it. And yet, they had a witness who'd seen him kneeling over the body and his shirt was covered in blood. It would look even worse for Clive if the victim was the same man he'd argued with just a couple of hours ago. There was one way to find out. He pulled out his phone and showed Mary Ellen the photo Alex had taken earlier.

"Was this the man Clive confronted?"

Mary Ellen's hand went to her neck and she croaked, "Yes."

"We'll get to the bottom of it." Rick tried to make it sound reassuring, but even though he didn't want it to, it sounded more like an accusation than anything else.

"Clive wouldn't commit murder! We have a four-year-old son. He wouldn't...do that...oh, God." Tears welled in Mary Ellen's eyes, and the numbness Rick had seen earlier was replaced by grief. She buried her face in her hands. Between sobs, she choked out, "That stupid, stupid man. Just when I thought we had another chance."

"Are you saying you two were getting back together?"

"There are times when he infuriates me to no end, but...I love him. I always have. And I always will. I don't think the man will ever change though, so I might as well reconcile myself to that and move on."

Mary Ellen wiped away the tears streaming down her cheeks with her fingertips. Her shoulders trembled, and Rick pulled her into his arms. He couldn't fault her concern one bit, especially if she was still in love with Clive. If he stood trial and was found guilty, he might never get out of prison. At least, not alive.

"I think you should take the rest of the night off. I can tell Ken what's happened and..."

"No. I need to work. My babysitter is already paid for and we barely get by as it is. If I don't work, I won't get paid. I will not let my son starve because his father..."

"We don't know that he did it," Rick said, but the words sounded hollow.

"I'll pray tonight that he didn't, but right now I've spent enough time worrying about that man and his temper. God knows I wanted to wash my hands of him before. Maybe this is what it will take to make it happen."

Rick watched Mary Ellen make her way back to the Crooked Mast. When she'd entered the restaurant through the back door, he returned to the other end of the alley. Adam was gone, and in his place there was a sheriff's forensic team. Rick texted Adam and got an immediate reply that Clive was not willing to speak unless he had a lawyer present and there wasn't much more they could do tonight.

Tomorrow, they would need to start tracking down witnesses. On his way back to the B&B, Rick made a mental note to speak with the Gardners, Mr. Gibson, and Amy Kama. When he closed the front door behind him, he saw there were lights on in the living room, and went to see if anyone was still there. Amy sat sideways on the couch near the fire. It was the same place she'd been in earlier in the day.

"Looks like you've found a favorite spot," Rick said with a smile.

"I don't think I can sleep. Marquetta and Alex and Madeline were so nice to me at dinner. I want to thank you all for taking such good care of me."

"I'm sure they were happy to have the company. Do you mind if I sit for a moment?" Rick gestured at the other end of the couch.

"Not at all. You probably have questions."

"I do."

She tucked her feet under her and sat a little straighter. "Like father, like daughter."

Rick cringed at the statement. "I hope Alex wasn't too much of a pest."

"It was no problem. She's precocious, but endearing."

Rick sat at the far end of the couch and planted his elbows on his knees. "Thank you. I do wish she'd keep her nose out of police business, but I can't seem to stop her. You said you didn't think you could sleep—is there something wrong with your room?"

"No. The room is quite comfortable. Ever since the incident in LA, I've had trouble sleeping. Seeing that man die tonight brought it all back. Whenever I close my eyes, I see it happen all over again."

Up until now, Rick hadn't noticed how drawn her face was. She had dark circles under her eyes and her pale complexion made her look anemic. "I'm sorry. I wish there was something we could do."

"It's okay, Rick. Really. I was much like Alex when I was young. Full of enthusiasm and curiosity."

"That would be her. Do you mind if I ask you a few more questions about what you saw?"

"Not at all. It's your job, right?"

He resisted the urge to tell her it was one he didn't get paid for. "Yes. From what I understand, Clive was hunched over the body when you first arrived?"

She shuddered, then stared vacantly across the room as though she were trying to remember the details. "He was kneeling next to it. But, truthfully? He could have been trying to help the victim."

"What do you mean?"

"He was on his hands and knees and very close. His shirt was covered in blood, and he looked kind of...dazed." She paused, pinched her lips together, and thought for a moment. "If he'd have been the killer, I would have expected him to run."

"Unless he realized what he'd done and decided to help."

"Possible, but why bother? The man was obviously dead. He'd lost a lot of blood."

Rick frowned, thinking back to the crime scene and the one critical piece of evidence he hadn't seen lying around. "Did you see a knife?"

"There was one on the ground next to the victim."

Good. That meant Adam must have taken it in as evidence. "I spoke to his wife afterwards, and she told me Clive owns a knife, but she didn't know if he had it with him. Maybe forensics will help clear this up."

Amy hugged her knees closer to her chest, then let out a heavy sigh. "It should."

"One last question. Did you see a mesh bag near the victim?"

She shook her head and frowned as she peered at Rick. "A mesh bag? You mean like one of those grocery bags?"

"More like a dive bag."

"No. Nothing like that. It was just the two men. Does this have something to do with the treasure Alex was talking about?"

"It could." In which case, the murder might have nothing to do with the confrontation Mary Ellen had witnessed.

"So the man I saw wasn't the killer?"

"Maybe. Or maybe this case is a lot more complex than it looks."

17

RICK

RICK TURNED AND CRANED HIS neck to see who was coming at the sound of approaching footsteps. He smiled when he saw it was Marquetta, and that she was carrying two glasses of wine. "Is one of those for me?"

Marquetta winked, then slanted her eyes to the opposite end of the couch. "This one's for Amy." She held out the glass. "Here you go. So you'd like a glass, too, Mr. Atwood? I'm surprised you're not still on duty."

"I think I'm off for the night," Rick said as he stretched his neck from side-to-side.

"Thank you, so much." Amy eased herself forward on the couch. "I'll let you two catch up. I can take this up to my room... if that's okay?"

"If you want," Marquetta said. "Or, Rick and I can go into the kitchen and you can just hang out here. That way you can enjoy the fire. And if you want company, come see us. You know where it's at."

Rick followed Marquetta, glad they'd have a few minutes to talk. He had so much to tell her. They pushed through the butler door and sat at the island, where Marquetta had left an empty glass next to the opened bottle.

"How'd it go?" Marquetta asked as she picked up the bottle and poured.

"Clive Crabbe may have killed our treasure thief."

"Seriously? Are you sure?"

"No, I'm not. In fact, that's what I wanted to talk to you about. I'm so happy you're still here."

"Amy was pretty upset. I think we got her feeling better. Mom went home a little while ago and that's when I sent Alex upstairs. Once we were alone, Amy said she'd like to sit by the fire for awhile, so I offered to get her another glass of wine. If you want, we can talk while I heat up some spaghetti for you."

Rick looked over his shoulder at the butler door. Out in their living room, a young woman who'd suffered her own recent tragedy was trying to sort out her life, and this murder had made things worse, not better. However, with a simple gesture of kindness, Marquetta had helped dull some of the pain. "You always know how to make people feel better, don't you?"

Marquetta laughed as she pulled two containers from the refrigerator. "Right now I know you need some dinner."

Her hair was pulled back and tied with a red scrunchie, and the way her lips curled up took Rick's breath away. She moved with such grace and fluidity in this little domain of hers. His heartbeat quickened. Why couldn't he just marry her right here and now? Why was he waiting?

Marquetta's smile fell as she spooned sauce onto the pasta. "I don't always know what to do, Rick."

"Is this about the wedding?"

She avoided looking at him as she loosely covered the bowl and placed it in the microwave. When she hit the start button, she turned, looked into his eyes, and bit her lip. "It's easier for me with other people. I've never been good about putting myself first."

Rick let out a short laugh, then rubbed the back of his neck.

Marquetta's brow furrowed and she crossed her arms over her chest. "What's so funny?"

He chuckled. "Me." He stood, went to stand before her, and took her hands. "I'm the one who's been an idiot. Don't you see? All this time, I've been making excuses and you've been trying to put my fears first. Maybe it was talking to Mary Ellen and seeing how much she still loves Clive, or maybe it was the way death has intruded once again on our lives, but I don't want to wait anymore." He pressed his finger to her lips and held her gaze. "If you're ready, I'd like to set a date for the wedding."

Tears brimmed in Marquetta's eyes. She swallowed a couple of times, and Rick feared she was having more second thoughts—maybe even enough to further delay things. "What about the B&B? And the business? The mayor's demands on your time? Now, this murder. There's so many things pulling you every which way."

"Tonight has made me realize that the problem wasn't time, the problem was my own fear. I was having trouble bringing myself to do what I wanted to do. And to paraphrase Rhett Butler, frankly, my dear, I don't give a rip about all those things. I care about you. Us."

"Yes," she whispered. "A thousand times, yes."

Rick leaned into her, wrapped his hand at the small of her back, and pulled her close. When the microwave beeped and they pulled apart, Marquetta's cheeks brightened.

"Well, Mr. Atwood, that was quite inappropriate."

He gave her a lopsided smile. "I hope so. Now, Ms. Weiss, when would you like to get married? Tomorrow? The next day?"

Marquetta cleared her throat and lengthened her spine. "Don't you realize a girl needs time to properly prepare for her wedding? I'll need a month," she said primly.

Rick groaned at the thought of waiting so long. "Not sooner?" The problem was that he knew the answer. With Giselle, it had taken more than a year to make all the preparations. The dress, the venue, the florist—those had been just the beginning. Between the appointments, commitments, and Giselle's constantly changing demands, it had been a year of what he considered extreme duress.

"If you'd like, I could take much longer. Say, six months...a year?"

"No. I can't wait that long. One month it is. Now, where are we going to get a venue on such short notice?"

Marquetta wrinkled her nose. "I know a guy. His name is Richard Atwood. He's a nice man once you get to know him. I'm sure that if I asked nicely he would let me use his gazebo for a very reasonable price."

Rick darted a glance out the French doors to the backyard gazebo. The lights were still on, and Rick could see it clearly. The downlighting bathed the structure and the surrounding gardens with an ethereal glow. Even in the daylight, it was one of the most beautiful spots on the grounds.

"I never thought of that," he whispered. "What a great idea."

"Actually, I can't take credit. It was Alex who came up with it. Mom wasn't thrilled, but the minute Alex said it, I realized it would be perfect."

"We do have a bit of a problem. We'll have to find a way to deal with all the guests. We're booked solid for months."

"Why don't we just invite them? There's plenty of room, and those who don't want to attend a wedding don't have to. We should have no problem lining up temporary help for the day. Mom's been busy making inquiries."

"Even though we hadn't set a date?"

"She thought it might remove some of the stress. And Alex, well, you know what an organizer she is. The B&B will probably run smoother that day than any other."

Marquetta laughed and it reminded Rick of tinkling bells. It was a sound he wanted to hear for the rest of his life. But as quickly as the emotional high washed in, it rushed out like the receding tide. His shoulders slumped and his stomach tightened.

"What's wrong? You don't like the idea?"

"When you laughed, I thought about how deeply in love I am with you, and that reminded me about Clive and Mary Ellen. Do you suppose they were like that once?"

"I'm not sure those feelings have changed. Theirs was a very hot romance, but their problem was always Clive's jealousy. He simply can't control himself."

"I will never do that to you," Rick said adamantly.

"Nor will I to you. At least, that's what we say tonight. But maybe after a few years, things will change."

"Things always change. It's just a matter of how we deal with it." Rick raised his glass and took a deep breath. Some of the weight he'd been feeling on his shoulders had lightened. He wanted to deal with this murder case and get on with his life. "Here's to us being strong enough to deal with change."

"Together." Marquetta clinked her glass against Rick's. Excitement tinged her voice as she continued, "I can't believe it. We're actually getting married." Suddenly, she stopped and her eyes opened wide. "Oh no! Your dinner!"

She turned to the microwave, but Rick grabbed her waist and pulled her close for one more kiss. "Now, woman, I'm ready to eat."

"Watch it, boss. You're treading on thin ice."

By the time Rick had finished eating, they'd checked the calendar, confirmed that, indeed, the B&B was booked solid on the day in question, but resolved to go forward.

"I guess I'd better let Alex know," Rick said as they were rinsing off the dishes and loading them in the dishwasher.

"If I'm not mistaken, this will make her evening," Marquetta said.

"I think I'll lead with, Alex, in a month you're going to have a new mother. If she wasn't already keyed up over the murder, I'm sure this will keep her awake half the night." Rick paused in the middle of drying the microwave container. "Speaking of Alex, there's something else we need to figure out. How to keep her from interfering in the investigation."

"Rick, you know that won't happen." Marquetta grimaced. "Besides, she's actually been a big help in the past."

Rick ran his fingers through his hair, then rubbed the back of his neck. "I can't believe you would actually condone Alex participating in a police investigation."

"I'm not, but I am trying to be practical."

"Then what exactly are you saying?"

"I think we need to give her something to do. Some minor aspect of the investigation that will occupy her mind and time and make her feel like she's contributing. You and Adam can do all the field work, but I can work with Alex to…do something."

While Rick hated the thought that his daughter would be involved at all, he knew Marquetta was correct. If Alex wasn't given a role, she'd make up her own. And that would be the worst possible scenario.

18

ALEX

Hey Journal,

Marquetta said I was asking Amy too many questions and
sent me up to my room. She said I was making a pest of myself.
For real? Amy said it wasn't so bad, but now I wonder if she
really meant it. With her being a cop and all down in LA, I
thought maybe she wouldn't mind, but I guess after shooting
that guy, she's still super upset. Anyway, I wanted to check on
some things so I didn't mind coming up here. It totally worked
out and I found exactly what I was looking for.

Adela said she thought there were gonna be skeletons on
the San Mañuel. But I remember that Flynn told me once
skeletons wouldn't survive in the ocean for more than a
hundred years or so on a wreck like the San Mañuel. My dad
always had to have two sources for a story, so I found a
website that had a video showing a pig body in the ocean. I can
tell you one thing, Journal, I totally don't want to die there!
Between the water and all the creatures who wanna feed on
you? Ewww. Flynn was right. Dying in the ocean is a totally
nasty way to go.

I also found Adela's Facebook page. Her bio said she was
going to USC, but it didn't list a major. The big thing is she's
like a real party girl. Her posts were all about parties and

fashion. She didn't post anything at all about what she's doing in school. I wonder if she's even still taking classes? I totally want to do some more checking, but I'm not sure how to do it.

Uh oh...my dad just knocked.

Gotta go!

Alex

"It's open!"

Daddy opens the door a crack and pokes his head in. "Hey, kiddo. It's after nine, why aren't you in bed already?"

"I lost track of time." I put my journal into the desk drawer and scoot over to the bed.

Daddy does his usual thing and comes over to sit next to me. He kinda fusses with the covers, then looks at me. "How was your night?"

"Okay. Amy told us all about the dead body she found. You're helping Chief Cunningham?"

Daddy messes with the covers again. "You don't waste any time, do you? Yes, I'm consulting with Seaside Cove's finest again. I've also confirmed it was your treasure thief who got himself killed."

"Did you find what he stole?"

"No. Alex, I'm concerned about this obsession you have with crime."

I ignore his comment 'cause I totally know where that's gonna go. Instead of waiting for him to start in, I sit up straighter and look at him. "Was it really Mr. Crabbe who did it?"

He gets that funny smile on his face he sometimes gets when he's not surprised about something and sighs. "It's too soon to tell, but I'm sure you know that."

"Do you have any other suspects?"

"Alex, I don't want to talk about this case."

His voice is real stern and that's a total bummer 'cause I know he's not gonna change his mind when he sounds like this. It might even mean he wants to ground me for going to Adela's room after he told me to stay away. Or maybe he's just gonna do like a preventative grounding. That would really suck.

"And no, I'm not going to reprimand you for going to see Adela after I said I wanted you to keep your distance."

"You're not?" That's awesome. I can't believe my luck.

"Actually, I'm here to tell you that Marquetta and I have set a wedding date."

"What?" My jaw drops. Is he like kidding me? I swallow hard and my eyes feel kinda watery. "For real?"

"Yes, kiddo, for real."

I throw both arms around his neck and hug him. This is the best news ever! When I pull away, it totally hits me. Marquetta's gonna be my mom. "I have to tell Sasha and Robbie and…"

"Hold on. It's too late for you to be contacting all your friends tonight. There will be plenty of time for that tomorrow."

"When's the wedding?"

"It's going to be May 17. It's the middle of the week, mostly because the logistics are easier."

"Awesome. We only have a month, Daddy. We have to start planning tomorrow."

"You have school tomorrow. And I do not want to get a call from Miss Redmond telling me you skipped class to do something else."

"No way. I love school. And Miss Redmond's awesome." I suck in a breath. "Oh, I totally have to tell her, too!"

"Okay, okay. I want you to go to sleep now. It's probably going to take you a while, so I'll stay here if you want me to. I could read to you."

I roll my eyes. "Daddy, I'm not four."

"Sorry, I sometimes wish you were. In some ways, life was easier then."

Oh, he is so wrong. No way was anything easier then. Daddy might not have had as much going on, but my real mom was always chasing a new part on Broadway or 'meeting with a producer.' Me and Daddy both knew what that meant. Things were so not easier then. But now, with Marquetta becoming my mom—I feel all warm inside. Things are gonna be awesome now. "You don't need to stay, Daddy. I'll get to sleep."

For the next couple minutes, he just sits on the edge of the bed looking at me. He strokes my hair a few times, then leans over and kisses me goodnight. I think he's sad 'cause he doesn't want me to grow up. I totally get that. It's fun being a kid, but there are so many more things I'll be able to do when I'm an adult.

I roll over on my side and think about the wedding. And maybe after that, I'll finally get my baby brother. I can teach him all my investigation tricks—and how to get out of trouble. We're gonna make an awesome team. I can dream about that tonight, right after I tell my journal the awesome news! I crawl out of bed, flick on my phone's flashlight, and grab my journal out of the drawer.

Hey Journal, me again. I've got so much to tell you...

19

RICK

IT WAS TIME FOR THE daily countdown, the final few minutes before Rick and Alex would take orders for breakfast. In addition to a choice between eggs with potatoes or oatmeal, Marquetta had a batch of individual quiches in the oven. Rick stood next to Alex just inside the butler door. Since the day they'd arrived at the B&B, this had become their morning ritual. It was one that had not gotten old yet.

"You're growing, kiddo. It won't be long before you'll be taller than Marquetta."

He caught Marquetta's gaze and winked. Alex nudged his hip and cut her eyes in Marquetta's direction.

"You could kiss her. The guests won't know." The corners of Alex's mouth curled up into an impish grin.

"Mind your own business, young lady." He took a another look at Marquetta, then turned his attention back to Alex. It felt like a weight had been removed from his shoulders. He'd noticed that, just like him, Marquetta was in an especially good mood. So was Alex. None of them had slept much, but that didn't seem to matter.

"You ready, kiddo?"

"Totally. I'll get my orders in, refill everybody's water, then get ready for school."

"Good girl. After the initial rush, Marquetta and I can handle it."

"What about Grandma Madeline? Isn't she gonna help today?"

"No, she's working at Howie's. So much for our part-time help. Guess I'll have to look for someone else."

"I could do more."

"No way. Not while you're in school. We'll figure it out. Let's go."

Rick pushed through the door with Alex right behind. He stopped when he came face to face with Marquetta's mother. She smiled at him, said good morning, then stood to one side.

"I'm sure Marquetta will be happy to see you, Madeline," Rick said.

"I hope so. I have news for her. Ta ta." Madeline turned and disappeared into the kitchen behind a swishing of the butler door.

Rick looked at Alex and pursed his lips. "I wonder what her news is."

Alex beamed at Rick, her eyes crinkling at the corners. "Yours was better!"

She darted away toward the dining room. They split the tables as they usually did. Alex took the far wall where early-morning sunshine beamed through the windows. This was one morning when the guests who had been lucky enough to score one of those tables could revel in the experience.

It was no surprise that Rick didn't see Amy Kama or Adela Barone. They both seemed to prefer coming near the end of the service. The dining room simply wasn't big enough to handle all of the guests at one time, so it worked out well that there were always a few who either didn't like feeling rushed by someone waiting for their table or slept in late. Phillip Gibson and his wife were seated at one of Alex's tables. This morning they'd snagged the table closest to the coffee and tea bar.

Everything moved smoothly until Alex got to the Gibsons. There, she seemed to get hung up. Rick wished he could tell if they were giving her a difficult time over today's special or if Alex might simply be lingering. Even when he'd finished taking his last order, Alex was still talking to them. Rick checked the time. Alex needed to finish up and get ready for school.

"Is there a problem here?" Rick asked as he approached.

"Nope. All good," Alex chirped and darted off toward the kitchen.

"We were just talking about last night's big event," Mr. Gibson said.

Rick peered at the man and said, "I don't understand."

"He's talking about the murder." Mrs. Gibson rolled her eyes. "My husband is a murder mystery buff, but he's never seen a real live dead body." She stopped, giggled, then added, "Somehow, I think that would be rather difficult, wouldn't it? Well, you know what I mean."

Her husband shot furtive glances around the room, then lowered his voice. "So you really are consulting with the police? That's exciting."

"It's pretty mundane, Mr. Gibson. I'm sorry, but I need to get my last couple of orders in. I just wanted to check on Alex. I'll be happy to talk to you later." As long as he was the one asking the questions, Rick thought as he left the dining room.

Alex burst through the butler door when Rick was a few feet away. "Beep, beep," she chirped as she rushed by him with a cart loaded down with fresh carafes of coffee, hot water, and orange juice. When she had a clear shot to the dining room, she looked over her shoulder and waggled her eyebrows, then motioned toward the kitchen with a quick bob of her head.

Rick sighed and pushed through the butler door. Marquetta set four plates on a tray along with two of Rick's first tickets. "Great," he said as he started to pick up the tray. Then, he returned it to the island, stepped over behind her and planted his hand in the small of her back. When she turned to look at him, he kissed her, then backed away.

"Inappropriate work behavior, boss." Marquetta winked at him and turned back to the stove. "Next order in about three minutes."

"What happened to your mother? I saw her come in, but I didn't see her leave."

"She wasn't very happy with me, so she left. Most likely she was hoping to grab another loaf of bread. Last night, she never did tell me what she was doing with it, so I hid the two loaves we picked up yesterday afternoon."

Rick snickered. "Brilliant. Simply brilliant."

He went back to the island, picked up the loaded tray, and backed out the butler door, still chuckling about the big bread mystery. He delivered the plates, saw that Alex had left, and took a deep breath. The early breakfast rush was the busiest part of the day, and with the exception of that minor slowdown with the Gibsons, they were off to a good start. For now, it was just a matter of keeping the ship on course.

By seven-thirty, the first round of guests had vacated the dining room and the second wave was trickling in. Whereas the first seating usually filled all six tables right from the start, the second consisted of a few stragglers and late risers. Rick took their orders, then headed back to the kitchen to catch up on dishes, refill beverage carafes, and restock the pastries.

The latest of the late risers today was Adela Barone. She straggled in at eight-twenty, gave the room a quick once-over, then settled at an empty table. Rick took her order, turned it in to Marquetta, then finished stacking the dishwasher. When he returned to Miss Barone's table with her breakfast, she gave him a perfunctory smile and asked if Alex was working.

"No, she has school today. During the school year, she helps us get started, then has to leave. I think you know where the coffee and tea are if you need a refill. I hope you have a great day."

After a dramatic huff and flipping of her hair, she said, "That Flynn O'Connor wasn't very nice to me, you know."

"I'm sorry you feel that way, Miss Barone. I didn't see Flynn afterwards, so I have no idea what you two discussed. However, you were making some serious accusations about her."

The comment earned Rick a dirty look, then another dramatic huff followed by a grimace. "Whatever."

Rick excused himself and returned to the kitchen. Marquetta was washing dishes, so he grabbed a towel and pitched in.

"So why wasn't Madeline happy with you?"

"To be honest, I wasn't very happy with her either." Marquetta rested her hands on the counter, then turned sideways to face Rick. "It's Wednesday. Today she's working for Howie Dockham in his shop. She'll be there all day."

"That's good, right? It'll give her something to do."

"Wednesdays, Rick."

"Oh." Rick's heart sank. There went the planned wedding date. "I don't suppose she's willing to make a change."

"I have no idea. Today is her first official day. She burst in here, all filled with excitement and couldn't stop talking about it. I was trying to tell her we'd set a date when she saw there was no bread. She said something and I told her we were out. She got in a huff and walked out."

If it were anybody else, Rick would have told them to work around the wedding date—but the mother of the bride? "I guess we'll have to figure something out tonight."

"We'll have to. How are things in the dining room?"

"Miss Barone has quite the chip on her shoulder this morning."

Marquetta set a washed and rinsed pot on the drying mat. "Why's that?"

"Last night's conversation with Flynn. I'll tell you all about it when we get a break. How's it going in here?"

"It's all under control. Tell me about Miss Barone."

Rick explained the brief discussion and was about to suggest they sit down for breakfast when the butler door opened. Adela Barone stood inside the door, her arms crossed in front of her, a scowl on her face.

"I felt ambushed," she said indignantly.

"I'm sorry you feel that way, Miss Barone. I can come to your table if you'd like to discuss this further, but guests aren't allowed in the kitchen."

"So some guests have special privileges. The ones you like?"

Rick accepted the attitude she was giving him with a grain of salt. The young woman had already caused enough grief in this house. He was not about to let her dish out more. Besides, what had she been doing? Stewing on this all night long? "Miss Barone..."

"You let that other woman in here last night. Why did she get to come in and nobody else can?"

Rick's irritation surged. He'd just about had enough of Adela Barone's childish behavior.

"Miss Barone," Marquetta said. "If you're talking about Amy Kama, she witnessed a murder last night. I think that warrants special treatment."

The young woman's jaw dropped open and she gaped at both Rick and Marquetta. "A...a murder?"

"That's right. A man was stabbed to death in an alley downtown." Tempted as he was to tell her he didn't think much of her attitude, Rick couldn't bring himself to do it. The longer she braced herself against the wall and gaped off into space, the more the color drained from her cheeks.

"It must have been awful," she croaked.

"I'm sure it was. Ms. Kama was the first to come across the scene."

Marquetta slipped by Rick and rested a hand on the girl's shoulder. "You poor thing. You look like you've seen a ghost. Come with me." Marquetta looked over her shoulder at Rick as she guided their guest back into the dining room.

Rick wasn't sure if he should follow or not. He was just irritated enough with that haughty little girl to lose his temper if she started acting all high-and-mighty again. Perhaps it was best to let Marquetta deal with her. Right now, he needed to check in with Adam. He dialed, the phone rang twice, then Adam answered.

"Do you still want to talk with Clive this morning?" Rick asked.

Adam paused. "I'd love to, but after his lawyer put the fear of God in him, I don't think Clive will be saying anything to anyone who's wearing a badge."

It was easy to hear the frustration bubbling over Adam's normally calm demeanor. This was not an emotion Rick saw very often in his friend. And while Adam, in his role as Chief of Police, probably didn't feel comfortable saying it, Rick had known him long enough that the message was clear—see if Clive will talk to you.

20

ALEX

Hey Journal,

I have to get ready for school, so I only have a few minutes. At breakfast I got the table for Mr. and Mrs. Gibson. He said he ate too much at dinner. Mrs. Gibson said he does that all the time. It kinda shows 'cause he's got a big belly. Anyway, he was out walking about the time of the murder.

He said that while he was on Front Street he saw a suspicious looking man come out of the alley and run across the street to the Rusty Nail. The man started looking through the bushes in the planter out front, but stopped and rushed away when he saw Mr. Crabbe. Mr. Gibson thought maybe they were gonna get into a fight or something 'cause the first man took off and Mr. Crabbe followed him. That's when Mr. Gibson got curious and went to check what was in the bushes. He told me he found a bag like the one I saw the treasure thief hiding at Dead Man's Cove. He said he didn't take it, but I kinda wonder if maybe he was lying. When I asked him to draw me a map, he got super hesitant. At least Mrs. Gibson was on my side, so he finally caved and drew out a map on a paper napkin.

I totally want to go check this before school, but there's not enough time. When we get recess, I'm gonna have Sasha go

*with me and we'll check it out. I figure I'm gonna need a
witness just in case there really is treasure in the bag. I don't
wanna tell my dad 'cause he'll do it himself and leave me out.
You know what, Journal? Sometimes it sucks being a kid.*

Xoxo

Alex

I finish brushing my teeth and get my hair combed out. I've
got a purple scrunchie that will be perfect for today. Once I've
got my hair fixed, I start working on my backpack. I add a
couple books, my laptop, and my lunch bag.

The map Mr. Gibson made for me is in my pocket. I pull it
out and look at it. This is awesome! I have my own real treasure
map! I just have to get to the treasure before anybody else does.
Maybe I should hide the map in my backpack? Just to be safe.
But I can't always see my backpack, so I'm gonna keep the map
right where I had it.

I only have a couple minutes before I have to leave for
school, but I can't resist taking one last look at the map. I know
exactly where that spot is. Me and Sasha. We're gonna rock this
treasure hunt. I can't wait until I can tell my dad we found the
missing treasure!

21

RICK

LOOKING OUT THE BANK OF windows over the kitchen sink, Rick surveyed the B&B's backyard. To his right was the gazebo, the place where he and Marquetta would be married next month, assuming there were no more surprises. To the left of the gazebo stood the Three Maidens Fountain. At six-foot high and equally wide, its water burbled constantly and garnered enthusiastic comments from the guests. Like the gazebo, it was a favorite spot for photos.

After a mild winter, the roses and hyacinth were already in bloom, signaling the start of spring. In a couple of weeks, the scent of lavender would fill the air. Rick took a deep, satisfied breath, and said another mental thank you to his grandfather for leaving him the B&B.

"Hey, you look deep in thought," Marquetta said softly.

Rick turned, pulled her into his arms, and held her close. "Just thanking Captain Jack for making me his sole heir."

"Me, too." Marquetta slipped out of his arms and picked up her mug. "I got Miss Barone settled down. It could be she's starting to realize she doesn't know as much about the world as she thinks she does."

"Maybe. But I still want to keep her away from Alex. If she keeps her distance, we'll get along just fine."

"Between the two of us, we should be able to keep them apart. The trick is going to be keeping Alex occupied. Besides, Miss Barone won't be here that much longer."

Rick took a deep breath and glanced toward the butler door. "Let's hope she doesn't burst in here again. Okay, sounds like a solid plan, now all we have to do is pull it off. Already I have a problem because Adam wants me to talk to Clive. He thinks he'll say things to me that he won't say otherwise."

"I'm worried about him, Rick. Without Mary Ellen there to steady him, there's nothing to keep him from doing something stupid."

"Like run?" Rick asked.

"No. Clive's too anchored in this community. We went to the same schools. He wouldn't run."

Rick watched Marquetta with raised eyebrows. His childhood friends were long gone, scattered all around the country, but Seaside Cove was a completely different world. "You went to the same school?"

"A few years apart, but we even had some of the same teachers. He's lived here all his life, Rick. His business is here. And so is his family."

"You said that you don't think he'd jeopardize losing his son."

"Would you risk losing Alex?"

"No. But in the heat of the moment, who's to say what he did?"

"I won't deny the possibility, but no matter what anyone else says, Clive Crabbe is devoted to that boy. He'd do anything for him."

"Even if he's facing murder charges?"

Marquetta shook her head. "Talk to him. You'll see what I mean."

"Okay. Let's assume you're right. Where would I find him?"

"When they first started having problems, Mary Ellen kicked him out of the house, and he moved into his boat—the *Mary Ellen.*"

Rick let out a little laugh, then said, "He named his boat after his ex-wife?"

"She wasn't his ex when he got the boat. Besides, I think it's romantic." Marquetta set down her mug and came to stand just inches away. She gave him an impish smile. "Would you name your boat after me if you had one?"

He grinned at her. "Yes. I'd call it *The Charming Vixen.*"

Marquetta's cheeks flushed bright pink. She smacked Rick on the shoulder and turned away. "You are being a brat, Mr. Atwood. Maybe I won't marry you after all."

Rick grabbed Marquetta's hand and pulled her back. "Oh, you'll marry me, all right. If you don't, I'll die a lonely, frustrated man who forever regrets letting the love of his life get away."

Marquetta looked at him out of the corner of her eye and bit her lower lip. She wrinkled her nose and said, "You really think I'm charming?"

"And gorgeous. And funny. And a million other things. Now, as much as I'd love to continue this conversation, I need to see if I can find Clive."

"Try the *Mary Ellen.* He should be there."

"I'll do that, right after we get all of our morning chores out of the way. I've got billings to work on and a couple of early checkouts to deal with."

It was almost nine by the time Rick made it to the Seaside Cove Harbor. The checkouts had taken longer than expected, he'd had a couple of questions from guests, and he'd wanted to answer the emails that had come in overnight. None of it was terribly complex, but the minutes dragged as he thought about Clive Crabbe and how time was slipping away.

On his way into the marina, Rick said good morning to Joe Gray, who was cleaning and polishing the wood on his houseboat. Although Rick dealt often with Joe about boat charters or tours for guests, this was one morning he would have preferred to avoid him altogether. Rick liked Joe well enough, but as his handyman had once said, Joe Gray could talk up a storm faster than a squall on the sea. At least this morning Joe seemed to sense Rick's impatience and after only a brief greeting, encouraged him to go about his business. It was business which, most probably, Joe already knew about.

A year ago, Rick wouldn't have had a clue, but now he could estimate the length of the *Mary Ellen* at about forty feet. Clive was not on either of the upper decks, so Rick climbed aboard. He opened the lower deck door and called out.

A gruff, 'just a minute,' came from below. When Clive appeared, his brown eyes watched Rick suspiciously as he wiped his hands on his overalls. His sparse and scraggly beard did little for him other than make his face look dirty. "What are you doing here?"

"I'd like to talk, if you don't mind."

Clive stroked his chin as though he were considering it, then said, "If it's about last night, my lawyer told me to say nothing without him present."

"The Chief didn't send me, Clive." Maybe that was a partial lie, Rick thought, but Adam hadn't actually asked him to come here. "Let's just say I have a personal interest in this. Alex was out at Dead Man's Cove without my permission and saw a man hiding something. Based on the photo she took, we've confirmed the victim is the same man Alex saw. Did this guy have any kind of package or bag with him when you found him?"

"Guess there's no harm in answering that kind of question. No. I didn't see any packages or bags."

The *Mary Ellen* rolled ever so slightly. While Clive seemed to rock naturally with the boat, the motion threw Rick slightly off balance both mentally and physically. If Clive hadn't seen the treasure, that opened a new can of worms. Did someone else take it? Was it stashed somewhere in town?

"Huh," Rick said. "So you never saw him with a bag of any sort?"

Clive shook his head firmly. "Nope. Not when I saw him."

"Which time, Clive? At the Rusty Nail?"

"Right. He was looking in those bushes out front, but he took off like a shot when he saw me coming. What's the big deal about this...package? Did he steal it from the *San Mañuel*?"

"We think so, but it just seems to have disappeared. I suppose he could have tried to sell it, but the only place in town he could do that would be Howie's Collectibles."

"Howie's straight as they come. He'd report something like that in a heartbeat."

Rick suspected what Clive said was true, but there was no harm in following up with Howie or in trying to find other witnesses who might have seen something. "I saw Mary Ellen last night after Deputy Jackman put you in the car. She was pretty upset."

Clive ran a hand roughened by days spent at hard physical labor through his hair. He slumped against the wall of the doorway. "This is awful. I feel terrible about what this is gonna do to her and Lenny. Just when we were gonna get back together, too."

So they had been talking about reconciling. "Is that what she told you?"

"Yeah, yeah. Mary Ellen's always been my rock. I was always the one screwing up, but we'd been talking it over and I told her how I changed and she was gonna take me back."

Rick suppressed a smile. Mary Ellen hardly seemed to be a rock. The lives of these two had more drama than a soap opera. "She told me she didn't believe you could have committed murder."

"I didn't!" Clive blurted. He muttered something under his breath, then added, "Stupid lawyers."

"Excuse me?" Rick asked.

"My lawyer. Telling me I shouldn't talk to the chief. I didn't do nothing. I'm telling you, I caught up to the guy in the alley. I was walking toward him when someone hit me from behind. Next thing I know, I wake up with a dead guy underneath me and a woman screaming that I'm a murderer. Then the cops showed up and hauled me off in handcuffs."

"So when you caught up to the victim, what were you going to do?"

"I just wanted to talk to him. That's all."

"Come on, Clive. I already know what happened at the Crooked Mast. You've admitted you were following him. Do you really expect me to believe all you wanted to do was talk?"

Clive looked away from Rick, then sighed. "I guess not. The truth is I wanted to beat the crap out of him. He was hitting on Mary Ellen in the restaurant and she didn't want the attention."

"She didn't. Or, you didn't?"

Clive glared at Rick, but didn't respond.

"Let's talk about what happened at the Crooked Mast for a minute. Things got pretty heated. Right?"

"Yeah. I kinda lost my temper."

"So what happened after Ken threw you out? Were you on the street at the same time? Did you argue again?"

"Ken made the guy pay his bill, then he told him he wasn't welcome. He made me wait a few minutes."

"In my experience, when tempers get that hot, it takes a while to cool down. What did you do after the Crooked Mast?"

Clive ran his fingertips up and down the side of his neck. "This isn't gonna sound good."

Rather than saying anything, Rick waited while Clive stood, his hands stuffed in his pockets, his eyes darting around the cabin like fireflies. With each passing minute, Clive appeared to grow more anxious. Finally, his resolve must have cracked.

"Okay, okay. I left some stuff out before. I was still so worked up I went looking for the guy. It's true, I saw him in front of the Rusty Nail. He must've seen me because he took off and I didn't catch up to him until the alley. It was already dark, but I saw him in the security lighting. He was coming my way. That's when I told him to leave Mary Ellen alone. He refused and it didn't look like he was gonna back down. I lost it and grabbed his shirt to shove him against the wall. We started swinging at each other, but we'd both been drinking so neither of us really did much damage to the other guy. All of a sudden, somebody hit me from behind."

"For someone who didn't do much damage, he left you with a pretty good black eye."

Clive fingered his right cheek and winced. "Yeah. Guess so."

In hopes that Clive would eventually say something to fill the gap, Rick again held his silence. Finally, his patience paid off.

"What else you want to know?" Clive demanded.

"The knife that was used? Was it yours?"

"I guess so. I forgot to take it off before I went into town."

"Do you always take it off?"

"Usually...sometimes, I forget."

How convenient. He just happened to forget the night a man was killed. "Clive, I have to tell you, this isn't looking good. Can you tell me anything to help me prove you're innocent?"

"Other than the fact that I didn't do it?"

"Yes. Other than that."

"There was someone there, Rick. I swear there was."

"I need details, Clive. How do you know someone was there?"

"This lump on the back of my head for one." Clive turned his head and pointed at a bandage.

"You sure you didn't get that from the fight?"

"I'm telling you, somebody hit me from behind!"

"Okay, okay. Any idea who this person might have been?"

"No, I never saw him."

"So it was a man? Think, Clive. If there was someone in that alley, they might not just be your alibi. They might be the killer."

Clive's shoulders slumped and he gazed sullenly at the floor. "I don't know for sure."

Talk about a lost cause. Rick remembered one of the old reporters at the newspaper and his description of guys like Clive —he called them a sad sack. Apparently, Clive was going to be useless in his own defense. The biggest problem was even more basic. Was Clive's story even believable? It seemed entirely possible he was just making up his mystery attacker to hide his own guilt.

22

RICK

THE WEATHERED BOARDS BENEATH RICK'S feet creaked as he walked toward the harbor exit. So many inconsistencies had come up in his conversation with Clive—his relationship with Mary Ellen, carrying a knife by mistake, and the murder victim not having a package on him. His inner reporter wanted to confirm all those statements—and he didn't really want Adam around when he started asking questions. This was a case where an extra body, especially when one was the Chief of Police, would make things more difficult.

After a right turn at the roundabout, Rick continued onto Azalea Street. Mary Ellen lived two doors down from Marquetta where Whale Avenue met Azalea Street. As he walked, Rick let himself absorb the atmosphere. Small, quaint Craftsman homes, most painted in bright colors ranging from yellows to blues and so many others. Each home said something about its owner.

When he passed Marquetta's house, he wondered who had selected the color scheme—a pale gray with dark and light blue trim. Had she chosen those colors? Or had that been something left over from when her parents lived here? With the exception of a window left cracked open in the kitchen, the house was completely closed up for the day, so Rick continued past without stopping.

Mary Ellen's home, which Marquetta said the couple had purchased shortly after they married, was in need of many things, especially paint. The base color, a once-bright yellow, had dulled and worn to the point where the wood might soon have to be replaced. The trim paint, which was a combination of white and blue, peeled and flaked in the areas exposed to direct sun.

As Rick climbed the stairs, he noticed other signs of a home in disrepair—a loose tread on one of the steps, torn window screens, a few plants that appeared dead or dying in the yard. If Mary Ellen did take Clive back, her first order of business should be to have him do some of the necessary maintenance. The screen door rattled mercilessly with each rap of Rick's knuckles.

Mary Ellen inched open the door and peered out through the crack. Her hair was in disarray, as if she'd just awoken. She blinked a few times and Rick realized that she'd probably worked late and not slept well.

"Oh, hi Rick. What time is it?"

"Sorry, I didn't mean to wake you. I forgot you'd probably worked late." He checked the time on his phone and winced. "It's nine-thirty. I'm so sorry."

"It's fine. Last night was a rough one. I hardly slept at all. After I got Lenny off to preschool, I came back and decided to nap for an hour or so. I have to work again tonight. What brings you here?"

"I talked to Clive this morning. He told me a few things that I wanted your perspective on."

"What kinds of things?"

"About the two of you and your future."

Mary Ellen rubbed her temples with the fingers of her left hand and grimaced. "Come on in."

She unlatched the door and stepped to one side.

"Would it be better to do this later?"

"No. I'd rather just deal with it." Mary Ellen's eyelids drifted shut for a second and she shook her head. "I'm already awake. Come on in."

"I'm so sorry I disturbed you."

"It's fine. Don't worry about it. What did Clive tell you?"

"He said you were reconciling. Is that true?"

Mary Ellen looked at the ceiling and blew out a slow breath. She gestured toward an old couch with a faded checkerboard design. "Have a seat."

As she sat on the far end of the couch, Mary Ellen reminded Rick of a pixie. He guessed she stood just over five-foot-two and was slightly built. In her younger days, she could easily have passed for a gymnast. This morning, though, she looked as tired and worn as the couch she sat on.

"My relationship with Clive has always been up-and-down."

"How so?"

"He'd..." She sighed and seemed to shrink into herself. "He never cheated on me, but he always had a mean streak."

Rick recalled how quickly the town gossips had figured out he and Marquetta were attracted to each other. Some, including Alex, had known they would be together long before he'd ever thought it possible.

"Mary Ellen, I'm not here to make you feel bad. I'm just trying to figure out if Clive was being honest with me."

"He was and he wasn't." She hugged her knees to her chest as she laughed. "How's that for a confusing answer?"

Rick smiled, then said, "Sounds complicated."

"Very. A few weeks ago we talked about getting back together. Then, sometime last week he started stalking me. He would sit outside in his car for hours. It just totally creeped me out."

"So you changed your mind?"

Her jaw tightened and she blurted, "Yes." After another grimace, she continued. "Last night when he showed up at the Crooked Mast, I told him I was done with him. I said I'd made a break and wasn't willing to chance it again. Maybe that was why he went crazy on that guy, you know? Who knows? What if I'm the cause of this murder?"

"You're not, Mary Ellen." Rick tried to sound confident, but the question had him wondering.

"If Clive really did kill that man, I can't have him in my life. Or my son's."

"I could certainly understand that. Look, whatever Clive did, he did of his own volition. Don't take responsibility for his actions. When we spoke last night, you said you didn't think he had done it. It sounds like you've changed your mind."

Mary Ellen turned around and grabbed a glass of water from an old end table. She cradled it between her hands and looked off into space. The room was sparsely decorated—a couple of photos on the wall, a TV, and two end tables with lamps. Though she kept the interior clean, there were also signs that she didn't have much money to spend. The area rug in front of the couch was worn and faded. The hardwood floors had dulled in spots and needed refinishing. All in all, it appeared to be the home of someone scraping by.

"Maybe I should go so you can get some rest," Rick said.

"No." Though she hadn't taken a drink from the glass, Mary Ellen returned it to the end table. "I was thinking about me and Clive. All the things we've been through. All the times he got jealous. How sweet he can be. One minute I think there's no way he's a murderer, then I think about his temper and, to be honest, if he's even the same man I married. I don't know what I believe about him right now."

"Can I ask you a couple of questions about the incident at the Crooked Mast?"

"I guess." Mary Ellen's eyes were glazed over, her tone, listless.

"Clive said the man in the restaurant was coming onto you. Is that true?"

"Yes. He saw my name tag and told me his mother's name was Mary Ellen. Then he told me his name was Tuck. The way he started the conversation...I don't know, it just sounded like a pickup line to me."

"Did Clive see this?"

"He was sitting at the bar. So, yeah, he could see what was happening, but there's no way he could have heard what we were saying."

"What happened then?"

"The man ordered. Every time I got near the table, he kept eyeing me. You know how some guys are. It's like he was watching my every move. The whole thing made my skin crawl."

"Was he drinking?"

"Oh yeah. It was happy hour, so he had a beer before dinner and another with his meal. He was getting a little more obnoxious with each one. He ordered a third before he even finished the second one. When I suggested he slow down, he stood and put his hand on my arm. That's when Clive came over."

Rick played the scene in his mind, picturing this mysterious Tuck standing next to Mary Ellen. He could see how a man with a jealous streak might feel a need to intervene. "So then they argued?"

"It started with them just getting in each other's faces, but it was obvious neither of them was going to back down. That's when Ken came over and told this guy Tuck he needed to leave. He made Clive go back to the bar and told him to be quiet."

"Did you see this Tuck leave?"

"Sure. He went out the front and turned left toward the marina."

Rick's pulse quickened. Maybe he'd found his witness. "Was he carrying anything? Maybe a bag or something?"

Mary Ellen's brows furrowed. "No. In fact, what's strange is he didn't even have a wallet."

"Are you sure?"

"Positive. When he paid for his meal, he pulled the cash from his front pocket. I didn't think about it at the time, but Clive never carried money that way—for sure not that kind of cash."

"How much money do you think he had?"

"It was kind of a thick wad. I have no idea how much there was, but he peeled off a few twenties for dinner and had plenty left. Isn't that kind of weird?"

Not if you'd just robbed the cash box at Ocean Surf, thought Rick. "You've been very helpful, Mary Ellen. I'll let you go back to your nap."

She gave Rick a grim smile as she stood, then walked him to the door, but paused when she placed her hand on the doorknob. "I've been so upset over this whole thing with Clive that I never thought to ask. How's Marquetta holding up?"

Rick stiffened at the implication. "To my knowledge, she's doing fine. Have you heard something?"

"Not really. Marquetta hardly ever talks about herself, so she hasn't said anything. It's just that with her mom being back in town...well, you know how it gets between mothers and daughters when there's a wedding coming up. Everything gets turned upside down."

"Everything's good." Rick did his best to hide his concern, but the truth was, things had been harder since Madeline had returned.

Mary Ellen looked down at the floor and winced. "Sorry, I shouldn't have said anything. I'm sure it'll be just fine."

Famous last words, Rick thought as he left.

23

RICK

RICK LEFT MARY ELLEN'S HOME, crossed the street, and turned onto Whale Avenue toward downtown. Magnolia trees line both sides of the street, adding an elegant and soothing ambience. He passed the office of his attorney, which was on the opposite side of the street, then turned left on Main. One block later, he entered the front entrance of the Seaside Cove Police Department.

As usual, the office was quiet. Adam sat behind his desk talking on the phone, but motioned for Rick to take the visitor chair in front of his desk.

"Yes, Madame Mayor. No, Madame Mayor, we won't let that happen." Adam rolled his eyes, looked across the desk at Rick, and said, "Good news, he just walked in. We'll get right on it. Bye." He hung up and let out a heavy sigh. "Thank God you showed up. I'm not sure how long she'd have gone on this time. She wants this murder wrapped up *tout de suite*."

Rick chuckled. "You know, it took me a week to break Alex of using that expression after she first heard the mayor say it. That might have been one of the longest weeks of my life."

Adam's somber expression softened and he muttered, "Kids. Someday."

"You'll be a great dad, Adam."

"I hope so. In fact, I hope I'm as good with my own as you are with Alex."

Rick sighed. "Sometimes I don't know. I wish I could give her more time. She's at such a critical age."

"They're always at a critical age, Rick. Well, let's solve this case so you can go spend time with Nancy Drew. At least we've finally got ourselves a name for our dead guy. The victim was Tuck Hall. He's got a record—a few burglaries and an assault. He never did any serious time."

"The name tracks with what Mary Ellen said. He told her his name was Tuck. I also talked to Clive before I came here."

"You've been busy. What did Clive say?"

"I couldn't get a firm reading on him. He claims that he and Mary Ellen are getting back together. He also swears he didn't kill this Tuck Hall, but he does admit the knife was his, and he says he followed him out of the Crooked Mast after their altercation. He also realizes he's not helping his own case."

"Boy, is that ever true."

"I'd also say those two have one of the most bizarre relationships I've ever seen."

Adam's eyebrows went up and he sat straighter. "How so?"

"After I spoke with Clive, there were a few things that didn't make sense, so I went to talk to Mary Ellen. She told me he'd been sitting outside of her house for almost a week. Last night when he showed up at the Crooked Mast, she'd had enough and told him she was done with him."

"So he was probably angry and wanting to beat the crap out of someone."

"His exact words," Rick said.

Adam planted his elbows on the desk and rested his chin on his hands. He took a long breath in, then let it out slowly.

"Clive's got himself in a big mess this time. Alcohol is definitely not that man's friend."

Rick frowned and waited for some sort of explanation. This sounded like a part of Seaside Cove's history Marquetta had never told him. "Care to elaborate?"

"It was the Fourth of July and I was a brand new deputy, so I was on duty during the festivities at the park. Clive and Mary Ellen were together then, and they were there showing off Lenny. One of the tourists in town had a little too much to drink and tried to get a little friendly with Mary Ellen. I didn't hear the comment, but it was something to the effect of she was looking hot for a new mom. Clive blew his top and punched the guy out. I had to haul him in and babysit him until he sobered up. I didn't know it at the time, but that wouldn't be the last time Clive's temper got the better of him."

"Mary Ellen said he's got a mean streak. Is that what she meant? Or do you think maybe he's taken his aggression out on her, too?"

"I doubt it. There are no signs he ever laid a hand on her. And I don't think Mary Ellen would stand for it if he did. But I do think Clive's not above taking on anyone who looks the wrong way at his wife." Adam shook his head. "Ex wife. So what are your instincts telling you?"

"If I were still on the crime beat in New York, I'd say we need facts, not just all these people telling us stuff."

"True, that. Witnesses are about as reliable as the weather forecast. I'm thinking we need to go back to the alley and figure out the logistics. That should at least get us started."

"It's two blocks away. What are we waiting for?"

They walked down Main Street, all the while weaving between sightseers and shoppers who simply weren't paying attention to where they were going. At Crusty Buns, Mary

O'Donnell had just delivered an order to one of the outdoor tables and was now answering questions from passersby. Across the street, Laurel was on the front porch of Hot Feet adding more shoes to the rack.

"If this keeps up, I'm going to need two new deputies," Adam said.

"You think the mayor will agree to that?"

"I doubt it. I can't even get her to sign off on one." Adam's voice drifted off.

While Adam gazed wistfully into The Bee's Knees, Rick admired Traci Peterson's huge display on the front porch. There were enough scented candles to fill the air with their fragrance.

"When are you two going to tie the knot?" Rick asked.

Adam broke into a stupid grin. "Six months, five days, and two hours."

Rick snorted and continued walking. "Congratulations. You've got it locked down to the hour. We're lucky to have even set a date. At least I hope we have."

"We'll both get there. Maybe our kids will be friends. The munchkin can babysit."

"I think she'd rather be out solving murders. I wouldn't be surprised if she opened her own private detective agency."

Adam laughed and slapped Rick on the back. "I can just see that one. We'll probably both be out of a job."

As soon as they turned into the alley, Rick noticed a woman standing with her back against the wall. She had her arms crossed in front of her. Tears dribbled down her cheeks.

"Ms. Kama? What are you doing here?" Rick asked.

At the mention of her name, Amy Kama did a double take and looked at Rick and Adam. "I don't really know." She scanned the alley, her face devoid of emotion. "I was walking along Main Street, just enjoying the morning when I saw the alley. Everything after that is a blur."

Rick was about to offer to take her back to the B&B when a man and woman approached. The woman was smartly dressed in a conservative top and slacks. The man wore jeans, a tee shirt, and carried a video camera that he hoisted to his shoulder when the woman told him where she wanted him to set up. Rick glanced at Adam, who cleared his throat loudly and approached.

"You're not doing anything here," Adam said. "I'm Chief Cunningham and we are in the middle of an investigation. There will be no filming for the time being."

The woman started to protest, but Adam hooked his thumb to his right. "I don't care who you are. I don't care what station you're from. You will not compromise my crime scene or my investigation by televising what might be sensitive information. You will also not question one of my witnesses or I will throw you in jail for obstruction of justice."

Undeterred, the woman asked, "Chief, do you think the murder might have something to do with the alleged theft of antiquities from the *San Mañuel*?"

"No comment and move it along. You're getting nothing until the time is right. Other than maybe spend a night in my jail."

The cameraman backed away and looked to the woman. Muttering something about small-town cops with big attitudes, she stormed away.

The woman who had been watching the interaction intently said, "Amy Kama, Chief. Thank you for the chivalry, but you know you can't really stop them. Right?"

"You know that, and I know that. But at least they're gone for now. Besides, I don't even have a real jail. Be on the lookout, Ms. Kama. There are plenty of others who'll be hounding you. I don't want them ruining your time in town. Now, why did you come back here?"

"I told you. I don't know. Maybe what I really needed was closure. Everything happened so fast last night." She rubbed her arms absently as she looked around. Suddenly, her expression grew more intense and she crossed the alley to the spot where the body had been.

Rick held up his index finger when Adam looked at him. He suspected his guest had crossed some sort of mental bridge between emotion and professional detachment.

Amy pointed to the sidewalk on Main Street and her voice took on a clinical tone. "I was about there when I looked in this direction and saw the victim. His head was against this wall and his arms splayed out to his sides. The man you arrested last night was kneeling over him right about here. When I first saw him, I thought he'd just committed the crime." She frowned and kneeled next to a dark spot on the alley asphalt.

"Did you think of something else?" Adam asked.

"The suspect did not have the knife in his hand, Chief." She took a few steps sideways and added, "It was right about here."

"That's where it was when I arrived on the scene," Adam said.

"Amy, could it be that he was trying to help the victim?" Rick asked.

"It's possible."

"And do you think you might have misinterpreted what you saw last night?"

"I'm not sure. Last night I let my emotions control me, but coming back here and seeing the scene in the daylight—those reporters—it reminded me we've all got a job to do. We can't really change who we are."

Rick briefly explained that Amy had been a court officer and described her involvement with the LA shooting, then asked if she'd seen anything else lying on the ground.

"Like what?"

"A bag or a box. Some sort of artifact."

"No. Nothing."

Adam paused his inspection of the spot where the body had been found and looked up. He motioned for someone behind Rick to move on.

Rick turned, saw Adela Barone watching from the street, and muttered, "What's she doing here?"

"She's been trying to cozy up to me today," Amy said with a shrug. "She's another one just chasing the story. Was there something in particular you expected the victim to have, Chief?"

"Some sort of a bag. It would have had an artifact—maybe more than one, inside."

"Alex saw the deceased hiding it on the beach," Rick said. "Adam and Deputy Jackman did a thorough check of the area."

"Right. We turned over every rock and found nothing."

"Then that means our victim must have grabbed his stash when he fled Dead Man's Cove," Rick said. "And since Mary Ellen told me he didn't have it with him when he was at dinner, he must have disposed of it somewhere between there and here. She also said he pulled a wad of cash from his pocket to pay the bill. He didn't use a wallet."

"That's consistent with what I found. Our victim didn't have a wallet, but he had a lot of cash in his front pocket."

"The murder wasn't a robbery," Amy mused as she looked up and down the alley. Suddenly she shivered and clutched her arms around her. "It comes in flashes. One second I'm fine, the next thing I know I'm seeing that poor man in LA bleeding out in front of me."

"If there's anything we can do at the B&B to help, please let me know. I'm sure this has been a terrible shock."

"Actually, the chance to dissect this murder kind of helps to distance me from all that. But maybe you're right. I'll let you two get to work. I probably shouldn't be here anyway."

When she was gone, Adam looked at Rick. "You know, if the mayor would let me fill my other deputy spot, I'd be tempted to hire her."

"I think she'd be a real asset to the town. Speaking of deputies, where's Jackman today?"

"Unfortunately, it's meter reading day. The town coffers will not abide a delay in getting those water bills out. Once Jackman finishes with the route, she'll have to turn the readings into the bookkeeper, who will probably harass her for an hour over her handwriting."

"You had the same problem, didn't you?"

"Yeah. I felt like I was back in fourth grade."

"Look on the bright side. Now that you're the chief, you'll never have to read a another water meter again."

"Unless the mayor keeps tightening the pursestrings. If this keeps up, I'll be a police department of one." Adam stood and stretched his neck from one side to the other. "We definitely need to check with Dennis to see if our victim is the one who robbed Ocean Surf's cash drawer. We can stop by and I'll show Dennis a photo."

Rick took ten paces toward the far end of the alley. He turned and looked back toward Main Street. The dumpster Amy had been standing next to the night before was under a security light that pointed toward the street. "Stay where you are, Adam." Rick said as he slipped into the nook just beyond the big green bin. He squatted down, then called out, "Can you see me?"

"No way."

133

Rick stood and pointed at the security light. "And with that pointing into Amy's eyes, there's no way she could have seen someone hiding here. It would have been possible for someone to hide while Clive argued with the victim, then smash him on the head, and stab the victim. When Amy showed up, he probably hid here until he could sneak away unnoticed."

"Assuming Clive's story is true." Adam said skeptically. "You really want him to be innocent, don't you?"

Rick, feeling suddenly deflated, muttered, "I do. For some reason, I like the guy."

"I do, too. But I can't let my personal feelings get in the way of this investigation. We're stuck with the facts."

"So let's begin by running those down. Why don't we start with Dennis at Ocean Surf? Let's see if our victim is the same one who committed that robbery."

24

ALEX

Me and Sasha have been best friends ever since my dad moved us to Seaside Cove. Sasha's kinda like me, super curious about lots of stuff. We're not like totally identical 'cause she likes to do things I don't. She's into yoga and dance. I guess dance is okay, but I don't have time for all those weird yoga positions that Sasha does. But when it comes to an investigation, we're both totally in.

That's why I wanted her to come with me to check out the lead I got from Mr. Gibson. If Mr. Gibson's right, the dead guy hid the treasure in the bushes in front of The Rusty Nail. The bag sounds lots like the one I saw the treasure thief hiding at Dead Man's Cove. What's super awesome is that nobody realizes the treasure and the murder could be related.

"I've never skipped school before, Alex." Sasha grins at me.

"Me, either, Sash. But technically, we're not skipping school, just recess. Besides, this is super important 'cause I wanna make sure we get to the treasure before anybody else."

"That's why you didn't want to wait until after school?"

"Totally. The Rusty Nail opens at lunch and there's gonna be people around. We gotta keep this on the down low."

The Rusty Nail is only two blocks from school, so it's a short walk. And we're hustling so we'll get there and back before recess is over.

Sasha stops all of a sudden and looks at me. "Do you think Robbie will panic if Miss Redmond asks him where we are?"

"Let's hope not. I told him what to say. So if he sticks to the story I gave him, it'll all be cool." Robbie's kinda like my boyfriend. He's got dreamy blue eyes and I'm totally gonna marry him when we grow up. But for now, we gotta get through sixth grade. "Come on. According to Mr. Gibson, it's right there."

I point at the bushes in front of The Rusty Nail. The restaurant does a lot of business at night 'cause it's less expensive than The Crooked Mast. Since it's the middle of the morning and the only store that's open is Ocean Surf, the whole street's quiet. This should be a super easy operation.

"Let's check it out." I grab Sasha's hand and we run the rest of the way. There's a planter with three hibiscus and a bunch of low growing bushes. Some of them are jasmine, but I don't know what the others are. When I step into the middle of the planter, my foot goes squish. "Yuck. The sprinklers must have been on."

Sasha makes a face and kneels down. She pushes the plants around while I step out to the other side of the planter. The leaves are all wet and my hand's getting super cold. It's worse than Dead Man's Cove 'cause now we have to go back to school and sit through class, but it'll totally be worth it if we find the treasure. I get some icky white stuff on my fingers when I try to check under one of the jasmine. So far, all we're finding are wet plants and spiders. Double ick.

"Hey, Alex?"

"What Sash?" She's probably gonna tell me messing around in cold, wet bushes is totally not her thing. I agree. It's not mine, either.

"Is your dad working with Chief Cunningham today?"

"Most likely. Why?"

"Because they were going into Ocean Surf and your dad saw me. He's coming this way."

I look down the street. Sasha's right. It is my dad. And he doesn't look happy. "Oh man, I'm gonna be in so much trouble."

25

RICK

RICK DID A DOUBLE TAKE when he spotted Alex and Sasha. He couldn't believe they'd skip school, but there they were in front of the Rusty Nail. He told Adam he'd be back in a minute and jogged toward the girls. Apparently, it had been Sasha who'd seen him first. Alex looked like she was considering making a break for it, but he hoped she knew that would only make things worse.

"Alex, Sasha. What are you doing here?"

"Hi, Daddy."

"Hi, Mr. Atwood."

Alex's tone had been casual, almost flip, whereas Sasha sounded hesitant and—dare he think it?—guilty. Rick focused in on Alex, the most likely instigator of this little escapade. "Don't you try to use a nonchalant tone on me, young lady. I want to know why you two aren't in school. Does Miss Redmond know you're here?"

Alex hung her head and sighed. "No."

Rick studied the girls. They were both a mess. The sleeves on their jackets were wet; they had mud on their hands, their jeans, and their shoes. Alex even had mud smears on her cheek. "Why are you both here?"

"Mr. Gibson told me he saw a man hiding something in these bushes last night. When he described the man he saw, it

sounded like the dead guy. I wanted to prove someone killed
him because of the treasure he stole."

Rick hated to admit it, but her motive for the murder
actually made sense. He wanted to be angry with her for
skipping school and for talking Sasha into coming with her, but
he also had to admire their tenacity. They'd obviously quite
literally 'dug deep' to find what they were looking for.

"Sasha, I'm surprised at you—letting Alex talk you into
something like this."

"I'm sorry, Mr. Atwood. We just wanted to check it out
during recess."

"I heard the bell a couple of minutes ago. Recess is over."

Sasha looked at her watch, grimaced, then hung her head.
"Oh."

"You should have told me your theory, Alex. The chief and I
could have done this."

"But Daddy..."

"No, Alex. There are no buts. You skipped school to check
out a theory that you should have told me about. What am I
going to do with you?"

Alex scrunched up her face. "Ground me?" A moment later,
she added, "Again?"

If only that would help, but Rick already knew how
ineffective grounding his daughter had been in the past. "You
two go back to school. The chief and I will come back here after
we're done at Ocean Surf."

"You won't find it," Alex said. "Somebody already got it."

Rick surveyed the bushes, then the girls. If their appearance
was any indicator, they'd been extremely thorough. "From the
looks of you, you're probably right. Alex, we'll talk about this
tonight. Sasha, I was going to call your dad and tell him what

you've done, but with your mother's medical conditions, your parents already have enough going on."

"So you're not gonna tell on me?" Sasha watched Rick with hope in her eyes.

"No. However, when you get to school, I want you both to tell Miss Redmond what you've done. Whatever she decides to do is up to her. The same goes for you, Alex. Now, get back to school before I change my mind."

The girls ran toward the schoolyard while Rick walked back to Ocean Surf. When he was halfway there, he stopped and checked over his shoulder to make sure the girls hadn't doubled back. Satisfied that they'd followed directions, he stepped up his pace and arrived at Ocean Surf where Adam was flipping through a circular rack of women's tee shirts. Adam held up two shirts, one in each hand. "Which do you think Traci will like more?"

"I thought you were going to talk to Dennis."

"He had a couple of big spenders, so I told him I'd browse while he schmoozed. He got a nice sale out of the deal."

"Looks like he's finishing up. By the way, the coffee-colored one. You know how your girlfriend loves her coffee."

"You're right. I'll pay for this and we can talk business." Adam surveyed the store, spotted Dennis at the back, and called out, "Dennis! Ready to roll, here."

"Gotcha, Chief. Nice choice on the shirt, by the way. You know how Traci loves her coffee."

Rick smirked at Adam, who rolled his eyes. "So I've heard. While you ring me up, tell me about this guy who robbed you."

Dennis went to the back of the store and stood behind the cash terminal. As he scanned the first tag, he said, "The dude stole an expensive Hawaiian shirt and one of my best pairs of shorts plus all of my cash."

"No. What did he look like?"

Dennis peered at Adam for a couple of seconds, then nodded. In a way, Rick felt sorry for the guy. He was supposed to be an excellent diver, but Marquetta had said that in his younger days, he'd done a few too many drugs and was now paying the price.

"He had dark hair, wasn't too tall. Maybe...five-ten? Medium build. Came in wearing nothing but swim trunks."

"You didn't think that was unusual?" Rick checked over his shoulder after asking the question. He felt uncomfortable because the three of them were standing at the rear of the store and both he and Adam had their backs to whatever was going on in the rest of the store. Basically, anyone could sneak up behind them and they wouldn't know.

"People come in dressed like that all the time in the summer. It is kind of strange for early spring, but I get all kinds. There was this one dude who came in..."

"Dennis," Adam snapped. "The guy who robbed you, remember?"

"Oh, yeah. Sure. I was busy with two other customers when he came in. He made eye contact, so I just thought he was another eccentric tourist dude or something. Ever since they found the *San Mañuel*, my business has been through the roof. I'm gonna have to hire someone soon."

Rick and Adam exchanged a glance, then Adam let out a breath and showed Dennis a picture. "Is this him?"

"Hey! That's my shirt! What happened to it?"

"The guy's dead, Dennis. He was stabbed," Adam said.

"Oh, yeah, right. I heard about that. So I guess the shirt has a lot of blood on it?"

"And it's got a big hole in the middle of it right about here." Adam tapped a spot below his ribcage.

"What about my shorts?"

"What do you think?"

Dennis screwed up his cheeks and muttered something under his breath. "Between the two I'm out another hundred bucks."

"This guy's got more problems than money, Dennis. He's dead."

"Well, I didn't have nothing to do with it."

"Never said you did. Now, how much did he steal?"

"I didn't have an exact count on what was in the drawer, but according to the receipts, I'd taken in about four hundred in cash for the day."

"Wow," Rick said. "That's a lot of tee shirts."

"Like I said, it's been super busy lately. And most of my business is credit card, you know? You've been swamped at the B&B, too. Right, Rick?"

"We have. So how did this guy get out of the store without you seeing him?"

"I told you, dude, it's like crazy busy these days. All he had to do was wait until my back was turned and...poof!" Dennis threw his hands out to the side and looked up. "It's like, over in a second. You know?" He stopped, snuck a peek beyond Rick and Adam, and said, "Uh oh. I got people. You need anything else, Chief?"

"That depends. Is there anything else you can tell us?"

"I don't think so...wait, what about my money? Did he still have it on him?"

"Most of it. He had three-hundred-forty-two dollars left. It's evidence for now, but I'll get it back to you as soon as I can."

"Thanks, Chief. Gotta split." Dennis darted off and wound his way between the forest of clothing racks to greet his customers.

"Was he that bad yesterday?" Rick asked.

"I was trying to take his statement, but he kept bouncing around like a ball in a ping pong match. I'm hoping it's just the stress of him being busier than he's used to. Hey, maybe your future mother-in-law would like a part-time job."

"She's already got one at Howie's."

"That's right. I heard about her spending a lot of time there. Is it true they've been going to the park and feeding the ducks every day?"

"What? No. Good grief. Is that where my French bread is going? To feed the ducks?"

"Oh. I thought you knew."

Rick grumbled. "Lucky ducks."

"Relax, buddy. Marquetta will rein her in before it gets too..." Adam stopped and his eyes seemed to track someone's movements at the front of the store. "What's she doing down here?"

"Who?"

"Mary Ellen."

Rick turned to look out the front door, but stopped at the sight of Adela Barone. She stood not more than ten feet away and was rummaging through a rack of women's tees. Ever since she'd checked into the B&B, he'd not once seen her in a tee shirt. He wouldn't be surprised if she'd been eavesdropping on their conversation.

"Something wrong?" Adam asked.

"I'll tell you later." Rick checked the front door. A couple of tourists strolled by, but there was no sign of Mary Ellen. "You must be mistaken."

"I don't think so. And It looks like she's on her way to the harbor. Come on. My curiosity just went into overdrive."

They waved goodbye to Dennis as they exited the store. Down the street, Mary Ellen was at the roundabout and just turning into the marina.

"What was that inside the store?" Adam asked as they walked.

"Adela Barone. First, she showed up at the murder scene. Today, she just happens to be in Ocean Surf at the same time we are. That's a little too much coincidence in my book."

"Relax, buddy. When I took her statement, she seemed very immature. She's probably doing the same thing as all the other tourists and trying to score some of the *San Mañuel's* treasure."

"Speaking about the treasure, I learned something from Alex and Sasha." Rick proceeded to fill Adam in on what the girls had told him. They agreed it would be worth talking to Phillip Gibson and searching through the planter on their own.

All the way to the marina entrance, Adam's assessment of Adela Barone bothered Rick. She'd supposedly come to Seaside Cove for a news story, but what if she was more than she claimed? He'd text Marquetta later and ask her to keep an eye on the mysterious Miss Barone.

Mary Ellen was deep into the marina when Rick and Adam arrived. She'd turned right, gone past the Ugly Worm Bait & Tackle, and was following the northernmost dock to the end. There was only one boat out there, and it belonged to Clive Crabbe.

"For a lady who doesn't want to see much of her ex, Mary Ellen seems to be walking right into the lion's den," Adam said as they passed Gray's Charters. "What kind of game do you think she and Clive are playing?"

"Fire and ice."

Adam frowned and peered at Rick. "What?"

"There's something not making sense about their stories. One minute Mary Ellen's madly in love and the next she's pushing Clive away."

Rick listened to the sound of their footsteps on the wood decking. Solid, but steady. Assured, yet ominous—maybe not for him and Adam, but most certainly for Clive and Mary Ellen. Especially if this visit had something to do with the murder.

26

RICK

STANDING NEXT TO ADAM ON the dock before the *Mary Ellen*, Rick could look right and easily see the B&B and the path leading down to the breakwater. To his left lay the vast Pacific Ocean. This little marina might not be much by big-city standards, but it was incredibly tranquil.

The sense of calm the setting invoked stood in sharp contrast to the shock he felt at their reason for being here. Just a couple of hours ago he'd asked Mary Ellen all those questions about her and Clive and not once had she mentioned that she would be seeing him this morning. Watching her stride purposefully through the marina, she'd seemed so determined. About what, though?

"I don't hear anybody yelling," Rick said.

"You sure about that?"

Rick listened to the waves lapping against the dock, then said, "Oh, maybe."

"That's what I thought, too." Adam climbed aboard the *Mary Ellen* and bellowed, "Seaside Cove Police!"

"Guess we're in it, now," Rick muttered as he followed.

Adam rapped twice on the cabin door and was reaching for the handle when Clive threw it open. He was shirtless, and at the sight of Rick and Adam, the color in his cheeks drained. Mary Ellen appeared behind him and put her hand on his shoulder.

The way her eyes moved reminded Rick of a moth drawn to a flame—each time her attention came back to Rick or Adam, it fluttered away as though singed by the heat.

"Mind if we have a word, you two?" Adam asked, his voice deep and sounding very official.

"Chief...I can explain," Clive stammered.

"Good, because I'm going to want the story from both of you. Rick, you take Mary Ellen and get her side while I have a little chat with Clive. And Clive, you'd better make this good—you've just moved to the top of my suspect list."

"But we haven't done anything," Mary Ellen protested.

"Unless you two start telling the truth I'm thinking of charging you both with withholding information in a police investigation. I might even throw in obstruction of justice. I'm also thinking Clive killed Tuck Hall in a jealous rage, so we can either talk here or in my office. The result will be the same. And this time, Clive, you will go to County. Quite possibly, Mary Ellen will to."

"Go talk to Rick, babe. I'll deal with the Chief."

"Wise decision," Adam said as he stepped aside to let Mary Ellen pass.

Rick got off the boat, then held out his hand for Mary Ellen. She took it to steady herself, stepped onto the dock, then hung her head.

She sniffled a few times and her eyes welled with tears. "I feel so stupid. I should've told you this morning."

"Let's take a little walk."

Rick led the way back toward the marina entrance. Mary Ellen stayed at his side, all the while watching the weathered beams beneath her feet as though they might reveal some fascinating truth.

"How long have you two been seeing each other?" Rick asked.

"Ever since the divorce. We got caught in this stupid cycle—he'd do something, then I'd try to punish him, then he'd get in trouble and I'd feel terrible. After that, he'd be on his best behavior and we'd do it all again. We got serious a few weeks ago after I reported him for stalking me. I felt terrible about him being arrested like that, so I came out here to visit him. He told me he'd been so lonely and felt better when he was near me, even if he couldn't see me or be with me."

"I thought you said you were done with him."

They walked until they were almost to the Ugly Worm, then Rick stopped. He didn't think Jennifer Martin would gossip about what she heard, but he didn't know her that well, either. It would be better to keep their distance and avoid giving Jennifer any temptation to eavesdrop.

Rick did an about-face. "We'll turn around here. I want to keep this completely private."

"Thank you, but it's probably already too late. Joe Gray saw me on my way in."

"He is plugged into the rumor mill."

Mary Ellen sniffled and rubbed at her nose. "It feels like me and Clive are destined to have one of those—what do they call it? Oh yeah, a dysfunctional relationship. That's why we were keeping this quiet. I'd made such a big stink over our divorce and how he couldn't let go that I'd have been the laughing stock of the town if people found out we were back together."

"Is that why you told me this morning he'd been stalking you again?"

She hung her head. "It seemed like a good way to cover our tracks."

"You're right, Mary Ellen. People are going to talk, but gossip never lasts long."

"Really, Rick? You went through it when you moved here. They even had that stupid marriage competition to see who could snag Seaside Cove's new bachelor."

Rick snickered. "Yeah, it did get kind of crazy."

"Kind of? That's being nice. I couldn't stand the idea of everyone pointing fingers and talking about us behind our backs. It was more than I could bear. If we lived someplace bigger, we'd just be this anonymous couple. Here, we'll be the talk of the town until somebody else comes along."

"So that's why you didn't tell me this morning? Because you were worried I'd gossip?"

"I know, I was being stupid."

"I don't gossip, Mary Ellen. Especially when it's about an investigation. Are you planning on getting married again?"

"Clive's asked. I told him I needed more time." She shrugged, then laughed. "I guess it won't matter now. Might as well go public."

"That's your decision. What I want to know is how this changes what you told me about the murder?"

"It doesn't. I told you the truth about all of it. I heard about it at work. That's when I went over to see what was going on. The minute I saw Clive being taken away, I knew he was the one the chief suspected. I tell you, Rick, Clive wouldn't do that. He wouldn't jeopardize what we've got. He promised me." She squeezed her eyes shut tight, then croaked, "He promised!"

"I know what you want, Mary Ellen, but Clive has gotten himself into a real mess. The best way to help him is to tell the truth. Last night you told me you hadn't seen Clive since the incident in the Crooked Mast. Is that true? Or did you sneak out back after the incident and talk to him?"

Mary Ellen shook her head and blinked back tears. "No, it was the dinner rush and I couldn't get away. I wanted to. All night I kept thinking how if I'd gone to him and told him the guy was just being a jerk, that man might still be alive. I kept thinking it was my fault."

Rick reached out and gave Mary Ellen's arm a reassuring squeeze. "From what you've told me, nothing that happened last night was your fault." He paused, then looked at her. "Unless there's something else you've left out."

"There is one thing. It's not about me and Clive, but it was something that guy said when I was waiting on his table."

"What's that?"

"It was strange. I'm not even sure it means anything, but he said 'they'll be coming for me' and that he had to leave town right away."

"That's it? He didn't say who he was talking about?"

"No, but the way he said it, it seemed like maybe he was afraid of someone."

Rick frowned, considered the implications, and didn't like the conclusion. "Could he have been referring to the boat that left him behind?"

"Then why would he have been afraid?"

"Maybe he was worried he'd get arrested."

"He didn't seem like the kind who would be too bothered by that, you know?"

Rick glanced involuntarily back toward shore. Alex. What had she stumbled onto?

"Apparently, he was right," Rick said as he watched Adam and Clive standing on the deck of the *Mary Ellen.*

Rick waited for Adam while Mary Ellen returned to Clive. If Mary Ellen was correct, was it possible Clive had landed himself in the middle of some sort payback for a double-cross? It could also mean the killer was long gone. Unless he still had business to deal with.

"What's the matter?" Adam asked as he approached.

"I'm not sure. Mary Ellen told me something about Tuck Hall. She thinks he was afraid of someone."

"You think? The guy's dead." Adam stopped and looked back toward the *Mary Ellen*, then looked at Rick. "Maybe," he said as they continued toward the marina entrance.

As they neared Gray's Charters, Rick felt a sudden wariness about speaking. With the exception of old boards creaking beneath their feet and the occasional clanking of sailboat rigging, the marina was quiet. How far would their voices carry? That one question made Rick reluctant to talk, and apparently Adam felt the same because they walked in silence to the exit.

When they were at the roundabout, Rick said, "What Mary Ellen told me was that Tuck Hall felt someone was coming for him. I asked her if he could have been referring to the dive boat, but she seemed to think that wasn't the case. Adam, whoever killed Tuck Hall might still be in town and might be willing to kill for whatever Hall stole from the *San Mañuel*."

"Let's assume you're correct. Where do you want to start?"

"How about we take a crack at that planter in front of the Rusty Nail? The girls didn't find anything, but who knows? Maybe we'll find a clue. Something they missed. And if we don't find anything, then we know somebody retrieved the bag after Hall was killed."

"Let's get to it," Adam said and picked up his pace.

Rick matched him stride-for-stride as they walked in silence. They had just passed Ocean Surf when Rick stopped and pointed at the line forming outside the front door of the Rusty Nail. With that kind of audience, who knew what might happen?

"Look at all those people, Adam. The restaurant's not open yet. Are you sure you want to do this now?"

Adam stopped to inspect the crowd. He let out a heavy sigh. "This has disaster written all over it. Doesn't it?"

"Most of the people in that line look like visitors. As you know. most of them are dying to get their own little souvenir from the *San Mañuel*. And, for all we know, the killer could be in that line."

"Let's do it. The longer we wait to search, the more likely it is we'll miss critical evidence." Adam snapped his fingers. "I've got an idea." He pulled out his phone and dialed.

27

ALEX

MISS REDMOND WASN'T TOO MAD at us when me and Sasha told her why we were late for class. She warned us that we shouldn't have left school, but she said since neither of us had done anything bad before she was gonna let us off with just a warning. That was a huge relief for both of us 'cause neither of us have ever been in trouble at school.

I'm super happy that things turned out like they did. Sasha was gonna spend the afternoon with me 'cause her dad had to take her mom to a doctor's appointment in San Ladron. If Miss Redmond hadn't been so nice, our whole afternoon could've been messed up.

I see Grandma Madeline walking up Main Street on our way home. When I tell Sasha I want to make a stop, she makes a face, but she follows me up the street to where we can park our bikes.

"Okay, Alex, but I'm supposed to get started on my homework. I guess a few minutes won't make any difference. You're not gonna tell her about this morning, are you?"

"No way. Grandma Madeline isn't on the need-to-know list. I wanna talk to her about the dinner we're gonna set up for my dad and Marquetta. I can't do it at the B&B 'cause they're always around. And Grandma Madeline hasn't been spending much time at the B&B, so it's been super tough."

Down the street, I see Grandma Madeline going up the steps to the porch of Howie's Collectibles. She slips around the couple looking at the display and goes inside.

"Come on. She must be working. Maybe I can talk to her." I tug on the straps of my backpack and walk faster.

All the businesses on Main Street are in old houses so they've all got front porches and the business owners set up displays to pull in customers. Marquetta told me that people lived on the second floor of the houses way back when the town was built. Seaside Cove was a little fishing village in those days, but then some rich people discovered us and the town became kind of a resort.

Mr. Dockham's got an old-timey table set up out front. It's got a white lace tablecloth and some super cute knickknacks on top of that. The lady standing there is pointing at a teacup while her husband is looking kinda bored. The lady looks up and smiles at me as we go by. I don't recognize her, so she's either staying at the Seaside Cove Inn or they're just here for the day. I smile at her anyway and tell her the little teacup is really pretty before I go inside.

Grandma Madeline is at the back of the store with Mr. Dockham and another man. They're laughing and talking, but they're not making a lot of noise. Mr. and Mrs. Gibson are here, too. It looks like they're arguing over whether they should buy the figurine he's holding.

When Mr. Dockham sees me, he waves, then says something to Grandma Madeline. She looks at me, smiles, and weaves her way toward us. "My, my. What happened to the two of you? You look like you've been in a mudslinging contest."

Uh oh. I hadn't thought about how we looked. We'd been able to clean up a little, but our jeans still have mud stains. "I thought I lost something in the bushes on the way to school, but

I didn't find it. Anyway, we saw you walking, and I wanted to talk to you about the wedding plans."

Grandma Madeline glances over her shoulder, then winks at me. "Well, if you give me just a minute, we're almost done here. This man is Mr. E.J. Bradbrook. He's a big antiquities dealer from Los Angeles and came to town after he heard about the *San Mañuel*. This is his third visit to the shop. He told Howie he's very impressed by much of the inventory."

It sounds like Grandma Madeline is impressed, too. She's like all smiles and her cheeks are rosy. I haven't known Grandma Madeline that long, but I do know she's totally impressed by rich people. Plus, she likes to talk...a lot.

"Excuse me, ma'am," Mr. Gibson says. "Do you work here?"

"Why, yes I do."

Grandma Madeline kinda puffs up her hair and puts on a super big smile. "What can I help you with?"

"Can you ship this piece for us?"

"Oh, my. That's very expensive. I'm sure we can. Let me talk to the owner." She hurries off to ask Mr. Dockham about the shipping. When she gets about halfway there, she stops and looks back to me. "We'll talk tonight, dear."

Mr. Gibson looks at me. "Your grandmother is a busy woman. Are you off school for the day, Alex?"

"We just got out. I wanted to talk to her now, but I guess it's gonna have to wait."

"It's totally gonna have to wait," Sasha says. "My dad texted me from the B&B. They got back early and he wants to know why I'm not there."

Rats. Getting Sasha in trouble twice in one day was totally not in my game plan. "We gotta run, Mr. Gibson. Nice to see you again."

Mr. and Mrs. Gibson wave goodbye as me and Sasha hurry out the door. We run up the street, unlock our bikes, and race back to the B&B. It only takes us a couple minutes to get there, but even from a block away we can see Sasha's dad pacing out front.

28

RICK

A YOUNG COUPLE CARRYING SHOPPING bags Rick recognized from one of the downtown stores joined the line outside the Rusty Nail. The seconds ticked by slowly as Rick waited to find out who Adam had called.

"Sally? Chief Cunningham. I need a favor. There may be evidence from last night's murder in your raised planter out front. Can you open early so we can search without any of your customers getting too curious?" He waited, listened, then grinned and gave Rick a thumbs-up. "One more question. Did any of your customers comment about a man hiding a bag in your planter out front last night?"

Rick strained to hear Sally's response, but couldn't quite make it out.

A few seconds later, Adam said thanks and disconnected. "She said this is the first she's heard of anyone hiding anything out here. That's a dead end."

Sally Costas opened the front door about thirty seconds later. She looked over the line, put on a big smile, and said, "With so many people anxious for lunch, how could we wait a second longer to open? Come on in, folks!"

Everyone in line cheered, then filed inside. When the last person had disappeared through the doorway, Sally gave Rick and Adam a thumbs up and followed her customers.

Adam hooked his thumbs in his belt, a smug smile on his face. "The perks of being the Chief of Police."

"Don't let it go to your head, Adam. It's just lunch."

Rick and Adam searched the raised planter, picking through the bushes and ignoring the prying eyes of new patrons as they arrived. When one middle-aged man with thinning hair and an impressive paunch stopped to watch, Rick suspected the man was going to be trouble.

"Mind if I ask what you two are looking for?" The man stood about three feet away, attempting to spy over Rick's shoulder.

"Official investigation, sir," Adam said. "Enjoy your lunch."

"Does this have something to do with that murder last night? What about the treasure?"

Adam stood. He had his sleeves rolled up, mud on his hands and forearms, and a scowl on his face. "Did you see anything you should report, sir?"

The man backed away, then sputtered, "Uh...no."

"Then enjoy your lunch, sir," Adam said as he knelt next to the planter and resumed his search.

The expression on the man's face fell as his wife grabbed his arm and pulled him away. "Stop making a pest of yourself," she hissed. "Can't you see they've got work to do?"

From behind his back, Rick heard a woman's voice. "You look like a regular big city hardnose, Chief."

Rick recognized the voice immediately. It was Flynn O'Connor, and he was surprised neither of them had seen her coming. He stood, gave Flynn a thumbs-up, then said, "That's what I told him."

"That's not exactly what you said." Adam stood, stretched his back, and smiled at Flynn. "How did you hear about this little shindig?"

"A little birdie told me there might be something in those bushes you're manhandling."

"That birdie's name wouldn't be Alex, would it?" Rick asked.

Flynn zipped her lips shut with her thumb and index finger, then winked. "I don't want to betray a confidence."

"No worries. I was actually thinking about telling her that contacting you was a good idea." Rick stretched from side-to-side, then knelt again. Tempting as it was to stand around talking, this search wasn't going to complete itself. "You going to help us look, Flynn?"

"Absolutely." She pointed at the opposite side of the planter. "Have you looked over there yet?"

"It's all yours." A movement down the street caught Rick's eye. He looked closer and realized it was Amy Kama. "I guess we're the town's entertainment for the day."

Adam knelt back down and returned to sorting through bushes. "Police work always draws a crowd."

"Isn't that the truth?" Rick said as he joined Adam. They continued their inspection, separating the delicate branches and leaves carefully to avoid damaging the plants. With the three of them working, they finished within about ten minutes.

"We've got zip," Adam said. "Unless you count dirt, plants, and a few pieces of garbage."

"I've got sticky hands from that jasmine," Flynn said.

Rick, who had been looking to see where Amy Kama had gone, inspected Flynn's hands, and noted a couple of white smears. "You must have broken one of the stems."

"No, I was very careful. It did look like someone had stepped on that one plant, though."

Rick knelt next to the jasmine Flynn had indicated and inspected it closely. "You're right. Someone's crushed this one. It might have been Alex or Sasha. I'm guessing we've found where your missing artifacts were stashed. Now we just need to figure out who took it."

"Rick, you said one of your guests told Alex about this?"

"Yes. Alex said it was Mr. Gibson. Do you want to be there when I talk to him, Adam?"

"You can handle it. I trust your instincts."

"I'd like to be a part of that conversation," Flynn said.

No way. Having Flynn involved was the last thing Rick wanted. She could get very passionate about the *San Mañuel's* treasure and he suspected the conversation with Gibson would require subtlety, which was not Flynn's strong suit. She might be a great archaeologist, but she wasn't the best people person.

"I'll keep you in the loop, but I think the fewer people who are in the room, the more forthcoming Mr. Gibson will be."

"Agreed," Adam said. "Sorry, Flynn, but I think Rick's right."

"That's probably for the best. I've got two interviews with reporters coming up. In fact, the first one is in ten minutes. I should get going. Oh, and Rick? Your Miss Barone sounds like she might be coming around."

"Really? Are you sure?"

"Not entirely, but I would love to get someone so young and enthusiastic on my side. Gotta run. Bye."

Flynn waved over her shoulder as she darted away. Rick watched her go, wondering what else Alex might have told her.

"You're thinking Mr. Gibson decided to do a little treasure hunting himself?" Adam said.

"Who knows? The guy is fascinated by it. He doesn't strike me as the larcenous type, but when you throw money into the mix, anything can happen. I'll call Marquetta and see if he's at the B&B."

They agreed that while Rick pursued Gibson for more information about the 'treasure' he'd seen buried in the bushes,

Adam would return to the station to check the man's background. The man might be squeaky clean, but both Rick and Adam wanted to be sure.

Rick called Marquetta's cell, told her what Alex had said, then asked her to check on Mr. Gibson.

"There's no need to check on him. He and his wife left to do some shopping downtown. They're probably just walking around."

"Great," muttered Rick when he pocketed his phone. "If I want to find Gibson, I'll have to canvass the downtown. He and his wife are shopping."

Adam's cheek quirked and he gazed in the direction of Main Street. "Our downtown's not that big, but it could take awhile. This Mr. Gibson seems to be quite involved in this whole mess, doesn't he?"

"Yes. He was at the crime scene last night. He knew about the treasure. I don't think he grabbed it, though. If he had, why would he have told Alex about it?"

"Good point. Then maybe he saw something he didn't tell Nancy Drew."

"You're never going to stop calling her that, are you?"

Adam shook his head. "Probably not. You have to admit, Rick. She's a good little investigator."

"Exactly," Rick said.

Adam screwed up his face and regarded Rick "You worry too much."

"You'd do the same thing if you were in my shoes."

"Well…" Adam's face colored and he smiled slowly. "I would. So are you hunting down Gibson?"

"I need to make a trip to the market anyway. Might as well kill two birds."

The two men parted with Rick taking the same path Flynn had and Adam going the opposite direction to the police station. On his way, Rick passed the Crooked Mast, Scoops n'Scones, and was in front of the Bee's Knees when he spotted the Gibsons across the street at Howie's Collectibles.

A sightseeing couple driving up Main Street was too busy gawking and pointing at the colorful buildings to watch for pedestrians or other traffic. Rick waited for the car to pass, then had to wait for another coming in the opposite direction.

The Gibsons turned up the street, the opposite direction from the B&B. Obviously, their shopping spree wasn't over yet. They waved off a reporter and his cameraman when the reporter tried to shove a microphone in Phillip Gibson's face. As the reporter approached another person, Rick kept wondering if the questions being asked were about the *San Mañuel* or Flynn O'Connor.

"Hey, Rick. How are you doing?" Traci Peterson called down from her front porch.

Rick faced Traci, who was placing a large vase filled with a colorful bouquet in the middle of her candle display. He did another check on the Gibsons. When he saw them standing at the curb waiting to cross the street, the anxiety in his shoulders relaxed. Excellent. They were coming his way. Rick stepped back from the curb and approached Traci.

"I'm doing good. I'm waiting for Mr. and Mrs. Gibson to get a break in the traffic. I need to talk to them."

Traci straightened up and rearranged a couple of flowers in the vase. "Uh oh. If you need to talk to your guests outside of the B&B, it can't be good. Adam told me you're working with him again."

"Apparently, Mr. Gibson witnessed what may be a key event last night. I just need to see if he remembers anything more than what we already know."

"Here's your chance." Traci waved, then nodded. "They're coming this way. Mrs. Gibson bought an entire set of my Naturescapes candles. She's having me ship them to their ranch."

Rick found himself suddenly speechless. How was it he hadn't known the Gibsons lived on a ranch? Because he'd been too busy, that's how. He'd been glossing over everything just to get by. He spotted the couple making their way across the street and let out a huff. "You know more about them than I do."

Traci smirked, then looked around and lowered her voice. "Don't tell Adam, but I'm a professional at getting people to talk. It's amazing what you can find out when you listen. I'll let you get to it. See you later."

As Traci ducked back into the Bee's Knees, Rick looked to his left. The couple stood on the sidewalk, engaged in a mildly spirited discussion. Judging by the fingers pointing in opposite directions, they were probably trying to decide which way to go next.

Rick sucked in a breath. If he wanted the most information from Phillip and Peg Gibson, why not disarm them first? He decided to follow Alex's example and Traci's advice and donned a cheerful smile as he approached.

"Mr. and Mrs. Gibson. It looks like you're having trouble figuring out what to do. Might I suggest a trip to my favorite Seaside Cove bakery? Crusty Buns is right there. It'll be my treat."

29

RICK

CRUSTY BUNS WAS ONE OF those businesses in Seaside Cove that was forever busy. Most of the tables were filled, but Rick did see one open in the back. He led the way to the ordering line and suggested his guests inspect the display case while he waited.

"The chocolate chip muffins are Alex's favorite. I personally love the blueberry, but everything here is excellent."

"Must be nice having so many delectable temptations all in one place. If it's as good as you say, I'd want to be here every day." Mr. Gibson patted his stomach and chuckled. "Yessir, every single day."

"Phillip, don't get too carried away. The money hasn't come through yet."

Her husband did a double take, obviously displeased that his wife had even hinted at their secret. He made some sputtering noises, then added, "Don't worry, Peggy. It won't be long now. Let's go see what we can see, okay?"

The line inched forward, allowing Rick time to wonder what money the Gibsons were talking about. Were they expecting a windfall of some sort? If it was from the *San Mañuel*, he could see only three possibilities. At best, they could be setting themselves up for a huge disappointment. Somewhere in the middle was the potential to wind up on the wrong side of the law. And, at worst, they could become the targets of a killer.

As usual, the wait seemed to take forever, but it was fun watching his guests ooh and aah over the display case. By the time they'd seated themselves at a table, Mary O'Donnell was already coming out with a tray laden with one chocolate chip and one blueberry muffin and one hot scone. The tray also included two house blend coffees and an herbal tea for Peg.

"Are you enjoying Seaside Cove?" Rick asked.

"Your little town is such a delight," gushed Peg. "This is the kind of place everyone wants to live."

Phillip cleared his throat. "Must be terribly expensive, though. Eh?"

"It's not so bad. Certainly no worse than LA. Of course, now that word about the *San Mañuel* has become almost national news, we're getting much busier. It's probably going to raise property values significantly."

"That's always a good thing." Phillip gave Rick a sly smile and rubbed his thumb and forefingers together.

"Maybe if you're the seller," Rick said, then caught himself. He was not here to debate economics. "Anyway, I inherited the B&B from my grandfather a couple of years ago. The truth of it is I hadn't seen him in years, so the whole thing came as quite a shock." Rick paused, took a sip from his mug, and said, "It sounds like you've had a little bit of good fortune, too."

The looks on their faces were almost comical. Phillip was looking much like a child with a guilty conscience after he'd raided the cookie jar, and Peg was glaring daggers at her husband.

"Well, there's nothing final," Gibson cleared his throat a couple of times, then took a big bite of his chocolate chip muffin.

Peg gave her husband another look of exasperation, then set her jaw. "Phillip gets ahead of himself. We shouldn't have said anything."

"We?" Gibson said indignantly.

"I understand." Rick picked up his mug again, mostly to enjoy the warmth of the hot beverage radiating through the ceramic, but also to put the Gibsons at ease. "When Captain Jack left me the B&B, it took months to reconcile everything. It was awful. One day I was up, the next, down in the dumps. So I take it your windfall's not from an inheritance?"

"No...um..." Phillip's voice faltered, then he blurted, "It was a stock deal."

"That's right," Peg chimed in. "A good one."

This time, it was Phillip who was shooting the daggers. These two seemed like such an honest couple, yet here they were, obviously hiding something. And not doing a good job of it. Unfortunately, unless they were willing to open up, he'd probably gotten all he was going to get about this supposed windfall. The last thing he needed was to start accusing them of something before he knew what they were guilty of. Instead, he'd look into the Gibsons, but he'd do it quietly.

Rick raised his mug. "Well, here's to a swift and positive resolution."

Phillip responded with an enthusiastic, "Here, here."

Even after Rick had dismissed the subject, Peg still seemed bothered. Perhaps she was the avenue to figuring out their real situation. Rick set down his mug and pulled out the small notepad Adam had given him. "As you know, I'm working with the Seaside Cove Police on the murder investigation. Alex told me you saw the deceased on Front Street. What time was that?"

"It was right about six, give or take. We went for the Early Bird Special at the Crooked Mast."

"It was very good," Peg added.

"Right. Great food in this town." Phillip looked down at his empty mug. "I want to get some more of this delicious coffee."

He started to stand, but Rick raised his hand and splayed his fingers wide. "Mary will bring it. She's very good about that." Rick waved to Mary O'Donnell, who was delivering an order a couple of tables away, then looked at Peg, "Would you like a refill?"

"I'm fine, thank you."

Rick gestured that they wanted one refill for Gibson. Mary waved to him and rushed away. "Now, where were we? Oh, that's right, you said you were walking near the Rusty Nail when you saw the man hiding a package in the bushes. Is that what happened?"

"Um...yes. I like to walk after dinner. We went for a nice stroll around the downtown area. It was very pleasant and some of the stores were still open."

What should have been a very plausible explanation of the evening's events had turned into anything but. Rick eyed Gibson. Only a moment ago the man had said they'd gone for the walk before dinner. And Peg hadn't been with her husband at the murder scene. "So you're saying this happened after you'd had dinner at the Crooked Mast?"

Mrs. Gibson skewered her husband with an intense stare. "No, no, dear. We saw the man before dinner."

Gibson swallowed quickly a couple of times, then said, "Right, Peggy. It was...um...after that I went for a stroll."

Rick made a note, smiled, then looked back at Gibson. "Of course. Walking after dinner is a good routine to get into. Why don't you tell me what you saw the man do?"

"Well, we were on Front Street when we saw him carrying a bag of some sort. He kept looking over his shoulder. It was like he thought he was being watched, or didn't want anyone to see what he was doing."

Rick turned his attention to Peg and raised his eyebrows. "Is that what it looked like to you, too, Mrs. Gibson? Or did you have a different impression?"

"No, Phillip is right. The man was definitely being cautious. I said at the time that he looked like he was a man with a secret to keep."

Rick regarded the couple, thinking perhaps they should look in a mirror to see what that looked like. "So what happened then?"

Gibson snuck a peek at his wife, then cleared his throat a couple of times. "As he was walking by the bushes, he stopped and looked up and down the street, then he bent down and stuffed his bag of whatever it was into a bush with a lot of white flowers."

"It's jasmine, Phillip." Peg patted her husband's shoulder and sighed. "It was the jasmine. Phillip's not good with plants. His idea of yard work is sitting in the back yard with a beer while he watches the grass grow."

"Not true, Peggy. Not true. I do more than that."

"Yes, dear. But I still love you."

Phillip snorted, then cleared his throat. "Anyway, that's about all we saw. We walked back to the Crooked Mast, had dinner, then went straight back to the B&B."

"I guess that means you were taking your after-dinner stroll when I saw you at the murder scene with the Gardners?"

"Um...yes. Is that their name? I don't really know them."

Didn't know them? Hardly. Rick had seen the two couples talking at breakfast and Gibson had been standing right by them at the crime scene. Was he lying about knowing another B&B guest? If so, why?

"When you saw the man hiding the bag, were there any other people around?"

Gibson stiffened and his brow furrowed. "Why do you ask?"

"The bag's missing," Rick said casually. "We think someone took it."

"Well...well, it wasn't me. There were several others around. Any one of them could have taken it."

"Of course. And did you see the man who hid the bag again?"

Gibson shook his head vigorously and blurted, "No, no. Not again until...the alley."

Rick raised his eyebrows and made a note to check with Ken Grayson about the time the Gibsons had finished dinner. How was it even possible that these two had been in the Crooked Mast at the same time as Hall and not seen him? The restaurant wasn't that big. Maybe Ken's receipts would shed some light on things. They would certainly confirm when all the players had been in the restaurant.

"This has been very helpful," Rick said. "Thank you. Both of you. Now, I have to run, but I hope you both enjoy the rest of your day."

As Rick left the table, he walked by Mary O'Donnell. "Keep an eye out for my guests, would you, Mary? I'm curious how they handle our conversation."

"Something rotten in Denmark?" Mary said with a grin.

"Could be."

"They'll not escape my attention."

"Thank you."

As Rick left, he heard Mary calling after him. "And say hello to that lovely little lassie of yours!" She gave Rick a final wave, then turned and made a beeline for the table where the Gibsons sat with their heads together and looking like they were having a heated discussion.

30

ALEX

SASHA'S DAD IS PRETTY COOL about us getting to the B&B after him,
mostly because they weren't supposed to be back for another
couple of hours. But, because he asked Marquetta if Sasha was
there, Marquetta knows me and Sasha got back late. That totally
gives me another one of those conunderum things. If I tell
Marquetta we stopped to talk to Grandma Madeline, she'll start
asking what we talked about. I don't wanna lie to her, so I'm
gonna keep it all super simple. What is it my dad always says?
Less is more? That totally works.

"Marquetta, I'm sorry we were late."

She looks at me and tilts her head to the side. She kinda
smiles and gives me a big hug. I can't wait until she really is my
mom and I can ask her for a hug anytime.

"Sweetie, what happened to you? You look like you've been
rolling around in the mud." She pushes me back just a little and
looks me up and down.

Uh oh. I should have gone straight to my room and changed
clothes. I guess my dad hasn't said anything to her yet. Maybe
he won't? It's worth a try. "Am I in trouble?"

"Not so far, but you haven't answered my question."

So much for not telling that part. "Me and Sasha were trying
to find the missing treasure."

"What missing treasure?"

"Mr. Gibson told me he saw the murdered guy hide something in the bushes just before he was killed."

Marquetta lets out a sigh and bites her lower lip. "Sweetie, you and I need to talk. There are some things you should understand. Do you want some hot chocolate?"

"Sure! I'm always up for hot chocolate."

"All right, then. I could use a cup of tea, so let's get those going and you can tell me all about this missing treasure."

While Marquetta brews her tea, I mix the cocoa and sugar with some hot milk and vanilla. I start with just a little milk like Marquetta showed me and gradually add more. While I'm doing that and she's waiting for her water to boil, I tell her what Mr. Gibson said and how Daddy found me and Sasha outside the Rusty Nail.

"So your theory is this treasure thief stashed a priceless artifact in the bushes and then went to dinner?"

"Well, when you put it that way..."

"Sounds like a bit of a stretch. Doesn't it?"

"I guess."

We pick up our mugs and sit at the island. After a few seconds, Marquetta puts her hand on mine. "I'm not saying you're wrong. Lord knows, you've been right enough times in the past. All I'm saying is you need something more than just Mr. Gibson telling you he saw this man hiding the same bag you saw at Dead Man's Cove. How do you even know if it was the same bag?"

"He described it and it kinda sounded like mine."

"You don't sound very convinced." Marquetta puts her hand at the back of my head and pulls me toward her. She kisses the top of my head and sighs. "You need more proof."

I let out a big huff, then sit up and take a sip from my mug. Hot chocolate totally makes everything better. "So you think I should give up on this treasure 'cause even if it was the same, somebody stole it?"

"That's not what I'm saying at all. In fact, it might be just the opposite. What I am suggesting is that you look at the big picture. Ask more questions. For instance, why, all of a sudden, are there so many reporters in town? And why is someone so intent on making Flynn O'Connor look dishonest?"

Sometimes, Marquetta amazes me. She's totally got this on so many levels. "What else?"

"Didn't Mr. Gibson say he saw the murder scene last night?"

"Yeah. That's what he said at breakfast."

"Doesn't it seem odd to you that Mr. Gibson would have been in the two most convenient places he could be, all within the space of a few hours?"

"Whoa. You're right. That's totally suspicious."

"And what about the murder victim? How did he get from Dead Man's Cove to our downtown? Adam and Deputy Jackman went over the area with a fine-tooth comb and found no sign of him. Did he walk? Did he call a cab?"

I laugh and tell her that's funny. "Seaside Cove doesn't have any cabs at all." But, Marquetta's right. I need to ask more questions. "Are you gonna help me again?"

"Your dad and I agree that there's no keeping you out of the police investigation, so I thought we'd do a little snooping on our own." Marquetta just watches my face and smiles at me.

I'm like in shock. Wow. Marquetta's gonna help me again. I give her a high-five. "That's awesome! When can we start?"

"I think we already have. Tell me what you know, starting with the man on the beach."

"He was wearing a wetsuit when I saw him and he was hiding the bag."

"What kind? Be specific, Alex. The details are important when you investigate."

"It was mesh. Bright green, kinda like that neon stuff. It had a black band around the top. He left it behind when he ran after me, but then we heard the sirens and he must've grabbed it before he disappeared."

"Has it occurred to you that maybe he didn't stay on land? Maybe he swam back to the boat."

"He couldn't have 'cause the boat left right when the sirens started. And Daddy and Chief Cunningham showed up right after that, so he didn't have time to put on his gear."

"If that's the case, where was it? Was there any sign of it?"

"No." Oh, man, why didn't I think of this before? "All his stuff was gone. He must've turned around sooner than I thought."

"Which means he went back in the water and that's how he avoided being seen."

"But he couldn't swim to town from there...could he?"

Marquetta shakes her head. "Not unless he's an expert rough water swimmer. But he could have gotten out of the search zone. Sweetie, what questions do you think your dad would ask with everything you've told me?"

Now I have to think like Daddy? "He was a reporter for a lot of years, so he's got way more experience than me."

"Are you making excuses?"

Rats. Marquetta never lets me get away with anything, but that's one reason I love her so much. She cares about me, and she wants me to be the best I can. And I don't wanna let her down. "I think he might ask how the man got from Dead Man's Cove to here without being seen."

"Right. He might ask another one, too. Any ideas?"

"Who was in charge of the boat?"

"Well, maybe. I was thinking bigger than that. Don't you think there's been an awful lot of strange things happening in Seaside Cove lately?"

"Well, yeah. We totally have a lot of strangers here right now." And then there's all the reporters. And the day trippers. And so many tourists! There's so much stuff going on. The lies being told about Flynn O'Connor. The treasure thieves. The murder. "You're totally right, Marquetta. There's so many things happening at once that I didn't even think about it all being part of some big plan. The captain got his boat out of there super fast when the cops were getting close. I bet he had a scanner and that's how he knew the Coast Guard was coming. These guys were like super organized."

"Most likely they left behind the murder victim so they could save themselves."

"Maybe they wanted to teach him a lesson 'cause he got greedy and tried to steal stuff for himself."

"Now you're looking at the big picture."

"Totally. That's why he got killed! Because he double-crossed his boss."

"So if you were doing this investigation, how would you 'crack this case,' as you would say?"

"I'd find out who's behind it all?"

Marquetta holds up her mug and I clink mine against hers. We've totally got this. If we find whoever's behind all the bad stuff going on, we're gonna find our killer. The Dead Man's Cove caper doesn't stand a chance against me and Marquetta! Girl power rocks!

31

RICK

AFTER LEAVING CRUSTY BUNS, RICK walked to the B&B in hopes he could grab a quick lunch before heading back into town to meet with Adam. They needed a plan, some way to move forward quickly and efficiently. Climbing the steps to the B&B's front porch, Rick recalled the first time he'd seen the century-old house. He'd been only about ten when his mother had introduced him to a crusty old man she said was his grandfather.

Rick could still recall the old man's steely eyes boring into his as he'd said, "Kid, everybody calls me Captain Jack. You, too."

Rick could count on one hand the number of times other than that visit when he'd actually been in the presence of his grandfather. It was one of the things that made his inheritance so perplexing.

On his way to the kitchen, Rick noticed how the staircase bannister gleamed, as did the hardwood floors. There were no guests in sight, but as he stood with his eyes closed, he heard two voices coming from the dining area. The man's voice was a rich baritone, the woman's, high pitched with a touch of creakiness to it. Unless he was mistaken, it was the Gardners.

Rick entered the dining room and asked if they minded answering a few questions.

John Gardner scrunched up his face and shook his head. "Not at all, but we didn't see much. We got there maybe a few minutes before you arrived. Nat? Anything you can think of that might help Rick?"

"No, not really." Natalie Gardner dropped a teabag into the trash, but her brow furrowed as she took a sip. "Phillip Gibson was there before us. We saw him and stopped to say hi. While John was talking to him, I noticed the other guest standing against the wall. Her name's Amy, right? Anyway, after that, we came back here. Too much excitement for a couple of small-town seniors like us."

"When you said hello to Mr. Gibson, did he have a green mesh bag with him?"

"No." Mrs. Gardner paused and tapped her finger against her lower lip. "He was carrying a cloth shopping bag."

"Thank you both for your time," Rick said. "I hope the rest of your stay is much less exciting."

The Gardners made their way out of the dining room, and their conversation shifted to what they'd do next and which of the town's two restaurants they'd try that night. When they were out of range, Rick heard Marquetta's and Alex's voices coming from the kitchen. He tiptoed to the butler door and pressed his ear against it. Although their words were muffled, unlike the conversation his stomach was now conducting, the discussion sounded serious. Forget eavesdropping, he was hungry. Rick pushed on the door and entered.

Both Alex and Marquetta smiled as he said hello. Alex jumped up and rushed to him. He pulled her into his arms and squeezed her tight as he gazed across the room at Marquetta.

"Never gets old," he said, then went to Marquetta and kissed her. "That doesn't either."

"I'm surprised you came back," Marquetta said. "Are you going to the market later?"

"Yes. I have more to do in town this afternoon. Right now, it's lunch time and Adam's tied up, so here I am. I was hoping to get something quick."

"How about a sandwich? I can work on that while Alex tells you all about...what did you call it?"

"The Dead Man's Cove caper." Alex scrunched up her face and shook her head. "That's kinda long. I need to make it shorter."

Rick held back a smile. Alex and her sleuthing might well be the death of him, but her 'operations' and caper titles always brightened his day. "You work on that. Remember, the headline is your hook. Does this little sleuthing operation have to do with you and Sasha this morning?"

"Kinda. But it also has to do with the murder. Me and Marquetta think..."

"Alex," Marquetta said, "If you don't jump to the end, your dad might have a better chance at following your...logic."

Rick smiled. "Imagine that. My daughter's name and the word logic used in the same sentence."

"Daddy!"

"Sorry, I couldn't resist. All right, kiddo, take me through it. From the beginning."

Rick's suspicions that the Gibson's were hiding something grew as he listened to the details of Alex's conversation with Phillip Gibson that morning. Marquetta laid a sandwich in front of him just as Alex was nearing the end. He took a big bite, relishing the flavors of mayo, mustard, and thinly sliced roasted chicken.

When Alex finished, he said, "So you two think all the reporters are in town to cover this fake story about Flynn and that the murder was some sort of revenge because Tuck Hall double-crossed his boss? It's a pretty good theory, actually. And to be perfectly honest, I had a discussion with the Gibsons that has me thinking Phillip Gibson knows more about this treasure than he's admitting. Somehow, I have a hard time seeing him as any kind of criminal mastermind, though."

"He's not that smart," Alex said confidently.

Marquetta snickered while Rick did his best to keep a straight face. He took a deep breath. "Actually, I agree. Alex, I am loathe to do this, but you got more information out of Mr. Gibson than I was able to. So, I think I might have an assignment for you."

"Awesome! Am I going undercover?"

"In a sense. Tomorrow morning, I'd like you to do the same thing you did today. Spend some time with the Gibsons and let's see if his story changes overnight. I also have an assignment for you, Ms. Weiss. I'd like you to get to know Miss Barone a little better. She lied to us initially about her reason for being here and this morning she kept showing up. It's almost like she was following Adam and me. I'd like to know if she's tied into this, too."

"It won't work," Alex said with a shake of her head.

"What won't work, Sweetie? You think I won't be able to get into her confidence?"

"She sees both of you as, like, my parents. She's gonna be suspicious if you start being super nice to her."

Marquetta put an arm around Alex's shoulder and gave her a little shake. "Aren't you just becoming the voice of experience? What do you think, Rick?"

"You could be right, kiddo. I really hate doing this, but I think I have to let you handle her, too."

"I can tell her I got in big trouble for going with her, but that after the murder you're too busy to watch me and I think we should team up to find the missing treasure. She'll think it's gonna help her prove Flynn is guilty of stealing." Alex spread her hands apart as she continued. "Once I've found out her secrets, I can close the trap on her and prove she's wrong!" Alex slapped her hands together, a wide grin on her face.

Rick chuckled, then said, "Nice plan."

Marquetta gave Alex's shoulder another shake, then sat up straight. "Very impressive, Sweetie."

"There's just one problem with it," Rick said. He might as well share his hunch. "Our Miss Barone isn't a reporter."

Alex shrugged and regarded him with raised eyebrows. "How'd you find out?"

"Wait," Rick said. "You already knew?"

"For sure. She wants a story she can use to help her get a job."

"Spill it, kiddo. How do you know this?"

Alex scrunched up her face and her tone became more tentative. "When I went to her room, I told her I was onto her not being a reporter. She totally lost it and told me she was a Journalism major at USC. She said she couldn't tell anybody why she was really here."

"That's consistent with what she told Flynn and me. And, it may be the closest thing to the truth we're going to get from her. I have a bad feeling about her, Alex. I do not think that young woman has a lick of common sense."

Rick ran his hand through his hair and sighed. All those late nights in New York working with Alex on his knee while his wife had been out chasing her acting career still haunted him. No longer was it because he knew what Giselle had really been doing, but because he'd helped ignite a passion for the truth within his daughter.

"I hate the idea of you being involved in a police investigation, but I'm proud of you and want to congratulate you for digging up some valuable information. The reason I feel like I'm in a bind is I get very worried about you. Murder is not something to be taken lightly and I don't think you realize how dangerous this could be."

Alex approached Rick and hugged him. "You won't let anything happen to me. You never do."

Rick's voice broke as he tightened his grip around her. "I won't always be able to protect you, kiddo. I'd do anything for you, but there will come a time when I won't be there and that's what scares me to death."

With her face still buried in his shirt, she hugged him more tightly. "I know, Daddy. I'll be careful."

How many times had he heard that? How many times had he thought he might lose her? It didn't even have to be murder—a simple illness, a careless moment with an approaching car, anything could take her away.

Rick looked over at Marquetta, who was dabbing at her eyes. The rims, red and brimming with tears, reinforced what he already knew. If anything ever happened to him, she would protect Alex whether they'd ever married or not. The truth was that from their first meeting with Marquetta, she'd been a better mother than his ex had ever been. It was one of the myriad reasons he fell more deeply in love with her day by day.

While he would have loved to turn this into a big family moment, the outside world was bearing down on them. "We have another issue to deal with, and that's the media. If you two are out, you'll need to be extra careful about who you talk to. It feels like we've got reporters lurking around every corner. The last thing we need is to say the wrong thing to one of them."

"Does that include Adela?" Alex asked.

"Especially her. We still don't know exactly who she is or why she's here, and until we do, we have to assume she's going to misrepresent whatever we say. Be aware of your every word when you're speaking to her." Rick regarded Alex steadily for several seconds. "Especially you, kiddo. If she says something negative about Flynn, you need to realize she might be baiting you."

"I'll be careful." Alex looked at Marquetta. "We both will. Right?"

"Right, Sweetie."

"Then we all have our assignments," Rick said. "I'll work the case with Adam. You two will work together to see what you can get out of Miss Barone and Mr. Gibson."

Marquetta frowned at Rick and kept shaking her head.

"What's wrong?"

"I just can't believe either of them are somehow tied up in this murder."

"Me, either," Alex said confidently.

"That makes three of us. But what I do think is that Mr. Gibson and Miss Barone have both gotten themselves in over their heads. It makes sense that this Tuck Hall was killed because he double-crossed someone he shouldn't have. Murdering a man over a small bag of artifacts, no matter what their value, is extreme. That means until we can figure out who the killer is, we need to keep our guests from getting themselves hurt. Or worse."

32

RICK

LUNCH WENT BY WAY TOO fast. Rick often wondered how it was that the good times in life sped by while the bad ones seemed to linger like a scab on a wound. On his way out the door, he kissed Marquetta and Alex goodbye, confident that Marquetta would keep Alex out of trouble. For his part, he had a new plan. This one, if it worked, would leverage the eyes and ears that had been dogging the locals with questions about Flynn O'Connor's integrity.

For the past three days, he'd been seeing reporters of one stripe or another roam the streets of Seaside Cove. They'd been interviewing many of the local residents, some who'd never met Flynn. From the feedback he'd heard, some of the reporters had been using very leading questions. The worst were the ones who had obviously come to town looking for sensationalism. He could see the headline now—'Crooked Archaeologist Steals Pot of Gold.' But there were several others—those from reputable newspapers and even a couple of TV stations, who were trying to do some legitimate investigative journalism. Those were the ones he wanted to find.

Rick's first stop was back at Crusty Buns. The old adage that armies ran on their stomachs never seemed more true than after a visit to Crusty Buns. The O'Donnells had a reputation that drew in all kinds of hungry soldiers. Mary O'Donnell had just finished delivering coffee and muffins to one of the outdoor tables when Rick caught her attention. She winked at him and stepped away from the tables and closer to the curb.

"Aye, you were right about those two. They're a devious pair, Rick."

A glimmer of hope filled Rick's chest. "I knew you could get me something, Mary. You're a godsend."

Mary shook her head and grimaced. "Don't get ahead of yourself. They kept all the details to themselves, but I did overhear the Mrs. tell that husband of hers he's bringing down all sorts of trouble. They're worried, but they're not willing to give up whatever they're hiding. Does that help?"

Rick recalled the theory he'd spent his lunch hour discussing with Alex and Marquetta. If they were right, the Gibsons could be placing themselves in terrible danger.

"Indeed it does, Mary. More than you know. You've confirmed what I suspected. The trick is going to be getting them to realize the money's not worth the risk. Thank you. Now, I have one other favor to ask you. Are any of the reporters coming into Crusty Buns? I'm looking specifically for the news people, not the..."

"Scum mongers?" Mary said, then laughed.

"Yes. Exactly."

"Aye, there's a TV crew in there now. Back table. You'll see the camera at the man's feet."

"Thank you again."

Mary pulled Rick into a warm embrace. One of the things he'd noticed when he and Alex moved to Seaside Cove was how many more huggers there were here than in New York. After a bit of culture shock, he'd realized that deep down, he liked the way it reinforced the town's intimacy.

"I have to get back to my tables. Angus will be beside himself if he sees me out here on the sidewalk cavorting with a younger man." Mary threw Rick a final wink as she dashed back toward the front door.

Standing on the curb, Rick looked up and down the block. Main Street, normally a quiet scene, was bustling with visitors— some carried bags from the local stores, others merely window-shopped or snapped selfies. The discovery of the *San Mañuel* had changed the town. He hoped those changes would be for the better. If they weren't, he hoped they'd be only temporary.

"This town could use a little shakeup, just not anything too major," Rick said to himself as he dodged a young couple walking arm-in-arm.

Like most of the other visitors, they were too busy pointing out the sights to be concerned about where they were going. Crusty Buns was still busy, no less of a madhouse than it had been on his previous trip. The white laminated tops of tables looked like giant mushrooms in a sea of people. From singles to small groups, the patrons all sipped coffee and enjoyed their small indulgences. Rick spotted the man and woman who'd tried to set up in the alley at a table in the back. They had to be the ones Mary was referring to.

The woman watched Rick warily as he wove his way closer to their table. She craned her neck forward and said something to her companion. The man looked over his shoulder at Rick, raised his eyebrows, then turned back to his companion. When Rick arrived at their table, the woman looked up with a pasted on smile.

"What can I do for you, Officer? Or is it Detective?"

"It's neither. I'm actually a private citizen who's consulting with the police on the murder investigation. Mind if I sit? I come in peace, by the way."

"Why not? We're just twiddling our thumbs while we wait to hear back from our news director. I'm Lana Moreno, this is Alastair Canes."

Rick found a nearby empty chair and brought it to the table. He introduced himself and explained his background as a reporter in New York.

Lana's face lit up. "I remember you. You were up for a...what was it...a National Journalism Award? That was a few years ago, right?"

Warmth radiated into Rick's cheeks. He never had dealt well with recognition. "It was Investigative Reporting. That's all in the past, though. Now, I live the quiet life of a bed-and-breakfast owner in a small town."

"And solve murders on the side," Lana said. "What if we did a story on you? I could talk..."

"No," Rick said, suddenly regretting his openness about his past. "That's not why I'm here. I stopped by to ask you if you've been talking to people about the murder. Have you found any credible witnesses?"

Lana draped her arm over the back of her chair, suddenly changing her attitude to one of indifference. "We've talked to a few people, but this is sounding like a one-sided conversation."

Those were dreaded words in Rick's vocabulary. Lana wanted something, and her cameraman was certainly not going to try to dissuade her. "It appears I've opened a door I may not have intended to open. But for the sake of argument, what do you want, Ms. Moreno?"

"I need a story. Something to make sure this trip isn't a total waste. Now, if I had information about the murder investigation, or even leads to the key witnesses...I'd be willing to share resources. You scratch my back, etc."

Alastair snickered. "Lana's very persistent. I let her do all the negotiations. Me? All I am is a glorified pack mule. If I were you, buddy, I'd suggest giving in now. Surrender is the easiest option."

"No." Rick pushed back his chair. He'd been in the game long enough to know that they needed him more than he did them. "I can see this isn't going to work. You two enjoy your stay in Seaside Cove and good luck getting anything out of the locals. Once they hear of your interest in making the town look bad, I doubt if any of them will talk to you."

"And how will you accomplish that?" Lana smirked.

"Oh, I won't. But that lady right there, she knows every single person in town. Most of them are her customers. And she does love to talk—especially about outsiders."

Lana's complexion turned blotchy and she sucked in a breath through her teeth. "All right. I'm sorry. I had to try."

"I didn't receive that investigative journalism award because I was stupid, Ms. Moreno. There's something going on in this town, and it resulted in a man getting murdered. It's also resulted in us being swamped with more news reporters than we've seen in the past hundred years. So, if you want part of that story, you'll do this on my terms. If you do anything to cross me or try to make this town look bad, you might as well pack your bags and never return to Seaside Cove."

Lana Moreno's cheeks tightened and she swallowed. "Wow. You're tough. How about we forget this whole little incident ever occurred?"

"I have a better idea. How about I walk over to the counter and tell Mary O'Donnell to crank up the rumor mill? After that, I could walk down the street two doors and talk to the mayor. She loves to gossip and to tell people what to do. So that's how long you have, Ms. Moreno. In a couple of seconds, I walk over to that counter, and you start getting doors slammed in your face. What will your news director say then?"

Lana gritted her teeth, but kept quiet. On the other side of the table, Alastair chuckled.

"Well played. I don't believe I've ever seen Lana flustered before."

"Shut up, Alastair."

"Don't worry, Lana. Mums the word." He gave her a wicked grin.

"Fine. We'll play it by your rules, Mr. Atwood. But if you're not bringing good information to the table, our deal's off."

"Ms. Moreno, my daughter is eleven. For her, negative consequences usually mean getting grounded. But once we become adults, the consequences in life get much more difficult to deal with. Do you understand what I'm saying?"

The last of Lana Moreno's tough exterior cracked. She bit her lower lip, then chuckled. "Congratulations on the award, Mr. Atwood. I'm pretty sure you deserved it. What do you want to know?"

33

ALEX

APRIL 19

Hey Journal,

I finally get to be an official part of the investigation! Isn't that awesome? I only have a sec 'cause my dad wants me to spy on Adela and find out why she's really here. I'm so pumped that I had to tell you!

After Daddy left, me and Marquetta talked about the best way to deal with Adela. Marquetta agreed that I could talk to her on my own, but she's gonna hang out and pretend to be cleaning so she'll be really close if something happens.

I don't think Daddy or Marquetta really get Adela. There's no way she's the killer, and I don't think she's got a clue who is.

By the way, I still haven't had a chance to talk to Grandma Madeline about the wedding. Now that she's got this job at Howie's Collectibles, she's super busy, too. She said we'd talk tonight. I just hope that happens!

Xoxo

Alex

I tap on Adela's door and take a final look down the hall at Marquetta. She's vacuuming and dusting. It usually only takes us a few minutes to do the halls, but she's totally making it take a long time. We also had a checkout this morning and the new

188

guests haven't arrived, so if Marquetta needs something to do, there's the final inspection of the Captain's Quarters, too. Who knows? Marquetta's super fast and detailed, so she probably has a list of things she can pretend to do while she's waiting for me.

The door opens a crack and Adela peeks out. "What do you want?"

"We need to talk."

"What about your dad? Won't he get mad at me for corrupting you?"

"No way." I giggle. "He's clueless."

She kinda snickers, but rolls her eyes and opens the door. "Make it quick. I'm expecting a call."

"Thanks," I say as I pass her.

She's wearing her sweats again and has her hair pulled up. Before I even get in the room, the pizza smell slams me in the face. The room's a total mess. She's thrown a couple dresses and some underwear on the bed like she expects somebody to pick up after her. Her phone's there along with a laptop. There's a wet towel on the bathroom floor, and a pizza box sitting open on the little desk. She barely ate half of it. It looks gross now. This is totally bizarre—I'm having to resist the urge to treat her like a little kid and clean up after her.

Adela looks around the room like she's embarrassed. I think she might apologize or something, but then she crosses her arms in front of her and glares at me. Wow. It's so totally sixth grade.

"Why are you here?"

"I wanna be friends. And I realized you had some awesome ideas about the whole treasure thing."

She frowns at me and kinda relaxes a little. "I did?"

"For sure. It was your idea to go out to Dead Man's Cove. If it wasn't for you, we wouldn't have found the guy stealing the treasure."

"Well, I guess I did get this started." Adela looks at herself in the mirror and picks away a flaky piece of mascara. "Oh, God, I look all pasty white. This town and all this stress are terrible for my complexion." She makes a face at the mirror, then talks while she's watching herself. "I still don't have a story. If I don't get something soon, this whole trip will be wasted."

Wow. She's like totally obsessed with herself. Adela's pretty, but not super hot. Seaside Cove is a small town and we get a lot of guests at the B&B. I've never seen any of the girls who've stayed here be so obsessed with their looks. Marquetta's a lot prettier than Adela, but what's totally cool about her is she doesn't even think about it.

Adela's phone rings and the display lights up. *Uncle Ethan.* That's right! He's the one she was talking to when I saw her outside. She snatches up the phone and hides it behind her back.

"I have to take this. You need to leave."

She practically shoves me out the door and locks it. Standing there, I can make out her voice, but no words. Marquetta appears at my side and motions that we should walk away.

"Things didn't go as you planned?" Marquetta asks.

"She's super hostile right now. But I think I might have a lead on why she's really here."

"Really? Do tell."

"Not out here." I grab Marquetta's hand and drag her toward my room.

34

RICK

RICK CONSIDERED LANA MORENO TO be a lovely young woman—
lively blue eyes, dark hair cut at the shoulder, and fine
cheekbones. She wasn't yet fighting wrinkles around her eyes or
mouth. In fact, she was perfect for the camera, partly because
she could turn on the friendly reporter or fierce warrior on a
whim. With all that going for her, Rick still didn't like her.

She had a lot to learn about sources—when to push, and
when to ease up. In this case, she'd picked the wrong person to
try and strong-arm. And since he now had the upper hand, it
was time to make use of it.

"Let's begin with why you were sent to Seaside Cove in the
first place," Rick said.

"That's easy. Millions of dollars in sunken treasure off the
California coast? Who can resist that kind of story?"

"That's crap and you know it. What is your news director
looking for? I'm sure he gave you specifics." Rick desperately
wanted to ask if they'd been told to investigate Flynn, but he
wasn't about to give away the cards he was playing. He'd find a
way to work that into his questions in an indirect way.

Lana and Alastair exchanged a quick look, then Alastair
raised one hand and shook his head. "I'm just the pack mule,
Lana. How you handle this is up to you."

"All right. My news director got an anonymous tip that the archaeologist in charge of the operation was trying to steal the treasure. He happened to know her—Flynn O'Connor, right? He asked her what was going on and she flat-out denied the accusations, but she also told him she was worried because someone might be trying to discredit her."

"Seems like a flimsy basis for a story," Rick said. "If your news director knows Flynn and trusts her, why would he give that tip any credence at all?"

Lana sighed, picked up her mug, and drained the last of her coffee. She smiled at Alastair and set the mug down in front of him. "Would you mind getting me a refill?"

"Sure, Lana. Whatever you want."

The words sounded sincere enough, but as the man turned away, Rick caught him muttering under his breath. Apparently, there was no love lost between these two. "I assume you wanted to keep this between the two of us?"

"Alastair's a good guy, but he's got career aspirations, too. He wants to get out of the field, and I suspect if he thought he could buy the promotion at my expense, he wouldn't hesitate."

Aha. There it was. The rivalry. Rick checked, saw that Alastair was third in line, and turned back to Lana. "He's not here now."

"Mr. Atwood, I'm the proverbial low man on the totem pole. I got this story not because it's such a great lead, but because it's not. Basically, my news director sent me here to keep me out of the way. He's probably hoping I'll fail so that the next time there are layoffs, I'll be the easy target."

"It's a tough business," Rick said, leaving off the other half of that thought—it was getting tougher by the day.

"Come layoff time, guess who they'll cut first? The underperformers. If I don't make this into something, it will eventually cost me my job. That's why I'm so determined."

Chairs scraped at a nearby table for four as two couples prepared to leave. They all chattered eagerly as they made their way toward the front exit. Watching them made Rick wish he and Marquetta could take Alex and go someplace just for fun. A little time away from the day-to-day rigors of running a business —and the stress of conducting a murder investigation.

"So what have you found? Anything?"

"Not much." Lana shook her head as she pulled her hair back. "I was hoping the murder would give me something, but nobody seems to know anything about it."

"What have you learned?"

She told him how they'd tried to interview the people gathered at the crime scene on the night of the murder, how most had said they were visiting because of a news story they'd seen about sunken treasure, and how none had witnessed anything to do with the murder. "The bottom line is we walked away with nothing. All we got were a bunch of people who were interested in being on the news so they could say hi to their Aunt Martha."

"I'd like to see the footage. It might help in the investigation."

Lana opened her mouth as if she was about to say something, but stopped and looked up. "Thanks, Alastair." She accepted the mug he handed her and cradled it between her fingers.

"What's up?" Alastair asked.

"We were just talking about the interviews from last night," Rick said. "I'd like to see them."

Alastair planted his elbows on the table and grunted. "What's in it for us?"

It was the question Rick had feared would come up when they got to this point. It's certainly the one he would have asked if he were in their shoes, and since Alastair apparently understood the power game Rick was playing, the stakes had just gone up. Without Adam's help, he'd need something big to make these two share their work. It was a tall order, especially since he had nothing concrete he could offer.

"I could get a warrant."

"Maybe," Alastair said. "But that takes time and it would definitely put us at odds."

Rick's heart pounded. He had to come up with a tidbit that would be irresistible. Something like what Alex was so good at. Like what he'd done when she was having trouble getting to sleep. There had been plenty of those nights in New York, and he'd gotten very good at spinning yarns about knights and wizards and fairy princesses who did fantastical things and lived happily ever after.

Actually, he didn't need knights or princesses, only what he already knew. If he combined that with Alex's theories about the murder and Phillip Gibson, it might just work. "How about an exposé of the story all these other reporters are chasing?"

"What exposé?" Lana scoffed. "So far all any of us have is some tip that's looking like some crackpot made it up."

"That's where you're wrong." Rick recalled Alex's enthusiasm at lunch. If she were here, she'd weave a full-fledged conspiracy theory out of ragged wool. Rick raised his hands and motioned with his fingertips for Lana and Alastair to huddle closer. He whispered just loud enough for them to hear over the background noise. "It's not a crackpot, it's a professional."

"A professional what?" Lana asked, her blue eyes wide with confusion.

"Treasure thief. You see, the Chief and I have been keeping this under wraps, but that anonymous tip your news director received is partially true. There's a conspiracy to steal the treasure of the *San Mañuel*, but it's not Flynn O'Connor who's behind it. We believe Tuck Hall's death is linked to that conspiracy and whoever killed Hall is behind the whole thing."

Lana snickered as she shook her head. "You really expect me to believe that?"

"Your choice. We can part ways right now, but when the story comes out, you are going to be very sorry you walked away."

Alastair picked up a leftover crumb from his plate, gave Rick an evil grin, then looked at Lana. "Don't be so quick to walk away. Bottom line is we got nothing to lose by going along with this. Worst case is you get to expose the cops in this town as incompetent."

Lana clapped her hands together and her confusion turned into a smile. "Alastair, that's brilliant. Game, set, match, Mr. Atwood. We're in."

35

ALEX

ALL THE WAY TO MY room, Marquetta keeps asking what I'm up
to, but I just keep shaking my head. I don't want to say anything
here in the hall in case Adela comes out. When we're inside my
room, I lock the door and look at Marquetta.

"I went to Dead Man's Cove with Adela 'cause I overheard
her talking on the phone to her uncle. He must've asked if she
was having any problems and she mentioned me."

"Why do you think she was talking about you?"

"She called me a little busybody."

"Mmmm...I see. And that bothered you, did it?"

Maybe I should've left that part out. I can feel my shoulders
slump and I look down. Calling someone a busybody is totally
not a nice thing to do. "Yeah. Kinda." I look up at Marquetta and
my throat gets a lump in it. Marquetta's so pretty and she's so
nice to me and she's gonna be my mom someday and... "I'm not
a busybody, am I?"

Marquetta wraps her arms around me and pulls me close.
"Maybe a little bit. Especially when you're doing one of your
investigations. It's not necessarily a bad thing, but you don't
want to go overboard."

Her warm hands massage my shoulders. I relax into her and
let myself listen to her heart beat. That's when I realize I don't
care what Adela thinks of me. I pull back from Marquetta and sit

on the edge of the bed. "They had to be talking about the treasure 'cause she got all defensive when I asked about it."

"One phone call doesn't prove much, Sweetie. We don't know that she's planning anything nefarious."

"What's nefarious?" I kinda stumble over the word, but I wanna know what it means 'cause Miss Redmond's already made me go look up conundrum. I wasn't spelling it right, but I did have the right meaning. Anyway, Miss Redmond always tells us a good vocabulary is valuable. She'll be super impressed if I come in with another new word—unless I misspell it, and then she'll make me look it up—again.

Me and Marquetta sit side-by-side. I lean into her, and she puts her arm around me. I can't even count the number of times I wished for this with her. And now it's happening. The room gets blurry and my face feels hot.

"It means wicked or criminal," Marquetta says. "You should look it up to get the full meaning—and the spelling."

I sniffle and wipe a tear from my cheek. I don't think my real mom ever would have cared about my grades like Marquetta does. "Nefarious. I totally will."

Marquetta lifts my chin. When she looks into my eyes, she kinda frowns. "What's wrong, Sweetie?"

"I...I was thinking about how nice this is. Just you and me talking."

She touches my cheeks and gently wipes away another tear, then kisses me on the top of the head. "We can do this whenever you want."

"Really?" I know she's told me we can always talk, but I guess I'm still not sure she won't change her mind. My real mom did—about both me and Daddy.

Now Marquetta's got tears in her eyes and she's sniffling, too. "I love you as if you were my own flesh and blood. I will never abandon you."

"Promise?"

She holds out her hand with her pinky extended. "Promise. With a pinky swear if you want it."

I wrap my pinky around hers and we just sit for a minute. "I love you, Marquetta."

"I love you, too, Sweetie." Marquetta swipes at her cheeks and takes in a couple of short breaths. "Now," she sniffles, "where were we? You were telling me you've got other reasons to think Miss Barone is lying to us."

"When I was in her room, she got a call from her Uncle Ethan. She kicked me out and told me she had to take it. He's gotta be the one who sent her here 'cause she said he told her about the *San Mañuel*."

"Lots of people stay in touch with their relatives when they're here, Alex. You know that. Besides, even if he did send her here, it might have been for some other reason."

"Like what?"

"I don't know. Listen, I'm not saying you're wrong, I'm just saying we need more proof before we can say Miss Barone's trying to steal the *San Mañuel* treasure or Adam considers charging her as an accessory to murder."

I nod eagerly. "That's why I wanted to come in here. I might have a way to get some proof. Adela's super self-centered. She's like obsessed with clothes and acts like this big fashion diva, but she just throws her dresses on the bed."

"And the fact that she's a messy guest tells us what?" Marquetta smiles at me and raises her eyebrows.

Other than her being a slob? I scrunch up my face 'cause I'm getting super frustrated. Marquetta's right. We need more than what I've got so far. "I dunno. Do you have any ideas?"

Marquetta looks over her shoulder at my desk and my laptop. Her eyebrows go up and she smiles. "I just might."

36

RICK

RICK'S PLAN TO TURN THINGS around by making a deal with Lana Moreno weighed heavily on his conscience. He'd seriously misjudged Alastair Canes. The man was not just a glorified pack mule; he was sharp as a tack. The only thing Rick could do now was tell Adam about the deal and hope for the best. Rick walked up a block to the police station. Inside, Adam sat at his desk, his attention focused on his computer screen.

When Rick finished his explanation, he asked whether he should cancel the meeting.

"You told them this is some sort of plot, huh?" Adam asked.

"I needed bait to get Moreno interested."

"Look, buddy, you've got way more experience dealing with the press than I have. If you think the deal you made will do the trick, I'm willing to go along with it. What do you need me to do?"

"They'll be at the B&B at seven," Rick said. "Why don't you come and bring Traci? The girls can visit while we meet with Moreno and her cameraman."

"I'm sure Traci will be up for that. She'll be glad to have a chance to do something other than sit home and watch old movies. By the way, the coroner hasn't finished the autopsy yet, but she did say it's obvious the victim died from a fatal knife wound. She also believes the person who did this definitely had training."

After leaving the police station, Rick made a stop at the market. All during his shopping and on his way back to the B&B, he pondered the coroner's preliminary findings. Maybe they'd learn more once the autopsy was complete, but for now, this merely confirmed his fear that they were dealing with a trained killer.

Even as he climbed the front steps to the B&B, he couldn't shake the idea that they had a killer on the loose in Seaside Cove. When he pushed open the front door, he nearly collided with the Gibsons and Amy Kama on their way out to dinner.

The Gibsons thanked him for holding the door open and rushed out, but Amy stopped and waited, looking as though she might want to talk. "Any luck on the investigation?"

"Not much. For a second there I thought you were having dinner with them."

Amy frowned, then smiled. "No way. She seems nice, but there's something very strange about that man. We just happened to be leaving at the same time. Actually, I was happy you walked in when you did. It gave me a reason to break away."

"Gotcha. Glad my timing was good. I'd better get going, I have a TV news crew coming by tonight to show us their footage."

"Hoping you'll see something the human witnesses don't recall? Smart move. Good luck."

"Wait." Rick held up a finger. "Actually, I did have another question for you. How are you doing?"

"Better. I think that right after I saw the murder I was just in shock. Now, I'm starting to feel more like my old self. In fact, in a way, seeing the entire scene reminded me that violence can happen anywhere and I wasn't necessarily to blame for what happened in LA."

"Sounds like you're making progress."

"I think so. At least, I hope so. Well, I'm on my way to dinner."

Rick wished her a good night and walked through the front rooms to the back of the house and the kitchen. Marquetta was standing at the island with Alex opposite her and Adam Cunningham to the side. There were also two of Marquetta's large stainless steel bowls on the counter.

"I come bearing fruit, vegetables, and butter," Rick said.

"You'd better have some eggs in there, too," Marquetta said.

"Just the man I wanted to see." Adam gestured at the stool where Rick usually sat.

Rick placed the two bags he carried on the counter next to the refrigerator. "Eggs included. You got here fast, Adam."

"I drove and called Traci on the way."

"I take it she agreed to let you accept my dinner invitation?"

"Yes. In fact, she should be here any minute."

Marquetta's bowl contained lettuce, tomato, and cucumber. Two stalks of celery and a bunch of radishes sat on the counter next to the bowl waiting to be sliced. Alex's bowl, on the other hand, contained a chocolaty batter. When she dipped her finger in to taste test and rolled her eyes, he was convinced it contained nothing remotely healthy.

"Fortunately, I already had a pan of lasagna in the oven when Adam showed up," Marquetta said. "Otherwise, Mister Atwood, you would have been buying take-out for everyone. You didn't tell me what we were doing."

"Oops. I'm just lucky my fiancée is a mind reader. What's your other reason for coming over, Adam?"

"It may not be related, but we've had an incident on Flynn's dive boat."

"An incident?" What in the world did that mean? Rick raised his eyebrows and regarded Adam.

"Somebody tried to blow up the *Blue Phoenix*, Daddy." Alex threw her hands wide and let out a loud, "Boosh!."

Adam quirked one cheek, then shrugged. "Kids. They say the darnedest things. They didn't actually try to blow it up, but it could have turned into some serious damage, and, it's even possible it could have led to an engine fire. Basically, someone tried to sabotage the engine on the *Blue Phoenix* and, if it hadn't been for one of the deck hands spotting a broken lock, that boat probably would have been stranded at sea. In a worst case scenario, she could have gone down."

"Any suspects?"

"Nobody saw a thing. Actually, most of the crew were ashore while Flynn dealt with a bunch of these reporters who are wandering around town."

"So somebody snuck onboard, sabotaged the boat, then got off? That's pretty convenient."

"Or well-planned. One of the guys stuck around to do some maintenance. When he went below for some more varnish, he saw that the engine room door was ajar. He tried to lock it, but the lock was broken. That's when he got suspicious. He went into the engine room and noticed some grease on the floor. He started poking around and discovered the engine had been tampered with. It looks like whoever did this wanted to disable the *Blue Phoenix* for at least a few days. I'm becoming a believer in this conspiracy theory of yours."

Alex immediately perked up and looked at them with wide eyes. "What conspiracy theory?"

"Well, kiddo, you actually gave me the idea."

"Oh, that one. It was Marquetta's idea first," Alex said and grinned at Marquetta.

"Really?" Rick asked.

"Don't be so shocked, boss. I'm not just a maid and a cook, you know."

"I didn't mean it to sound the way it did. I just never thought of you as being so devious."

"Neither did I," Adam said. "Maybe I've been using the wrong consultant."

"No," Marquetta said firmly. "I'm perfectly happy being a consultant to your junior detective."

Alex exchanged a high-five with Marquetta, then beamed at Adam. "Do I get a badge?"

"No," Rick blurted.

"Sorry, munchkin, but you have to be at least eighteen to get a badge. Come see me in seven years." Adam turned to Rick and asked, "Are we on the same page?"

"As far as Alex becoming a deputy in seven years, no. But, as far as this case goes, I think so. After I spoke with Lana Moreno and her cameraman, I realized that the reporters are here almost as a distraction. I think they're part of this plan we're talking about."

Adam's attention flicked toward the butler door. When he seemed satisfied that the four of them were the only ones who would hear their conversation, he looked back to Rick. "We need to keep this under our hats, but so far it looks like it started with an anonymous tip to the news media telling them that Flynn is crooked. After that, the news media swarmed the town. They basically tied up everything and created all kinds of confusion."

"And then me and Adela found the treasure thief," Alex said.

"Right, kiddo. On a day when Flynn just happened to be out of town, this apparently rogue treasure hunter showed up. I think you're right. He must have been stealing from whoever hired him. Since he wound up dead that night, his boss must have discovered the double cross. Who knows? Maybe the murder was also a warning to anyone else who might have had similar ideas."

Adam held up a hand and began to count. "So we've got an anonymous tip to the press, a coordinated effort to do a fast in-and-out on the *San Mañuel*, and then a killing of one of the treasure thieves from Dead Man's Cove. Actually, if Alex and Miss Barone hadn't gone out there, they would have gotten away with stealing whatever they could and nobody would have been the wiser."

"And who knows how many times they might have come back?" Rick said.

"So what you're saying is that by showing up at Dead Man's Cove, your daughter and Adela Barone disrupted this grand plan." Adam fingered his chin while letting his green eyes flick from Rick to Alex. "If you're right, then your theories about Miss Barone must be incorrect."

"It would seem so." Rick let out a sigh that was long and slow and filled with exasperation.

"She's totally up to something," Alex said adamantly.

"How, kiddo? If she hadn't goaded you into going out there, nobody would have known about the thieves and Tuck Hall would probably still be alive."

"She's hiding something, Daddy. Maybe she was supposed to meet her accomplice and I got in the way. On the phone, she told her uncle she could handle me."

Marquetta cleared her throat. "What if Alex is right? What if Adela is somehow tied into this? Rick, I have a suggestion that might work for everyone. What if Alex and I continue to look into Adela while you and Adam handle your main suspects?"

He'd love to, if only they had some. But, the suggestion did help ease Rick's tension. That could be the perfect solution. With Marquetta 'consulting' to Alex, she'd keep her away from the direct path of the investigation. With Alex sidelined, it would be a load off his mind. "What do you think, Adam?" Rick asked.

"That could work." Adam's green eyes regarded Rick. "We've got a lot to do and unless Miss Barone comes back on the radar, there's no reason for us to be spending time on her. And this way, if she is somehow related, Markie and Alex can let us know. Sound good to you?"

"Works for me," Rick said. "Alex, Marquetta, are you good with that?"

"Totally." Alex exchanged another high-five with Marquetta. "You'll see, Daddy. We're gonna rock this."

That was not the response Rick had expected—and now he regretted his haste in dismissing Adela Barone as a suspect.

37

ALEX

WHILE MY DAD AND CHIEF Cunningham talk about the investigation, me and Marquetta go back to making the salad and dessert. Marquetta finishes chopping the veggies while I pour the batter for chocolate banana muffins into the molds. We don't get a chance to talk until we're cleaning up.

"Marquetta? Do you think Adela's involved?"

She bumps my hip with hers. "What? Are you having second thoughts about this deal?"

"No. Well, maybe a little. She's gotta be involved. She just has to."

"That could be, but what if it's unrelated to the murder? How will you feel then?"

My cheeks burn a little 'cause I so don't want to be wrong. "At least I'll know."

"And you'll prove she's not a suspect. That will help Adam and your dad, too." She hands me the last big bowl. It's eight quarts and last year when we got here I didn't think I could ever hold onto it. Now that I'm more at home in the kitchen, I totally love it, along with everything else about the B&B.

Dinner is kinda fun. It can be a little lonely being the only kid in a roomful of adults, but Traci's always nice and Marquetta always seems to have me in her thoughts. The closer it gets to seven, the more I feel kinda antsy. Getting to watch all the news footage is gonna be awesome. I'd like to see if Adela's in any of their shots. But when the reporters show up, everything falls apart.

"No," Miss Moreno says to my dad. "Our agreement was to let you and the chief see the footage. This was not supposed to be news night in Seaside Cove. Besides, I have questions for both of you. And I don't need spectators while I'm doing an interview."

"An interview was not part of our agreement," Rick said.

"My news director is totally against this meeting unless I get that." She crosses her arms over her chest, then looks at Chief Cunningham. "Would you be willing to make a few comments later, Chief?"

"I'll tell you when we're done, Ms. Moreno. Until then, let me know if you're not planning to cooperate, and I'll get started on that warrant."

"Fine," she huffs. "We'll do it your way."

My dad cocks his head toward the door. "Alex, I'm sorry, but you and Marquetta and Traci will have to do something else until we're done here."

Marquetta grabs the bottle of wine and cocks her head toward the door. "Come on, girls, let's go hang out in the living room with a warm fire."

My heart is super heavy as we leave. There's no way me and Marquetta and Traci are gonna get to stay. And there goes my plan to see if Adela was hanging out around the murder scene.

"Well, she's a bossy one," Traci says, then laughs as she sits on the couch that's opposite the one me and Marquetta use.

Marquetta pours more wine into Traci's glass. "I would guess Ms. Moreno has to fight for everything she gets. On the other hand, I hate being kicked out of my own kitchen."

Marquetta wants to sit close to the fireplace, so I grab the other end of the couch where I can watch the flames flicker. The fire is nice, but I'm super bummed out. "How am I gonna make any progress if we can't see the evidence?"

"What evidence is that, Sweetie?" Marquetta cocks her head to the side and looks at me.

"The video those guys took. I was hoping to see who was trolling the murder scene."

"Ah, your sneaky mind was working overtime." Marquetta laughs.

"I don't know what they're so protective of," Traci says.

"Maybe they don't have anything and they know it," Marquetta says.

"You think? What about you, Alex? I guess you think there's something worthwhile in all that video footage."

If we weren't sitting in the living room, I'd tell Traci I was hoping to see if Adela was there. But where we're sitting, our voices could carry up to the second floor. Any of the guests could hear us, and that wouldn't be cool. It would be super bad if Adela happened to hear me say I was looking to see if she'd been interviewed or if she was lurking around the crime scene.

I start to tell Traci that I do think there's stuff in the video when I see someone coming down the staircase. First it's the shoes, then the legs, then the frilly pink dress.

Adela shoots a look over her shoulder towards us, probably to see who's down here, then looks away. I'll never get information out of her now, but that doesn't mean I can't get information about her. I watch and wait until the front door closes behind her.

"What are you thinking about, Sweetie?"

Adela's gone. Probably to dinner. She won't be back for at least an hour. There are three of us, but the room's kinda quiet, so I lower my voice. "I still think she's hiding something."

"Let's say that I'd trust her a lot more if she hadn't lied about why she was here, and then dragged you into what could have been a dangerous situation."

I bite my lower lip, then smile at Marquetta. "She just went to dinner, you know."

"What's so unusual about that?" Traci asks.

"I think I know," Marquetta says. "Explain yourself, Alex. Now."

I get a fluttery feeling in my stomach. Maybe I'll get in trouble for this, but I hope not. "Well, she did leave a wet towel on the floor of the bathroom. And if it sits there for too long, it could damage the floor. I just thought it might be good to check on it. Or see if she's damaged anything in the room 'cause she's so careless."

"I see." Marquetta stretches out the last word, then cranes her neck to look at the front door. "We do have an obligation to keep the house in good condition for the next guest. Maybe we should check for damages."

"Oh, my God," Traci mutters. "Adam's going to flip."

38

RICK

RICK AND ADAM STOOD BEHIND Alastair Canes and Lana Moreno, who sat next to each other at the kitchen island. The plan was to have Alastair, who'd already opened up a folder on his laptop, navigate while Lana narrated.

"Where do you want to begin?" Lana asked.

Adam gestured at Rick with an open hand. "It's your show, buddy."

"What did you get prior to the murder?"

Alastair craned his neck around to look at Rick. "It was mostly background on the town. We'd just gotten in that afternoon."

Talk about coming way late to the party. Most of the other reporters had been here for a couple of days at that point. "Why were you so late getting to town?"

Lana dismissed Rick's question with a flip of her hand. "I told you, our news director knows Flynn O'Connor and didn't believe the tip. Alastair, show them the intro footage."

"Right." Alastair navigated to the first file in the folder and opened it. "Lana wanted to start out with the Seaside Cove Police Department in the background. We found this spot on the opposite corner on Main Street."

Alastair double-clicked the file and a video began to play. Lana's pleasant introduction to the town sounded much like the beginning of a travelogue with lots of nice adjectives interspersed for effect.

"As you can see, that was recorded at two-fifteen," Lana said as she pointed at the timestamp on the video. "We'd driven in from San Ladron and were hungry, so we grabbed a sandwich at the market and got to work."

"Did you get anything besides fluff before the murder?" Rick asked.

"I tried a couple of man-on-the-street interviews and didn't get much there, either. After the murder, we tried a few of the people in the crowd, but nobody admitted to seeing anything. Run the three that we got, Alastair."

The first person interviewed was Joe Gray. In his typical roundabout method, Joe described what a peaceful town Seaside Cove was and how he couldn't believe someone had committed murder on the streets of the town.

"Not helpful," Rick said. "Joe runs a boat charter service down in the marina. He's also one of those people who likes to promote the town whenever he can."

"No wonder he sounded like a Chamber of Commerce ad. Who did we do second, Alastair?"

"That was Gibson." Alastair clicked the link to start the video, then pointed at the man on the screen. "Isn't he one of your guests?"

"He is." Rick immediately noticed two things. First, Peg Gibson was not with her husband. Second, just as the Gardners had described, Gibson was carrying a cloth shopping bag.

"I'm with Phillip Gibson, a visitor here in Seaside Cove. Mr. Gibson said he was out for a walk when he heard a lot of commotion. Would you describe what you discovered when you got here?"

"There was a man hunched over the body. He was covered in blood and looked really shaken up—like maybe he'd just been in a fight or something."

"Did you feel as though you were in danger at that point?"

"Well, maybe." Gibson cleared his throat the way he had when he'd wanted to end the interview at the Crooked Mast. "I mean, if the guy was a killer, what would stop him from doing it again?"

"Was he carrying a weapon of any kind? Maybe a knife?"

Gibson sputtered a few times, then said, "Well, maybe."

"And the man you saw, was he the one the police took away?"

"Definitely."

"Thank you, Mr. Gibson." Lana turned back to the camera. "We'll keep trying to find witnesses to this brutal crime. Lana Moreno reporting from Seaside Cove."

"Did the station run that interview?" Adam asked.

"My news director wasn't happy about it. He said I put words in the man's mouth, but it was all we had, so he went with it. The third interview was even less helpful. Some guy in a wheelchair who was all freaked out over this murder spree."

"One incident does not a spree make," Adam grumbled.

"Alastair, would you replay Gibson's interview for me?" Rick waited as the video began, watching as the camera zoomed in on Gibson. "Stop! Right there," he blurted.

Adam looked sideways at Rick, then craned his neck to look closer. "What are we looking for, buddy?"

"Check out his hands and knees. There's mud, and he looks a lot like Alex and Sasha did when they were searching that planter in front of the Rusty Nail."

"Holy cow. I didn't even notice. Sharp eye."

"Very," Lana said as she inspected the image on the screen. "I didn't think anything of it when I was interviewing him. I just thought he'd been gardening or something. What's so important about some dirt on his knees?"

"If it hadn't been for my experience with my daughter and her friend, I might have missed it, too. Our Mr. Gibson lied to me about his after dinner walk."

"I agree," Adam said. "He may not be our killer, but he sure must know something about the missing artifacts."

"Wait!" Lana's eyes widened and she gaped at Rick. She pulled a notepad and pen from her purse and jotted down the date and time. "You have missing artifacts? What do you mean? Are you saying the line you fed us this afternoon is true?"

"It's looking like it." Rick chose his next words carefully as he continued. "We believe the man who was killed was a diver hired to do some recovery work by a treasure hunter. The police broke up the diving operation, but the victim escaped with a mesh bag we believe contained artifacts he'd brought up."

Lana looked up from her notes. "What does that have to do with Gibson?"

"He told me he was coming into some money, but then he made it sound like it was a stock deal or something. But if he found that stolen treasure and realized what it was, it would explain a lot. Why he's been so fidgety. Why his wife thinks he's jumping the gun spending money."

"Which room is he in?" Adam asked.

"He's in the Foresail Room. But they left for dinner a little while ago."

"I'll check to see if they've gotten back yet." Adam pointed a finger at Lana and Alastair as he stepped away from the group. "You two stay here. Rick, keep an eye on them."

"No problem. And by the way, just to be clear, this is private property and you do not have my permission to interview guests on the premises."

"We had a deal!" Lana snapped.

"We still do. And you'll still get your story, but the B&B is not part of the deal. While we're waiting, why don't you show me the third interview?"

Alastair shrugged, then turned back to his laptop. "No problem." He clicked the link to open the video.

"Is this another one of your guests?" Lana asked as the camera zoomed in.

"No. That's Howie Dockham. He runs a local antiquities shop. I never figured him for the melodramatic type."

The butler door opened and Adam came in wearing a grim expression on his face. "Traci told me the Gibsons haven't returned yet. We'll have to wait for them."

"So what are the girls doing? Just sitting in the living room people watching?"

"Uh, no. As a matter of fact, Traci said Alex and Marquetta went upstairs to check something out."

Rick regarded Adam for a few seconds, alarm bells sounding in his head. He desperately wanted to go find Alex and Marquetta. He didn't dare say a word with Lana and Alastair in his kitchen, which meant he could only wonder what his daughter was up to until he could make a break. Unfortunately, he was going to have to sit through more video footage that would do only one thing—waste more time.

"What about the crime scene? Did you get footage there?" Adam asked.

Alastair started a clip in which the camera panned the alley and came to rest on the body of Tuck Hall. A few seconds later, it captured Amy Kama standing off to the side watching intently as Clive was led away by Deputy Jackman.

"Stop!" Rick called out, then pointed at Amy. "Can you zoom in on her face?"

"Sure. You see something?"

Rick studied Amy's face for a minute, then said, "I don't know. She just looks so intense." He shrugged and let out a deep sigh. "You have any other footage that's worthwhile? Or are we at a standstill?"

"We did a few interviews today, but after our news director saw them, he told us to focus on law enforcement." Lana looked at Adam. "Can I send Alastair out for his gear, Chief?"

Rick's jaw tightened with the realization that in his desperation to find information, he'd made a terrible deal. The cords in his neck felt like steel springs stretched to their limit. How stupid could he have been?

"No, Ms. Moreno, you may not. You've shown us nothing to indicate you have any valuable information whatsoever. This meeting is over."

"Wait a minute, Chief. We had a deal."

"No, Ms. Moreno. The agreement was that we would review the footage and go from there. From what you've shown us, you've brought nothing to the table. I see no reason to waste anymore of your time or ours."

"But…"

"Good night, Ms. Moreno. I'll call you if I change my mind."

Rick waited until he was sure Lana and Alastair had left, then said, "I hate getting on the bad side of the press."

"I know, but we can smooth that over in the morning. I saw the look on your face when I told you about Alex and Marquetta. You think they're up to no good."

"Oh, yeah. They are. And I'm pretty sure you do not want to know what they've been doing."

"Forget it. I definitely want to know what scheme Nancy Drew came up with this time. Let's go."

39

ALEX

MARQUETTA KNOCKS ON THE DOOR to the Jib Room. "Housekeeping." There's no answer, so she slips the master key into the lock and gives me a sideways look. "Why do I let you talk me into doing this kind of thing?"

Ewww. How do I answer that? Maybe I shouldn't. Yeah. Less is more, right? I grab her hand. My heart is pounding like it's gonna explode in my chest. "We don't have to. Not if you think it's wrong. I don't wanna cause a problem."

She looks at me for a couple seconds, shakes her head, and smiles. "Oh, it's definitely wrong, but if there's a wet towel on the floor, we should see if it's doing any damage." She takes a deep breath, pushes open the door, and we go inside.

The room looks better than it did when I was here before. "She still hasn't made the bed, but at least she hung up the dresses. And she picked up her underwear."

"This was the last room I cleaned this morning. I remember seeing her leave around ten or so. I came in, made the bed and changed the towels in the bathroom." Marquetta walks into the bathroom and looks around. "Here's the one you saw, Alex. You're right, it's damp, but it's on the tile, so it should be okay until morning."

A soft chime comes from Marquetta's phone. She reads the display and winces.

My heart is still pounding so hard it makes me wonder if Marquetta can hear it. "Is Adela coming back?"

"No. Adam was going to come up here to talk to Mr. Gibson, but Traci told him she'd seen them leave for dinner. Adam went back to the kitchen. Nothing to worry about."

Wow. Marquetta's totally cool. I thought that would have been enough to make her want to leave, but she looks like she's into spy mode now. I inch closer to the bathroom to see what she's so interested in. It's a small box and it looks like she's reading the label. "What's that?"

"A prescription for migraine medication. There are three pills missing from this pack, and one of the wrappers is in the trash. I wonder if that's why she went back to bed after I was here this morning? The poor girl must have had a migraine and had to rest." Marquetta puts the box back where she found it. "Have we answered your questions, Sweetie?"

I look around. There's nothing of Adela's on the little desk except her laptop. On her way to the door, Marquetta stops and opens it up. The screen comes alive, but everything's password protected. Marquetta makes a face. I didn't see that one coming. I'm gonna have to start locking my laptop whenever I leave my room.

"I think we've seen enough. Let's get out of here before someone discovers us."

I'm totally cool with that. Even though I'm with Marquetta, the idea of getting caught in a guest's room kinda freaks me out. I go to the door, open it, and check the hallway. There's nobody in sight so I start to breathe easier. Marquetta joins me, makes sure the door is locked, then looks down the hall.

"Are we going back downstairs?" I ask.

"Not quite yet. Stay here." Marquetta walks quickly back to the second-floor landing. She whispers, "Traci? Are we still good?" She waits, then flashes a thumbs-up and comes back to where I'm standing. I never realized it before, but when she wants to be quiet, Marquetta can walk without hardly making any sound at all. She grabs my hand and pulls me along.

"Where are we going?"

"We have one more room to check." Marquetta stops in front of the Foresail Room, knocks once, and announces us just like she did at the Jib Room. There's no answer, so she slips the key into the lock and we duck inside.

"This is the Gibson's room," I whisper as Marquetta closes the door behind me. I totally don't believe we're doing this. Marquetta's usually so straight, and now she's like this super sleuth. "This is like the biggest rush ever."

"Don't get used to it, Sweetie. Let's be quick. Check their laundry bag for clothes that might have dirt or mud stains."

Marquetta checks the rest of the room while I'm searching through smelly laundry. "What are you looking for?"

"Signs of your missing treasure."

I pull a pair of pants out of the laundry basket. "Marquetta? I think these are the same mud stains from the Rusty Nail."

"Okay, so we know he must have gone looking for the treasure. The question is, did he find it? You said the man on the beach had a mesh bag?"

"Totally. It was a bright green. Kinda that glow-in-the-dark type color."

Marquetta begins pulling open the armoire drawers. There's no mesh bag. No lost treasure. Her phone chimes again. "Oh no. Traci just texted me a 9-1-1. We need to get out of here. Fast."

40

RICK

RICK HAD A STRONG SUSPICION he knew what Alex and Marquetta had been up to while he and Adam had been busy with Lana and Alastair. And while he didn't like the idea of sneaking into guest rooms, he also knew the purpose was well-intentioned.

"What did you just do, Traci?" Adam's voice held a definite edge to it as he strode toward his fiancée.

Rick rushed forward and got in front of his friend. "It's not her fault. You know who's behind this. If you want to get mad at someone, take it out on me."

Traci's voice quavered as she spoke. "I'm not four, Rick. You don't need to take the blame for me. I'm sorry, Adam. I'm sure you're disappointed in me." Traci straightened her shoulders and looked directly at Adam. "But technically, nobody has done anything illegal."

Rick suppressed a snicker. If that didn't sound like Alex talking. "She's right. Maybe it would be best if you two stayed down here by the fire while I dealt with this?"

Footsteps came from the stairway, and Rick turned to see who was coming. As he suspected, it was Alex and Marquetta.

"Dealt with what, Rick?" Marquetta asked.

If there was ever a time when Rick felt the walls had ears, this was it. Standing in the middle of the living room right next to the stairs was definitely not the place to be asking if they'd broken into a guest's room. "About where you two have been."

Marquetta draped a protective arm over Alex's shoulder. Alex was uncharacteristically silent and leaned her head against Marquetta. His daughter's feigned indifference alone was enough to confirm his suspicions.

"We were just doing a little turn-down service. That's all," Marquetta said casually.

Rick pressed his lips together to keep from bursting into laughter. A turn-down service? Since when had they offered that? Probably since his daughter had concocted the idea. He looked at Adam and cleared his throat. "Yes. Um, the turn-down service. We've been trying it out on a...selective basis."

Traci raised herself up on her tiptoes and kissed Adam's cheek. "See, silly? I told you there was nothing to worry about."

Adam looked down at Traci and sucked in a breath, then let it out slowly. He kissed her back and said, "Well, Miss Peterson, it appears you have done nothing illegal—this time."

"Why don't we adjourn to the kitchen so we don't disturb any of the guests?" Rick asked.

"Good idea, buddy. I'm curious to hear how this 'turn-down service' is working for you and if it's going to become a regular thing."

Alex started to say something, but Marquetta shushed her with a squeeze of her shoulder. "Let's go to the kitchen, Sweetie. I'm sure Adam's curiosity is killing him."

Rick entered the kitchen last, being sure to check the downstairs area for guests who might overhear their conversation. Satisfied they were alone, and that they'd left everything in the living room tidy, he let the butler door slip closed behind him.

Marquetta held up the bottle of Chardonnay they'd started at dinner. "Would you like the last of the wine, Rick?"

"I think I may need it. In fact, we might need another bottle. So, which room did you 'turn down'?"

"The Gibson's," Marquetta said.

"Oh."

"And Miss Barone's," she added.

Rick groaned, then took his wine glass from Marquetta and sipped. "Any others?"

"No, just those two. And, quite honestly, it wasn't that productive."

"I see. Meaning?"

To Rick's right, Adam stood silently, a somber look on his face, but obviously interested in any new information that might surface.

Marquetta flipped her hand nonchalantly and said, "Miss Barone suffers from migraines and Mr. Gibson got his pants dirty."

"Wait." Adam craned his neck forward, his brow furrowed. "What do migraines have to do with anything?"

"This morning I made the bed in her room. When Alex was up there, the bed was unmade, there were clothes strewn on top, and underwear on the floor. She must have come back to her room at some point, stripped down, and climbed into bed— probably after she popped a migraine pill. The question I have is what triggered the episode?"

"So you think you know what she did, just not why." Adam stroked his chin and took a deep breath, then let it out slowly. "Do you two have any ideas what this trigger might have been?"

Traci put her hand on Adam's forearm. "People have various triggers, Adam. It could be anything from changes in the weather to some particular food—or stress."

"Stress is a big one," Marquetta added.

"Could it be what happened at Dead Man's Cove?" Alex asked.

"Maybe, but that was the day before. Rick, you saw Miss Barone at breakfast. Did she seem okay to you?"

"I didn't spend a lot of time with her, but she seemed perfectly normal—standoffish, haughty. Overall, I'd say she was fine."

"I know she was," Traci said. "She came into the Bee's Knees about ten-thirty."

"Was she alone?" Marquetta asked.

"For sure. And she was in a pretty good mood, too."

"So, what could have happened after that to trigger a migraine?" Adam looked at Traci. "You saw her at ten-thirty?"

"About. I didn't check the clock."

"Tell you what. I'm going to call a couple of the merchants and see if she was in any of the other stores." Adam pulled a notepad from his pocket and jotted something down. "Now, what about the Gibsons? What's this about dirty pants?"

Marquetta nudged Alex with her elbow. "Your discovery—on both counts. You tell him."

"The bag I saw at Dead Man's Cove was a super bright green. Because Mr. Gibson said he saw the dead guy put it in the bushes at the Rusty Nail, me and Sasha were sure it was gonna be there. When it wasn't, I started wondering if Mr. Gibson went back and stole it. Since we were in the room, we looked for it, but it wasn't there. All we found were the dirty pants. It totally has to be the same mud me and Sasha had on us when my dad sent us back to school."

Rick noticed that Adam had been taking notes during Alex's little monologue. When she finished, Adam gave her a thumbs up. "Makes sense, munchkin."

Alex's face lit up with a satisfied smile. She pumped her fist once. "Yes! I knew it."

"Don't get too carried away. I'm not saying Gibson actually stole that bag, only that it's a possibility. I'm going to need to talk to Mr. Gibson and see if he'll tell me anything. And even if he did steal the missing artifacts, it doesn't mean he committed murder."

"So when are you gonna talk to him?" Alex asked.

"I guess that depends on when he and his wife get back from dinner. He deserves the opportunity to tell me his side before I start drawing conclusions. Now, did you find anything else?"

"That was it," Marquetta said. "It's not much to go on."

Adam regarded Rick with concern etched on his face. "What's going on with you, buddy? You look like you're deep in thought."

"I can't help but think these are pieces in a larger puzzle."

"With the larger puzzle being that conspiracy we were talking about?"

"The *San Mañuel* and it's treasure are certainly the prize. If we could find this missing bag, it might help answer that part of the question. I just don't like all these different things happening at once. First, it was the press getting this bogus tip about Flynn being crooked. Then Adela Barone showed up and dragged Alex off to Dead Man's Cove. Now we've got treasure thieves, sabotage on Flynn's boat, and a murder. It's all just too coincidental. Don't you think?"

Adam let out a long sigh and shook his head. "I'd feel better about all these links we're drawing if we had some sort of proof."

"What kind of proof?" Alex asked.

"I'll know it when I see it. That's all I can tell you."

Marquetta chuckled. "I've known Adam since elementary school, Sweetie. What it really means is right now he's as confused as everyone else."

It wasn't hard to see that Marquetta was right, and Rick hoped they could figure out what—or who—was the link to all the pieces before it was too late.

41

ALEX

Hey Journal,

I'm super bummed out. I was totally sure me and Marquetta would have cracked the case when we snuck into Adela's and the Gibson's rooms. The truth is, we can't prove anything! At least I didn't get grounded. It was totally like I had one of those get-out-of-jail-free cards 'cause I was working with Marquetta and Daddy can't ground her! LOL

By the time I came up for bed, Chief Cunningham and Traci were getting ready to leave and the Gibsons still hadn't gotten back from dinner. They must be having an awesome time 'cause they haven't stayed out so late before. I'll talk to them in the morning and see if they'll tell me anything.

It's getting late, Journal. My dad will be coming up soon, but I kinda wish it would be Marquetta instead.

Somebody just knocked on my door. Gotta go!

Xoxo,

Alex

Marquetta pokes her head in the door, and I get a big smile on my face. I wave for her to come in and lay my journal on the bed. She closes the door behind her and sits next to me. She looks at the journal, then at me, and strokes my forehead. Her fingertips are warm and soft.

"You're still writing in your journal?"

"All the time. It's awesome to have a place where I can be me."

"And not worry about anyone criticizing you?"

I bite my lower lip and my face gets kinda hot. "Yeah. Marquetta? Is that being selfish?"

"No, Sweetie, it's not selfish at all. Now, you've had a big day and should get some sleep."

I know. And it was almost a super big disaster. "I was hoping it would be you instead of my dad."

"Why's that?" Marquetta grins at me. "Are you worried you might get in trouble for our little escapade?"

I can feel the heat in my cheeks again. "Maybe. But..." I look away until she puts her fingers under my jaw and turns my head to face her. "My mom never did this."

Her smile fades and Marquetta frowns at me. "I am so sorry for what your mother put you through, Alex. I hope the hurt will fade in time."

The room gets kinda blurry, and now I've got the sniffles. "It is, already. Thanks to you."

Marquetta kisses me on the forehead and straightens my blanket. "You know, when I mentioned coming up here to your dad, he said you'd told him you were getting too old to have him tuck you in."

I don't know what to say, so I just shrug and look away.

"It's okay, Sweetie. Your dad will always be here for you. And I hope I can, too."

"Do you think..."

Marquetta waits for me to finish my question, but when I don't, she asks, "What?"

"Do you think you and Daddy will get married soon?"

"I hope so. With all my heart. But we have to do this in our own time."

And wham! Just like that, I get it. I didn't before, but I do now. "The more me and Grandma Madeline push you guys the harder it is for you."

"The truth is, I'm not looking for a big wedding. But, I do want a perfect one. And that means your dad and I need to work out what we want."

"Not what me or Grandma Madeline want."

"Exactly. Now, you need to get some sleep."

She fusses with the covers kinda like my dad does, but not exactly the same way. As I snuggle down, I think about how nice it would have been if Marquetta had been my real mom. My life would be so different.

"Marquetta? Would you tuck me in again tomorrow night?"

She smiles at me. "It would be my pleasure, but you have to promise me one thing."

"What's that?"

"Well, two things. First, you'll tell me if you ever get tired of me doing this?"

I shake my head. "I never will."

"If you do, just tell me. But the other thing is I don't want you going off to investigate on your own. I will help you in any way I can, but we have to do things as a team. Okay?"

"Okay. But I can still do research, right?"

"Are we talking about doing things online?"

"For sure."

"That's no problem. But from what Adam and your dad are saying, there's a dangerous man somewhere in this town, and we don't want you getting anywhere close to him. You sneaking off on your own is not an option. Got it?"

"Promise." I sit up in bed and let the covers drop as I throw my arms around her neck. "I can't wait until you're my mom."

Marquetta holds onto me a little longer, then eases me back down. Now she's got the sniffles, too. "Can you keep a secret?"

I bite my lower lip and nod.

"I can't wait, either."

When Marquetta turns out the light and closes my door, I lay in bed looking at the ceiling. A crack of light seeps in around the drapes. My heart is so happy I think it's gonna burst. I finally get why Marquetta and my dad have been taking so long to arrange the wedding. I guess if I was getting married, I'd want mine to be perfect, too.

I close my eyes and think about what Marquetta said. I can do online research. Like maybe check out Adela's social media. Yeah. Totally. I'm gonna do that tomorrow. I hope it's gonna help us figure out who Adela really is.

42

RICK

EVEN THOUGH RICK AND ALEX had lived in Seaside Cove for more than a year, Rick still hadn't adjusted to spring mornings along the coast. Sometimes, it seemed as though the days, with their dreary cloud cover, dimmed the sunrises until they blended into one monotonous cycle of gray mornings and gloomy days. The worst were the ones when the overcast never burned off and sunset was also nothing more than a fading of the light until the sky dimmed to black.

At five-thirty, Rick closed and locked the door to his room. While passing through the dining room, he noticed light peeking from beneath the butler door and heard the faint sounds of Marquetta at work.

"Good morning," Rick said as he entered.

Marquetta looked up from the cutting board before her. "Hey. How'd you sleep?"

"Not very well." Rick put on his apron, then went to fill a mug with coffee. "I waited up until midnight, but the Gibsons never showed."

Marquetta laid down her chef's knife and bit her lip. "I hope nothing's happened to them. Did you check their room this morning?"

"No. I didn't have a good excuse to go knocking on their door at o'dark thirty. I'll watch for them at breakfast. I need to let them know Adam will be here at eight-thirty and wants to talk with them."

As he busied himself with the morning routine of helping to prepare breakfast for the guests, Rick couldn't stop his thoughts from returning to Phillip and Peg Gibson. Marquetta was right—he hoped nothing had happened to them. Alex arrived to help with the initial rush of breakfast orders just before Rick opened the dining room at six-thirty. She looked far more awake than he felt, and he'd had two mugs of coffee to get himself going.

Rick kept a close watch on Alex, who continually scanned the dining room as if she were looking for someone. When the two of them returned to the kitchen, Alex looked up at Rick.

"I don't see the Gibsons, Daddy. They're usually the first ones here."

"They were out late last night, apparently. I've been watching for them, too."

"Maybe I should check on them?"

"No, Alex. They deserve their privacy. At least until eight-thirty when Adam will be here to interview them."

By seven, the first wave of guests had been served and Rick gave Alex a thumbs up, their signal that he'd be able to handle the rest of the shift on his own. Instead of darting off to the kitchen for her own breakfast, Alex came and stood next to him.

"What's going on, Daddy? The Gibsons still aren't here, Miss Kama's not here, and neither is Adela."

"I don't know, kiddo. We'll get it figured out. Now, you have to get moving. You've got school today."

At eight-thirty, Rick closed the breakfast service, restocked the coffee and tea carafes, and went to the kitchen. To his surprise, Adam was already there. He stood next to Marquetta, an apron covering the front of his uniform, a dishtowel in one hand and a plate in the other.

"I didn't realize we had a new hire," Rick said. "Did you check his references?"

"He's a hard worker. Inexperienced, but he caught onto how to dry a plate quickly," Marquetta said. "His hourly rate is cheap, so I'm not complaining."

Adam rubbed his stomach and winked at Rick. "Bacon, eggs, and fried potatoes. Man, you guys know how to live."

"I never saw you come in," Rick said.

"I came around the back way. I didn't think you needed your guests thinking the place was being raided or something."

"Don't kid me. You wanted breakfast first. Lucky you, I'm getting oatmeal," Rick grumbled. "Hey, the Gibsons, along with a couple of the other guests, never showed up for breakfast. I'm actually starting to get a little worried about them."

"Go," Marquetta said. "I can handle this."

Rick and Adam looked at each other with raised eyebrows, then ditched their aprons and hurried out of the kitchen. To Rick's surprise, Amy Kama stood at the coffee carafe sipping from a mug. She stifled a yawn, and blinked a couple of times.

"Sorry," she said. "I couldn't sleep last night."

"Remembering your incident?" Rick asked.

"No, actually, I've been thinking about this murder. Chief, I think there might have been someone else in the alley besides Clive Crabbe when I arrived. I'd blocked it out, but I could swear I heard someone's footsteps—like maybe they were walking away or something."

"Walking away? With everything that was going on, that's pretty calm," Adam said.

"I know, Chief. That's what bothered me. Whoever it was must have been on the other side of the dumpster in the shadows."

"That's consistent with the theory we've been kicking around," Adam said. "It would also back up Clive's story that someone hit him from behind and knocked him out. Can you think of anything else?"

Amy shook her head and sighed. "Not really."

"Thank you, Ms. Kama. If you remember something, please let me or Rick know. Sorry, I'd love to talk further, but right now we need to go speak with one of Rick's guests."

"That wouldn't be the Gibsons, would it?"

"As a matter of fact, it is." Rick cocked his head to one side and let his curiosity take over. "How did you know?"

"They left around two. I finally gave up trying to sleep and came down to sit by the fire somewhere around one o'clock. I hope you don't mind, Rick, but I turned on the gas log. I turned it off when I went upstairs."

"No worries," Rick said. "You said they left around two?"

"Yes. They came in around quarter to, scurried upstairs, then came down about fifteen minutes later. I was so shocked because they had their bags with them. It looked like they were in a huge hurry."

Adam made a note in his pad, then, with a grimace, shook his head. "How long were you down here?"

"I went back to my room about two-forty-five. And, no, they didn't come back while I was here."

"Hope your room was prepaid, buddy."

"I doubt that we'll have a problem. But I do need to go check for damages and see if they left anything behind. Amy, did they say anything?"

"Not to me. It didn't look like they were too happy with each other. Especially, the Mrs. She was very put out with her husband. Is he a suspect?"

Rick glanced at Adam, who answered Rick's unasked question with a nonchalant quirk of his cheek. Apparently, Adam had no problem in sharing information with Amy. Come to think of it, she might even have a suggestion or two on how they could proceed.

"We don't think he committed the murder, but we think he witnessed something. He may also have found a mesh bag containing some artifacts stolen from the *San Mañuel* dive site."

"Oh, I heard about that in town yesterday. Lots of people want to find it. Right?" Amy exaggerated an eye roll and laughed. "Is it like that all the time around here? Everybody all hyped up on rumors about sunken treasure?"

"It takes some getting used to," Rick admitted with a smile. "Did you hear the Gibsons say anything about it?"

"It could be what the Mrs. was so upset about. She was going on about unnecessary chances and how this trip had turned into a disaster thanks to her husband's greed. Even though she was whispering, I could tell she was ragging on him pretty good."

"Anything else?" Adam asked between scribbles.

"Not that I can recall."

"Thanks, Amy. Keep this up and Adam will want to put you on the payroll."

She raised her eyebrows and regarded Adam. "Do you have an opening, Chief?"

"Maybe, Ms. Kama. Come talk to me later today."

"Why don't you two talk right now? I'll go check on the Gibsons. If they really did skip out last night, there's no rush. I'll check the room and wait for you to come up."

Rick went up the stairs and straight to the Foresail Room. He knocked twice, then announced himself and eased open the door. It looked like Amy was right. The Gibsons had pulled off a quick getaway. Shaking his head, Rick walked around to inspect the room.

The bedspread was rumpled and folded over on itself to form a triangle. A couple of hangers had been left on top of the sheets and blanket. In the bathroom, Rick found towels on the floor that still looked damp. Overall, it wasn't as bad as it could have been. They hadn't destroyed anything. Assuming they didn't try to skip out on the bill, everything would be fine.

Rick went back to the bed, picked up the hangers, and placed them on the rod where they belonged. Returning to the bed, he inspected it closely. The sheets were still tucked in. Everything neat, except for the bedspread. Nobody had even slept here. And if what Amy told them was correct, they hadn't intended to sleep here either. So why start to pull down the covers? And why only turn down one corner?

Taking the corner that had been turned down, Rick pulled it back to the top of the bed and recoiled at the sight of a large dark spot in the middle of the white duvet. That had to be mud from the planter in front of the Rusty Nail.

He pulled out his phone, dialed Adam's number, and without any preamble, said, "The Gibsons have gone on the run with that bag we've been trying to find."

43

RICK

RICK INCHED CLOSER TO THE bed, his anger surging as he inspected the mud stains on the white duvet. Most guests were careful about what they put on the covering, but apparently the Gibsons had no such inclination. At the sound of someone knocking, Rick stopped mentally cursing Phillip Gibson and greeted Adam at the door.

Adam looked around the room, spotted the stained duvet, and said, "I thought you were going to wait for me."

"Sorry. When they didn't answer, I opened the door, and when I saw the empty room, I got caught up in seeing if they'd done any damage." Rick pointed at the duvet. "Looks like they set that bag on the bed. We'll have to take it into San Ladron to be cleaned."

"Let's hope it doesn't cost you an arm and a leg." Adam snapped a photo of the duvet, checked it, then took another. "Sorry, Rick, but I'm regarding the Gibsons as fugitives. I want to take this in as evidence."

"Sure. I'm hoping it's not ruined."

"I also want to give the room a good once-over before I release it. It shouldn't take too long. I'll take a few more photos and…"

Adam stopped at the sound of his phone chirping loudly. He pulled the phone from its holster and frowned as he read the display. "What's he want?"

"Who?"

"Joe Gray. This can't be good."

Rick inspected the room again as Adam listened and made facial expressions that were the best visual representation of a groan he'd ever seen.

Adam ended the call with a curt, "I'll be there in five minutes."

"Now what?" Rick asked.

"There's been another sabotage attempt on Flynn's boat. This time, one of the crew members was injured. I'd send Jackman, but she's at a training session in San Ladron. I definitely have to talk to the mayor about freeing up my budget. This is ridiculous."

With that, Rick had to agree. Even his own arrangement with the mayor to help Adam was driven in part by Francine's unwillingness to spend money. He took a final look around as he closed the door and made sure it was locked.

"I'd love to stay here and help Marquetta get this room back into service, but there's not much we can do until you release it. I'll go with you. If we can document what happened on the *Blue Phoenix*, you can come back here and wrap this up."

Adam headed straight to the marina while Rick gave Marquetta a quick recap of the situation. Despite her reassurances that she could handle the B&B and that he should not worry, Rick felt a twinge of guilt as he exited the front door. The walk to the marina took only a few minutes, and Rick immediately saw Adam standing on the dock next to the *Blue Phoenix* talking to Joe Gray.

Joe's voice carried over the small marina background noises. Once Joe got wound up like he was now, he sounded like a small dog yapping in the middle of the night. Even the waves lapping against the dock pilings couldn't take the edge off his rant.

"And I'm telling you, Adam, you need to close off the road out of town, because this guy is still here."

"I can't just close off the only road in and out of Seaside Cove, Joe. But, since you got a photo of the man who did this, we might be able to find him—if we act fast. Send a copy of the photo to Devon and have him put out a special edition of the *Cove Talkers Newsletter*. All he has to do is publish the photo with a message that the man is armed and dangerous and for anyone who sees him to contact me immediately."

Joe grinned. "Consider it done, Chief. Devon's going to love this," he said as he walked away, already typing out a message on his phone.

"You made his day," Rick said.

"You know Joe. Loves to be involved. Loves his gossip. Now, let's talk to the crew and see what we can see."

Adam started toward the *Blue Phoenix*, but Rick stopped him. "Here comes Flynn."

"Oh, crap." Adam watched Flynn stride toward them, then added, "She looks mad enough to spit peas."

When Flynn was about ten feet away, she snapped, "I got a call saying my deck hand has been injured. What is going on in this town, Chief?"

"We're working on figuring it out, Flynn. The problem is, this is a lot bigger than we initially thought it was."

Adam explained the theory that someone was executing a coordinated plan to ruin Flynn and gain access to the *San Mañuel*. By the time he finished the explanation, Flynn was gritting her teeth.

"I will protect that site until my dying day. There's so much history down there. I cannot and will not lose it to some two-bit treasure thief." She waved to a man standing on the deck of the *Blue Phoenix*. "Now, if you'll excuse me, I need to talk to Captain Struthers."

No sooner had Flynn spoken than the man she'd waved to came down the gangway to the dock. He wore a US Navy ball cap and a dark blue windbreaker and introduced himself to Rick and Adam, then directed his attention to Flynn.

"We have a serious problem. The intruder was a lot less subtle this time. He was armed when he boarded, went straight to the bridge, and smashed up my navigation panel. Telly got a jump on him, but the intruder pistol-whipped him with a Glock 37 and threatened to shoot the next man who tried to stop him."

Adam looked closely at Captain Struthers. "A Glock 37? That's pretty specific. Are you sure?"

"Captain Struthers was a Navy SEAL, Chief. He knows his weapons, and he knows how to use them."

The captain gazed at Flynn with the eyes of a patient parent. "No need to go into all of that, Flynn. But she's right, I do know one end of a gun from the other. Besides, the model is etched on the barrel. Pretty hard to miss it."

"A lot of people might just see a big gun pointing at them and panic," Adam said.

Struthers shook his head. "Not on my crew. These men have all seen battle conditions. I'd trust my life to any one of them."

"And they to you, Captain," Flynn said.

"Thank you, but I underestimated the intruder. I'm posting an armed guard immediately. We weren't expecting hostile activity in this marina, but we'll deal with it. They won't get aboard again."

Captain Struthers did not strike Rick as the kind of man to take unnecessary chances with his boat or crew. So how had he gotten caught off guard a second time? "Just out of curiosity, why didn't you post a guard after the first sabotage attempt?"

"I did. The intruder approached, asked for permission to come aboard, then pulled his weapon. My man wasn't armed. And I can tell you this, the guy you're looking for, he's well trained. He knows what he's doing and I have no doubts he'd shoot to kill."

44

ALEX

ALL DURING SCHOOL, I KEEP thinking about Grandma Madeline
and how hard we've been working to get Daddy and Marquetta
married. It wasn't until after my talk yesterday with Miss
Redmond and then Marquetta last night, that I got it. We can't
rush them. Besides, the reason I wanted the wedding sooner was
so Marquetta could be my mom. But I've realized nothing will
change because she already is, at least, in our hearts. All the
wedding's gonna do is make things official. And now I have to
get Grandma Madeline to understand that, too.

The minute Miss Redmond dismisses class, I head for the
door. I've already told my friends I have to rush downtown after
school. Grandma Madeline is probably working, so I ride to the
bike rack near Howie's Collectibles and lock up my bike. The
sun feels good on my face as I walk toward the store.

Mayor Carter stops sweeping the sidewalk in front of Scoops
'n Scones and waves to me from across the street. As I pass Hot
Feet, I see the owner inside showing some cool sandals to a
couple of customers. She sees me and waves, too. I never
thought I'd like Seaside Cove when we first moved here, but now
it feels like a real home.

I don't see Grandma Madeline until I've climbed the steps
onto Howie's front porch. She's inside talking to a customer. I
stop and look up and down the street. The downtown area is all

pretty old houses that have been turned into shops, and I know all the people who run those shops. Seaside Cove is totally my home. It's where my dad is. And Marquetta. And Grandma Madeline. They're my family, whether my dad and Marquetta get married or not.

The customers Grandma Madeline was dealing with come out of the store and leave. A second later, Grandma Madeline is standing next to me. The little lines around her gray eyes crinkle into a smile.

"What are you doing here, dear? Do we have time to strategize?" She raises and lowers her eyebrows.

"That's why I came to see you. We need to talk."

She clucks a couple times and frowns. "Oh, sounds serious. What's wrong?"

I take a step closer and wrap my arms around her. When she hugs me back, I let myself settle into her for a few seconds. Grandma Madeline's a little on the heavy side, so it's kinda like settling into a comfy pillow. "My teacher, Miss Redmond? She said something yesterday about my dad and Marquetta getting married."

"What was that, dear?"

"She said we shouldn't push them because it only makes it harder for them."

Grandma Madeline takes me by the shoulders and looks at me. "I thought you wanted a baby brother, Alex?"

"I did...I mean, I do. But my dad says he married my mom too soon. He said neither of them were ready and how it put a strain on everything. Then, when my mom got pregnant with me it made things even worse. I don't want Marquetta to hate me 'cause we pushed them into getting married before they were ready."

"I see." Her voice gets kinda curt. "Well, I would dearly love to have a grandbaby, but I'm certainly not in favor of my daughter getting pregnant before the marriage."

"But, it's not what we want that matters. They have to make their own decisions." I look at her and let out a heavy sigh. "I know you're not really my grandma. Not yet, anyway. And I totally want to have you as my grandma, but I think we need to wait for them to catch up."

She takes a deep breath and pulls me in for another hug. "You're right, dear. Whether they're married is not going to change the way I feel about you or your father. Or what my daughter's doing with her life. What matters is their happiness. Marquetta has a mind of her own, much like you. If I didn't know better, I'd swear you popped out of her womb."

Ewww. That's kinda gross, but I get her point.

I look up at her and raise my eyebrows. "So we're gonna be patient?"

She lets out a big sigh. "I suppose. And by the way, you may continue to call me grandma if you like. I love you dearly and, I have to admit, it does have a very nice ring to it."

We exchange another big hug, but she breaks it off and sucks in a breath.

"What's wrong?"

"You need to be careful, dear. There's a dangerous man on the loose in town. A special *Cove Talkers Newsletter* came out a short time ago. This man forcibly boarded a boat at the marina and assaulted one of the crew. It's all terribly frightening, and I think you should go home right now."

The *Cove Talkers Newsletter*? I pull out my phone and check messages. Sure enough. Mr. Van Horne sent out a special edition with just a photo of a mean looking man and a few sentences about the *Blue Phoenix* and what Grandma Madeline told me.

"I gotta go. Bye!" I run down the stairs and head toward my bike.

"Where are you going, Alex?"

"Home," I yell over my shoulder as I run toward my bike. I stop to tell her I'm looking forward to seeing her tonight at dinner. She blows me a kiss, then I turn around and run the rest of the way.

The ride home only takes a couple minutes. When I get to the B&B's front sidewalk, I take the little decomposed granite path that shoots off to the side and goes around the house. The sea breeze has picked up this afternoon like it always does and it makes it feel extra cold in the shade.

When I get to the shed where I keep my bike, I rest it against the wall and pull out the key my dad gave me. I open the lock, get my bike put away, and then close up the shed.

The wind whistles through the bushes and the trees. Our gazebo isn't far away. It's got eight sides with a floor that's raised about two feet off the ground. There's a white canopy covering the top and white lattice around the base to keep out small animals or little kids, but there's something wrong with the lattice. Part of it's out of place. No. Wait. It's broken.

We can't see this side from the house, and I was in a hurry when I left for school this morning. I also didn't notice that the bushes around the base look like someone trampled them.

Somebody's been here.

I look around. There's nobody in sight. What if they're hiding? Watching.

It could be the man Grandma Madeline told me about.

Maybe I should call for help? But if he was here, wouldn't he have grabbed me already?

My heart races, and I take a step toward the gazebo.

45

RICK

WITH THE B&B WORK behind them for the day, Rick and Marquetta went to Rick's office to grab a bit of solitude. Rick sat behind his desk checking out the special edition of the *Cove Talkers Newsletter*. Marquetta sat opposite him in one of the plush leather visitor chairs, which squeaked with her every movement.

"Devon sure got that out quickly. Let's hope it helps," Rick said.

"I never really thought about our little newsletter having a useful purpose before, but almost everyone in town reads it. If that man shows his face anywhere, Adam will hear about it."

"I sure hope so." Rick closed the lid on his laptop and regarded the coffered ceiling.

"What are you thinking?"

"Oh, nothing about the newsletter. I was just remembering how much I hated this room when we first got here. I mean, come on, mahogany bookshelves and a coffered ceiling in a private office? I thought it was completely overstated opulence."

Marquetta scanned the room and sighed. "I believe you called it a man pandering to his own vanity."

"Ouch. Throwing my own words back at me. That hurts."

"You're forgiven."

The playful smile and wink Marquetta gave him sent a flush of yearning into Rick's veins. The sooner they became man and wife, the better.

"When you got here you knew nothing about Captain Jack," Marquetta said. "But now I think you're starting to understand him. He was a man of so many contradictions."

"And one who was very meticulous about every detail when he remodeled. It took awhile, but now I appreciate that this room is more than a pretentious library with old books and fancy furniture. I've also realized it's a way to connect with my grandfather and commemorate his life."

"Captain Jack tried to act so rigid, but he had a huge heart, Rick. He took good care of me and my mother. He used to tell my mother he was coming up here to think, but she once told me it was his way of saying he was going to take a nap."

Rick chuckled. "It's a good room for that. It's become my refuge where I can maintain complete focus. In fact, right now, I need some focus to figure out a brilliant way to wrap up Tuck Hall's murder and stop the attacks against Flynn."

He looked up at the ceiling again. It's dark beams formed a complex, interwoven pattern, kind of like his grandfather. Captain Jack, so gruff on the outside, had been tormented by insecurities Rick had never realized until his grandfather was gone. The debt from his grandfather's remodel had almost sunk the B&B at one time. But these days, with the town suffering from an overabundance of tourists and the B&B filled to capacity, the weight had been removed.

"You're pretty deep in thought, Mr. Atwood. Or maybe you're the one who needs a nap."

"No," Rick laughed. "I was just thinking about how well the B&B is doing these days. Part of the credit for our success goes to Captain Jack. His remodel turned this into an upscale destination that draws visitors back year after year."

Skepticism showed in Marquetta's eyes as she gazed at him. "Really? You didn't look like you were thinking about business."

"Looks like I'm busted. You're right. It was more than that. There are only two other places for visitors to stay in town, Mrs. Chambers's little B&B and the Seaside Cove Inn."

"I don't see why you'd give the Inn a second thought. Ray's got a lot more rooms, but his place is cheap and caters to..." Marquetta stopped and her lips parted. "Are you thinking this man you're looking for is staying there?"

"It's possible. If he's from out of town, where else is he going to stay? Mrs. Chambers only has two rooms, but Ray has fifty. He's not going to know all those people."

"He doesn't even try. Ray's strictly a get-them-in, get-them-out kind of guy. He might remember a face, though."

"Exactly what I was thinking." Rick dialed Ray's number, feeling his anticipation grow as he waited.

"Seaside Cove Inn." Ray growled, his tone both gruff and curt.

"Ray, this is Rick Atwood. Do you get the *Cove Talkers Newsletter*?"

"Of course. Why?"

"Have you seen the special edition Devon put out earlier today?"

"Must be some big goings on for it to come out on a Thursday. Besides, it's been busy and I haven't seen email at all. One of my maids called off sick."

"I understand. But you should take a look at it. There was another incident of sabotage on Flynn O'Connor's boat. One of her crew was hurt, but Joe Gray got a photo of the culprit as he tried to get away. That's what the special edition is all about. This guy's armed and dangerous."

There was a long pause, then Ray grumbled, "Hang on a sec."

Rick waited as he listened to the sounds of tapping on a keyboard. About thirty seconds later, Ray let out a long sigh.

"He's here. Staying in 203. I knew there was something off about him, but he had a reservation. Paid in cash. You want me to call Adam?"

"I can give Adam a heads up. So the guy hasn't checked out yet?"

"Tomorrow morning. Tell Adam that if he does come to get him, don't shoot up my room. I don't need repair bills or upset customers. Gotta run."

The line went dead and Rick looked at Marquetta. "I guess you heard that. I'll call Adam and see what he wants to do."

"If this man is armed, you shouldn't be there, Rick. It could be dangerous."

"Deputy Jackman's out of town, so Adam's probably going to need the sheriff."

Rick made the call, passed on the information Ray had given him, then asked how Adam intended to handle the situation. He was relieved to hear Adam was taking no chances and would be calling in additional manpower.

"It looks like I'm off he hook on this one," Rick said when he disconnected. "Now, I guess we just wait for the word on whether they make the arrest or not." The steady tick-tock, tick-tock of the old grandfather clock standing against the wall filled the room. Rick watched the pendulum swing slowly from side to side. He glanced at Marquetta and smiled.

"What?" Marquetta asked.

"Do you remember when you showed me how to wind that clock?"

"I couldn't believe a grown man didn't know how to do that."

Rick felt a small flush of heat in his cheeks. "I'll let you in on a little secret. I played dumb just so I could have you alone for a few minutes."

"Oh my, Mr. Atwood. I do believe you've just revealed one of your deep, dark secrets."

"I have, Ms. Weiss. Care to reveal one of yours?"

"No, I don't think so. A girl needs her privacy, you know. Besides, Alex should be home any minute."

With a final look at the swinging pendulum, Rick let out a deep sigh. "Okay. Let's go downstairs. I want to catch her when she comes in. The last thing I need is for her to be getting wind of the big bust and visiting the Seaside Cove Inn."

46

ALEX

WITH EACH STEP I TAKE toward the broken lattice, my heart
pounds faster. When I'm a few feet away, I stop and look
around. There's a ton of places someone could hide out here. I
wouldn't have a clue if they were watching or...

I bite my lip. I'm still not sure if I should go get help. No.
Because if there is somebody out here, by the time I get back
with Daddy or Marquetta, whatever was left behind could be
gone. And there's totally something under there. I can see the
outline of what looks like a green blob just inside the lattice.

Whoever hid that there totally smushed the azalea in front of
the opening. It's little branches are broken and laying on the
ground. I take a couple more steps, then kneel down to get a
better look. Yuck. There's an old spider web clinging to part of
the lattice closest to me. I hate spiders. Just thinking about their
little legs crawling on my skin. Double yuck. I shiver to get rid of
the creepy crawly feeling and look closer.

It's super bright green. Mesh. Oh my God! It's gotta be the
missing treasure. I reach in and grab the bag. The material feels
soft, but grimy. It's like its caked with mud or something gross. I
don't care if there's a creepy old spider on it or not! I yank on
the bag and pull it out.

There's a little clink when I lay it on the grass in front of me.
It looks like a whole china plate inside along with a few smaller

pieces that look like they're broken. I hope I didn't do any damage when I yanked on it. My heart is pounding so hard I can't think. This totally has to be the missing treasure.

Holy moley. This is, like, four-hundred years old.

And it's here. In front of me.

My jeans are getting cold and damp from the grass. I shiver against a chill that runs down my spine. Should I open the bag and look inside? If I do, I could break something. But I can't leave it out here. I have to take it inside and call Flynn. She'll wanna come over and check this out to see if it's real.

I look around again. There's still no sign of anybody, so whoever hid the bag left it. It had to be the Gibsons. That means Mr. Gibson must have found this in the planter and took it before me and Sasha got there. This must be what he was calling his big windfall. Wait a minute. They weren't at breakfast this morning. What if this wasn't everything? Maybe there was more stuff that they took with them.

Or maybe the killer saw him take the bag and followed him. The Gibsons might even be dead. But Mr. Gibson totally would have given up the treasure if it would have saved his life. Unless the killer hasn't gotten here yet. Or I interrupted him...

Footsteps crunch on the path. A chill runs down my back. Someone's coming.

I suck in a breath and look back at the opening under the gazebo. The footsteps are getting closer. It makes my skin itch to think about crawling under there. I reach for the bag, but I'm too late.

"Stop right there, Alex."

47

RICK

RICK STEPPED OFF THE DECOMPOSED granite path and onto the grass near where Alex sat on her knees in front of a lime-green mesh bag. "What have you got there?"

Alex threw her head back and heaved a giant sigh. "I thought you were somebody else."

"Sorry. I didn't mean to scare you." Rick squatted next to Alex to see what she'd found. "Is that it? The bag from Dead Man's Cove?"

"I think so. Mr. Gibson hid it out here."

Rick looked at the opening in the gazebo. The crisscrossing slats were broken in two spots. It wasn't much of a surprise given that the lattice was at least twenty or thirty years old. If Gibson hadn't tried to pry it back to loosen it, it would have gone at least a few more years. Now, the handyman had to repair it. Another expense, most likely at the hands of Phillip Gibson.

"Come on, let's get you inside. Do you want me to carry that?"

"I totally don't want to break it." Alex held the bag out in Rick's direction.

"Given how old it is, I don't blame you," he said as he cradled it in his hands.

They walked to the house, Rick holding the bag in both hands while Alex walked next to him, all the while telling him to be careful. In looking at what Alex had entrusted to him, he didn't think it looked like much more than a muddy bag with a few ceramic shards and what might be a complete plate.

Marquetta met them on the back patio. As she watched them approach, she pointed at what Rick carried. "Is that what I think it is?"

"I found the missing treasure!"

Alex rushed forward and started to wrap her arms around Marquetta's waist, but Marquetta gently grabbed her shoulders and pushed her back. "You need to get cleaned up, Sweetie. Use the sink in the laundry room."

"But I need to call Flynn!"

"You can do that right after you wash up. Now, scoot." Marquetta sighed and grimaced as she eyed the bag. "Put it on the island. That will be the easiest to clean afterwards."

"A lot easier than a duvet," Rick said. He walked past Marquetta, hoping bits of mud or the four-hundred-year-old ceramic didn't fall to the floor. He laid the bag on the smooth countertop, then went to the kitchen sink.

While Rick washed his hands, Alex called Flynn. The three of them sat around the island for the next ten minutes staring at Alex's find while they waited for Flynn to arrive. When she walked in, she placed her backpack on the island next to the mesh bag.

Alex watched, her eyes wide and her elbows resting on the polished island's surface. Her voice was eager as she asked, "What's in the backpack?"

"A few things to help with a preliminary inspection. Now, what have we got here?" Flynn leaned over the mesh bag without touching it. After a few seconds, she grimaced, then opened her backpack and pulled out a pair of nitrile gloves.

"Where did you say you found this?" Flynn asked absently as she reached into the backpack again.

"Under the gazebo," Alex said.

Flynn placed a neatly folded tarp on the counter next to the bag, then laid two paint brushes and a jeweler's loupe next to the tarp. "This is what we were looking for in front of the Rusty Nail?"

"We think so," Rick said.

"One of our guests stole it and hid it under the gazebo," Alex added.

"We didn't actually see Mr. Gibson do that, did we, Alex?" Rick gazed at his daughter until she rolled her eyes and her shoulders slumped.

"No. We didn't. But it totally looks like the bag I saw out at Dead Man's Cove."

"I'm sure these pieces weren't this dirty when the diver brought them up. They're a mess now. We'll have to get some of this muck off." Flynn handed a pair of gloves to Alex. "Put those on. This is all we'll need to do a preliminary cleaning. I figured that since this is your find, you deserve to be around for this part. Afterwards, I'll take it to the lab for a thorough analysis. The first step is to transfer it onto the tarp."

Rick held the bag while Marquetta wiped down the white granite. Flynn and Alex waited until Marquetta had finished, then smoothed out the tarp.

"When we're done I can fold this up and sift the contents to make sure nothing is lost," Flynn said.

"That's super smart," Alex said.

"The technique has been around for a long time. Archaeologists don't like letting even one little chip or bone fragment get lost. We account for everything." Flynn raised and lowered her shoulders and grinned. "Now, are you ready to help me clean up these pieces?"

"For real?" Alex's face lit up and she nodded eagerly. "Totally. What do I do?"

"First thing is to put on those gloves and watch me for a minute."

She extracted an intact plate and three fragments. All of the pieces were an off-white base with delicate blue ink drawings. The pale blue color of the ink appeared to be identical on all of the pieces.

Flynn handed a paintbrush and a rectangular fragment to Alex, then pointed at the design. "See this blue ink? It's typical of the Ming Dynasty. See how delicate and intricate this scene is? That's also typical of the period. The blue is called an under-glaze, and you could say it was the standard for the time in China."

As Alex inspected her piece closely, Rick swallowed hard at the sight of her wonder. After all, it wasn't every day an archaeologist let you handle a piece of history, possibly one that was priceless, in your own kitchen.

Flynn brushed the surface of the plate, only letting the bristles gently touch the glaze. "Do you see how the glaze has deteriorated? The surface is almost like a matte finish now. That's most likely because it's been under water for hundreds of years. Now, brush away some of the muck like this."

Rick watched in fascination as more of the design slowly materialized beneath the thin layer of grime and dirt.

"You don't want to wash them?" Rick asked.

"Not under these conditions. We'll do a full cleaning and inspection back at the lab, but we can get a good idea of what we're dealing with in a few minutes. Kind of like triage in a hospital."

Rick's phone pinged with a message from Adam. After he read it, he pocketed his phone. "Adam's got Vincent Pulley in custody, and he thinks the story he's getting is bogus. He wants me to talk to Pulley, too. They're still at the Seaside Cove Inn. I have to go."

The color in Marquetta's face paled as she looked at Rick. "Please be careful. If that man really is a killer…"

Rick stood in front of her and took her hands. "It's okay. He's in custody. He's unarmed. Hopefully, this won't take too long." He kissed Marquetta, gave Alex a hug, and said goodbye to Flynn on his way out the door.

No sooner had he turned onto Front Street, than chaos enveloped him. In addition to Adam's 4x4, sheriff vehicles were parked on both sides of the normally sedate, tree-lined street. Emergency lights flashed in a chaotic dance of red and blue while two sheriff deputies stood in front of one vehicle talking.

An involuntary shudder crept down Rick's spine as he passed the sign advertising "clean, affordable lodging" in front of the inn. Rick recalled Marquetta's cautionary goodbye as he climbed the wooden stairs to the entrance. Ray Villari paced back and forth in the lobby, an angry scowl on his face.

"About time you got here."

Rick eased back a bit and looked at Ray. "I just got Adam's text a few minutes ago."

"Whatever. Follow me." Ray motioned with his head toward the door to the inner courtyard and walked away.

"Okay," Rick muttered as he hurried his pace to catch up.

He found Ray standing next to the pool pointing at a room on the second floor that was swarming with activity.

"Yeah," Ray grumbled. "I got people complaining right and left. Adam wants to see you up there."

He turned away and stormed back into the office, leaving Rick standing alone. Ray was never what Rick would call a cheery sort, but this was over-the-top even for him. Rick wound his way around the pool and through the courtyard. The lush green of this interior garden was, in his opinion, the best feature of the Seaside Cove Inn. Otherwise, it was just another cheap motel with a grumpy owner.

Rick spotted Adam coming out the door of Room 203. He was followed by a man in handcuffs who was guided by a sheriff's deputy. Adam acknowledged Rick with a quirking of his cheek and motioned for him to approach. Rick stepped to one side as the man in custody and the deputy filed by.

"Thanks for getting here so fast," Adam said.

"No problem. That guy who was just led away in handcuffs, isn't he the one you wanted me to talk to?"

"It is, but I don't want to do it here. Ray's griping that we're chasing away his upscale clientele."

Rick chuckled. "Ray doesn't have upscale clientele. Maybe that's why he's in such a mood."

"He's not mad at you. He doesn't like it when people shoot up his rooms."

Rick's eyes widened. "There were shots fired?"

Adam grimaced and craned his neck from side to side. "After getting off a couple of rounds, Mr. Pulley decided he really couldn't outgun a SWAT team. Fortunately, we didn't have to actually have them here."

"Really? A guy who forces his way onto a boat with a gun just gives up when the cops threaten to bring in SWAT? Doesn't that strike you as pretty easy?"

"Absolutely. We all felt the same way. It was almost as though he didn't mind getting caught."

Rick looked around the complex. Or, that he'd gotten orders from someone else.

48

ALEX

HANDLING A FOUR-HUNDRED-YEAR-old piece of porcelain is super awesome. It's like holding history in your hands. It's too bad my dad had to leave 'cause he looked like he was totally into this, too. My fragment has four sides. The top curves out just a little, but the other three sides broke really straight. There are birds in the design and what looks like a lake. Whoever made this was super talented.

"I never realized how beautiful this stuff could be," I say.

Flynn nudges my elbow with hers and winks at me. "Watch out or you'll give up crime fighting to go on a dig with me. Once it gets in your blood, you're hooked."

Marquetta has been sitting on her regular stool with her elbows resting on the island. She's been watching everything that me and Flynn do. "Are you finding a new passion, Sweetie?"

I turn the piece over. It's got some sort of artwork on the back. "I dunno. This is fun, but I don't think I'd want to do it forever."

"I'm crushed," Flynn chuckles, then points at the back of my piece. "You see what's on the back? It's part of the information that will help us date these pieces. Think of it as a watermark on a photo. Different eras used different marks to signify the location, reign, date, etc. Because of the breaks, your piece doesn't have the full marking, but we might be able to match it up with something else already on file."

The butler door bursts open. Since none of the guests are supposed to be back here, I expect it to be my dad, but it's Adela.

"Oh, sorry," she says. "I didn't mean to interrupt. I was just taking a shortcut to go out back."

Marquetta gets up and looks Adela in the eye. "Miss Barone. I thought we'd explained that the kitchen was off limits to guests."

"Sorry. I guess maybe I forgot..." She stops and looks at the island. The color in her cheeks gets kinda blotchy and her mouth drops open. "Is that the bag the man on the beach had?"

"Hey, Adela. It is. I found it."

All of a sudden, all her attention is on the pieces of porcelain me and Flynn are holding. I can see her finally get it. We found the missing treasure. She starts to take a step forward, but Flynn clears her throat and shoots Marquetta a look.

Marquetta steps in front of Adela and squares her shoulders. Marquetta might only be about the same height and build as Adela, but she can be a lot more intimidating when she wants to be. I've seen her totally face down some big guys, and Adela's no match for her.

"Miss Barone. I must insist. The kitchen is off limits to guests. Now please, if you don't mind."

Marquetta takes another step forward. Adela automatically steps back, then mutters something and darts out the door.

"Whatever do you suppose that was all about?" Marquetta asks when she turns back to us.

"I bet she wants to steal these pieces."

"If only we knew for sure, Sweetie."

"Thank you for chasing her out," Flynn says. "I get skittish when people I don't know are around artifacts." She looks down at the pieces we're holding and sighs. "Even if they're not worth that much."

"What?" I blurt. "These aren't worth anything?"

Flynn shakes her head. "They have value from a historical standpoint. And they'll certainly make their way into the museum archives, but they're not display quality. They're really nothing special. Part of the problem is the level of corrosion. We'll take more time with them and get them fully cleaned, but I suspect the glaze has degraded too much for collectors to consider them valuable."

But the piece in my hand is so pretty. And it's like four-hundred years old. Four-hundred years. That's a super long time to be laying on the bottom of the ocean. I guess it was too much for it. "So the guy who stole these died for nothing?"

"I wouldn't say he died for nothing," Flynn says. "But, if he was thinking he'd found his fortune, then, yes."

Holy moley. This is like the worst motive for murder ever.

49

RICK

VINCENT PULLEY SAT IN A straight-backed chair in the Seaside Cove Police Department's interrogation room. Though the situation was perfectly safe—Pulley was secured to his chair; he was on the opposite side of a small table; and Adam sat next to Rick—just being near Pulley was enough to make Rick anxious.

With prematurely gray hair and intense brown eyes, Pulley looked to be a hard man, the kind who had grown up on the streets and who'd learned how to survive. A stone-faced sheriff's deputy stood to one side, his watchful eyes seldom straying from the prisoner.

So far, the interview had brought up nothing new, but what seemed odd to Rick was that Pulley had not asked for an attorney. If Adam hadn't explained his plan to lay a trap, and how Rick was an integral part of the plan, he wouldn't have expected to even be here during this interrogation. Adam's plan seemed smart enough, but would it convince Pulley to tell the real story?

Adam had a yellow notepad in front of him and had been jotting notes all along. "Mr. Pulley, why did you board the *Blue Phoenix* and damage the engine?"

"Told you that already. A guy hired me to do it."

"You didn't ask him why he wanted you to break the law?"

Pulley's right cheek pulled back slightly. It was one of the few signs that he was confident he'd walk away with nothing more than a slap on the wrist. As he attempted to reposition himself—a difficult task given the shackles he wore—Rick wondered if he was actually uncomfortable or if he was just stalling for time.

"In my line of work, you don't ask a lot of questions," Pulley said.

Adam made a note on his pad, then planted his elbows on the table. "So what exactly is your line of work, Mr. Pulley?"

The right corner of Pulley's mouth curled back further, revealing a pair of gold crowns. "I'm kind of like a handyman. I do odd jobs for people."

"People you don't know?"

Pulley shrugged. "Sometimes."

"So if a stranger walked up to you on the street and told you he wanted you to kill a man, you'd be okay with that? Did you commit murder in my town, Mr. Pulley?"

"What?" Pulley's smile disappeared and he tried to jerk upright, but his restraints stopped him. He cleared his throat. "Who said anything about murder?"

"We know you forcibly boarded the *Blue Phoenix*. Witnesses will testify that you're the one who assaulted one of the crew members when he tried to stop you. So you clearly have no problem with violent behavior."

"That ain't murder." Pulley's mouth curled into a nasty scowl.

"You're right. It's not. But there's more than that. You see, this is a small town. There are eyes and ears everywhere. And people are very willing to help each other out." Adam looked sideways at Rick. "How's your list of witnesses coming along?"

"I'm working on it, Chief. I'd say another day or so and it will be all nice and tight."

"Excellent." Adam looked back at Pulley. "We're putting together a list of witnesses who will put you at the scene of a recent murder. You are, after all, the most promising suspect in my investigation."

"I didn't kill that guy."

"See? You do know more than you're admitting." Adam stared across the table at Pulley.

"How so?"

"I didn't say anything about the victim being a man."

"That don't prove nothing. I just heard people talking about it. That's all."

"What people?"

"What do you mean?"

"It's a simple question, Mr. Pulley. What people did you hear talking about the murder?"

"I don't know. I guess it was somebody in a restaurant."

Adam nodded and looked sideways at Rick. "That makes sense. Right?"

"I guess," Rick said, then looked at Pulley. "What restaurant?"

"I...don't know the name of it."

"That's understandable," Rick said with a chuckle. "We have so many."

"Rick, why don't you call Ken at the Crooked Mast and Sally at the Rusty Nail and ask them if they seated Mr. Pulley on Tuesday night? Be sure to get the time and his table number, too. If he has an alibi for the time of the murder, he'll be one lucky guy."

"All right! I didn't have any dinners out. I was supposed to hang out in my room so I wouldn't be seen in public. I met this guy in San Ladron a few days ago and he asked me to board the boat and damage the engine. That's all I know."

"So you were just hired off the street by this guy you'd never seen before to commit a felony. That's the story you're going with? Sounds weak, Mr. Pulley. Very weak." Adam turned to Rick. "How many witnesses do you think we'll have?"

"I'd say at least five." Rick started to count on his fingers, then added, "Maybe more."

Beads of sweat dotted Pulley's forehead. His eyes were now flitting around the room. The sheriff's deputy was still looking alert, but impassive, and Rick wondered how he did it. Even if he had years of practice, Rick doubted if he could ever stand by like a robot just waiting for something to happen.

"You sure you don't want to amend your story?" Adam asked as he watched Pulley for some sort of reaction.

One of the beads of sweat dribbled down Pulley's temple. Rick kept quiet, but it appeared Vincent Pulley's confidence was eroding fast.

Pulley's jaw worked from side-to-side as he appeared to consider his situation. "What's in it for me?"

"For one, it might keep you off death row. As I said, you are, right now, our primary suspect, and I think the DA is going to love it when I hand him..." Adam stopped and turned to Rick. "How many witnesses was that?"

"Five or six. All very credible."

"Yeah, the DA's going love the idea of locking you away for a very long time. Unless she's got someone else to focus on, of course."

Rick's phone vibrated with a message from Marquetta. Apparently, the Gibsons had turned up in San Ladron when they'd stopped for gas. They were being held pending notification from Adam that they should be released. In fact,

Phillip Gibson had called the B&B hoping Rick would intervene with Seaside Cove's Chief of Police.

When Rick looked up from reading the message, he saw Pulley, who seemed fixated on the phone. Though he didn't know what exactly Pulley was expecting, the man's interest did provide an opportunity. Maybe he thought the sheriff had captured his boss? It was worth a shot. Rick held out the phone so Adam could read the screen.

"Here's a development that might change things. They made the arrest an hour ago." Rick looked across the table at Pulley and added, "Not good for you, Mr. Pulley."

"What is that?" Pulley demanded.

"You know how it goes, the first one to talk gets the deal," Rick said. "And since you seem somewhat reluctant, the chief might as well start processing you."

Adam nodded. "Looks like your time to make a deal is up, Mr. Pulley. "

Finally, it appeared they had the leverage they needed. Pulley's breaths were coming faster and his eyes kept flitting between Rick and Adam. Unless he was mistaken, Rick was sure Vincent Pulley was about to break. The only question was, could they get his confession before he discovered this was nothing but a ruse and they had nothing connecting him to Tuck Hall's murder?

50

RICK

RICK HAD TO ADMIT THAT Adam seemed to have judged Vincent Pulley correctly. Impressive. As was Adam's poker face, which he kept firmly in place as he made a final note on his pad.

"Well? What's it going to be Mr. Pulley?" Adam asked.

Pulley's confident smirk, which had faded as the threats had escalated, slowly returned. "You know what, Chief? You almost had me. Stuff your deal. If you had something, you wouldn't be giving me another chance. I want a lawyer."

"Your loss," Adam said, then told the sheriff's deputy to take Pulley in.

Rick and Adam sat looking glumly at each other as their last hope for an easy solution was taken out of the building.

"Thanks for trying. We almost had him," Adam said.

"If he sits in custody for a while, maybe he'll change his mind."

"I doubt it. He knows the system too well. My mistake was asking him that last time if he was willing to deal. I should've bluffed and ordered him booked for murder. Enough of that. We still have a case to solve. And we seem to be back to square one."

"Do you think Pulley could have been the one who did it?"

Adam looked down at his notepad and shook his head. "Pulley's no stranger to the system, but he's never been charged with murder. Besides, if you'd just killed a man, why would you put yourself into an obviously exposed position by boarding a boat just to disable it? It doesn't make sense."

"I agree. I think our killer is someone who's a lot smarter than Vincent Pulley."

"Someone who's pulling his strings?"

"Exactly. I'll do some research, too. Maybe between both of us we can turn up some connection to whoever hired him. Now, what do you want to do about the Gibsons?"

"I'd like to drive to San Ladron and talk to him in person, but I don't have three or four hours to kill."

"Why not do a video call?" Rick asked.

"Good idea. Let's see what we can set up."

Less than thirty minutes later Rick and Adam were looking into the face of Phillip Gibson. Rick's anger over Gibson's quick departure softened when he saw Gibson's haggard appearance. He looked drawn and tired and seemed to have difficulty focusing.

When Adam paused to make a few notes, Rick asked, "Mr. Gibson, how are you holding up?"

"Terrible. I've...I've never been in jail before."

"Well, you're not actually in jail, Mr. Gibson. Not yet, anyway. We have some additional questions about that bag you hid under my gazebo."

Gibson groaned and hung his head. "I'm sorry about the lattice. It just kind of broke."

Rick took a breath to soften the edge he knew would be in his voice. "Were you in a hurry?"

"Yes. Peg was adamant that we needed to get out of town. She kept saying the treasure was going to bring us nothing but trouble."

"It appears she was correct. If you were in such a hurry, why were you out until two in the morning?"

"Peg kept saying she didn't think it was safe for us to stay in Seaside Cove, so we drove to San Ladron for dinner. By the time we finished, we were both so worried that we drove around for a while, then came back here and searched the grounds for a place to hide the bag. We got the lattice moved, then went back to our room and cleared it out. Peg waited in the car while I took the bag out back and hid it."

Rick caught himself clenching his teeth. He tried to relax, but between the cleaning of the duvet and the repairs to the gazebo lattice, he'd have been better off having the room empty. "Why'd you put it under my gazebo, Mr. Gibson? Surely there were easier places."

"We didn't think anyone would find it there. At least, not right away." Gibson hung his head and croaked, "We thought if we got rid of it and left town, we'd be fine."

That seemed pretty naive. At a minimum, whoever killed Tuck Hall probably wanted to have a very serious chat with Phillip Gibson. "You do realize that until we solve the murder, you're still in danger, right?"

"I know. They killed that man for it."

"Did you see the killing?"

"No. All I saw was the victim hiding the bag in the bushes earlier that evening."

"In front of the Rusty Nail?"

"Yes. We saw him hide it, then hurry on. I didn't think anything of it at the time, but after we got back to the B&B, I started wondering what was in the bag. I couldn't figure out why someone would hide something in a place like that unless they were in trouble and it was valuable. We'd been hearing rumors about the Dead Man's Cove missing treasure, so I thought maybe that was it. I made an excuse and went back. That's when I found the bag and brought it back to the room."

"And what did you do with the bag, Mr. Gibson? Other than lay it on my clean duvet?"

Gibson winced and looked down to the side. "I'm sorry about that, too. I got sloppy when we were trying to get out of the room. Peg really chewed me out for being so careless. You're not going to charge me for it, are you?"

Unfortunately, Rick doubted if he'd ever collect from Gibson for the damages. And right now, he and Adam had a bigger issue to deal with, Tuck Hall's murder. "I'm still thinking about it, Mr. Gibson. Tell me what happened next."

"We looked through the bag. It was an old plate and a couple of fragments."

"How many fragments?"

"Three. Peg was getting on me about the bag being hidden in the bushes for a reason. And when she started saying it had already cost one man his life—I got worried. I didn't want to die. You have to believe me. We put it under the gazebo because we knew somebody would find it sooner or later. All we wanted was to buy some time."

"Mr. Gibson, do you realize I could charge you with handling stolen property?" Adam demanded.

"Stolen? I didn't steal it. It was right there on the ground in that planter. I saw the guy hide it and then when he turned up dead...that's when I went back to check on it."

"Did you take the bag before the murder? Or after?"

"It was before I knew about the murder, but the guy was already dead."

"How do you know that?"

Gibson buried his face in his hands. When he looked up, he had tears in his eyes. "Can't we just forget this happened, Chief? You've got the bag and the artifacts back. You don't need to go after me. Right?"

"Wrong," Adam said firmly. "And I'll tell you why. You, Mr. Gibson, know more than you're letting on. You've lied during the course of a police investigation, and I believe you either saw the murder or know who committed it. If you want me to consider obstruction of justice as a charge, I'm happy to do that. It would be better for you, though, if you just told me everything. Right now."

"I can't ever catch a break, you know? All my life, that's all I've wanted was one decent break, but every single time something happens. Okay, Chief, you win. I'll tell you everything. What do you want to know?"

"Let's start from the beginning. And this time I want the truth."

"Peg and I left the B&B at five-thirty. We had a six o'clock reservation at the Crooked Mast, but we wanted to get there early. Peg hates to be late for anything."

Adam jotted down the times on his pad, and when he finished, looked at the screen. "Go on."

"We got to the Crooked Mast at five-forty. I know because I made a comment about being five minutes early for our fifteen-minute-early time. Peg agreed we could take a short walk and check out the menu at the other restaurant."

"The Rusty Nail?"

"That's it. The one on Front Street. It only took us a few minutes to get there and that's when we saw this man putting something in the bushes. Neither of us wanted to get involved, so we turned around and went back to the Crooked Mast. We were in and out in about forty-five minutes."

At least that part was consistent with what he'd said earlier, thought Rick. It was also about the time Tuck Hall had tried hitting on Mary Ellen. "So you were at the Crooked Mast from about five-forty-five until about six-thirty?"

"Yes. And right after the hostess seated us, the guy I saw hiding the bag walked in. They put him a few tables over from us. I kept thinking he'd recognize me, but he didn't pay us any attention. He was too busy flirting with that waitress."

"Mary Ellen?" Rick asked.

"We had a different girl. I don't know her name. But I'll tell you, that whole thing was causing quite the stir."

"How so?" Rick asked.

Gibson cleared his throat, then looked from side to side. He took a deep breath, then continued. "You could tell he was making her uncomfortable, but things got out of hand when her husband came over and started making threats."

"Can you be more specific?" Rick asked.

"He said if the guy didn't leave his wife alone, he'd kill him."

"Were those his exact words?"

"Well, no. Peg remembers this kind of stuff better than I do, but I do remember her making a comment after we heard about the murder. She said she thought the husband looked like the kind of guy who'd been in a lot of fights—I think his name was Clive. That's what the manager called him when he had to intervene. Anyway, he must have caught up with the guy who was hitting on his wife."

Rick felt a stab of disappointment at the implications of Gibson's statement. Was it possible that Clive had let his jealousy go too far? Maybe he was guilty and the whole conspiracy with the treasure was unrelated. No. He couldn't have misread the situation that badly. "Think carefully, Mr. Gibson. Did you see the husband leave the Crooked Mast?"

"Everybody in the place saw it. The manager made the one who'd started everything leave first, then he made the husband leave a few minutes later. Wasn't more than three or four minutes between them, I'd say." Gibson stopped, and a frown creased his brow.

Rick recognized the look from countless interviews he'd done over the years. With any luck, they might be about to get something new. "What are you remembering, Mr. Gibson?"

"It's funny, because a third man left right after the husband."

"What do you mean? A third man? Do you know who it was?" Rick asked.

"No, but he almost had a coronary when the murder victim walked in. He also kept watching him. I told Peg and she said I was imagining things. But I know what I saw. Those two guys knew each other from somewhere. And it didn't look like either of them was happy the other one was there."

51

RICK

DESPITE THEIR BEST EFFORTS, NEITHER Rick nor Adam could extract a decent description from Phillip Gibson about the mysterious third man at the Crooked Mast. The only thing they knew was the man had neatly cut, blondish gray hair and that he'd been very upset when Tuck Hall walked in. It appeared the only way to get additional information about him would be to call Ken Grayson and ask if he remembered anything. If Ken didn't know, he'd ask his staff, but unless the man had made some sort of scene, they would probably get nothing more than they had now.

Sensing that Adam was equally irritated with Gibson's answers, Rick decided to move on to later in the evening. "Let's talk about after you left the restaurant."

"We went back to the room and I told Peg I'd eaten too much and that I needed to walk it off. I went to the car and picked up one of our big reusable shopping bags. We've got a few that we hardly ever use and..."

"Mr. Gibson," Adam said sternly. "Please, stick to what happened."

"Sorry. Right. I went back to the Rusty Nail and rummaged around those bushes. The bag I'd seen the man hide was still there, so I figured it was fair game. I pulled it out and stuffed it in the shopping bag, then cut over to Main Street."

"Did anyone see you do this?" Adam asked.

"At the time, I didn't think so, but when I got over to Main Street, I saw someone about a block behind me. He was still there half a block later, so I joined the crowd at the murder scene."

"What happened to the man who had been following you when you joined the crowd?"

"I don't really know. I was trying not to look at him, but I think he turned around and went back the way he came."

Adam grimaced and let out an irritated huff. "Did you recognize this man, Mr. Gibson? Or are you going to tell me you don't remember what he looked like?"

"He...he was too far away. Besides, I don't know anybody in town except for the staff at the B&B."

"Let me rephrase my question. Had you seen him anywhere before?"

"I have no idea. I didn't get a close look at him. And since I was trying to not let him know I saw him, I couldn't describe him."

Adam rubbed the back of his neck and let out a deep sigh. He looked at Rick. "You got any questions?"

"Actually, yes. Mr. Gibson, you said the man who hid the bag was being watched by a third man at the restaurant. Was that third man the one who was following you?"

"It probably was. He seemed very interested in the bag."

"How do you know he was interested?" Rick asked.

"Well...um...he had to be. Right?"

What a terrible witness Gibson was. So few facts, so much conjecture. Rick made a mental note to call Ken at the Crooked Mast. He and his staff might be the only way to figure out who the third man was.

Adam looked at Rick, the lines on his forehead creased and his eyebrows knitted together. "Looks like we can wrap this up."

There was a note of resignation in Adam's voice that concerned Rick, and rightly so, he thought. They were running out of options. "What do you want to do with the Gibsons?"

"Fair question," Adam said. "Mr. Gibson, I'm going to speak to the sheriff and have you released, but I want you to drive straight home and remain available for further questions. Do you understand?"

"Yes. And thank you, Chief. I guess we really made a mess of things."

"Just don't make me regret my decision to not charge you." Adam ended the call with Gibson, then messaged the San Ladron Sheriff Department. When he'd finished, he gave his notes a quick review and grimaced. "We didn't get much from him."

"Other than a mystery man who followed him around, probably saw him take the bag, and who is most likely our killer. Unless, of course, Clive has been lying to us this whole time and he took it—or maybe it was Vincent Pulley. I'm sure he's lying to us about at least part of this."

Adam huffed again, then rubbed his face with his hands. "You're supposed to be my consultant and helping me solve this case, not reminding me that all we have is squat."

"Sorry. Look, Adam, I don't know what the Gibsons have to do with this other than maybe the husband got greedy and took the wrong thing, but my gut tells me Pulley's in this up to his neck and he's somehow tied to this mystery man."

"Agreed." Adam read through his notes, absently clicking his pen until he looked up at Rick. "Would you mind doing some checking on Vincent Pulley tonight?"

"No problem. Do you want me to call Ken and ask him if he can help us identify this third man?"

"I'll talk to Ken. It's five-thirty, so he isn't going to be happy about taking time out from the dinner rush to answer questions. I can put a little pressure on him while you focus on Pulley. We can compare notes in the morning."

With his role assigned, Rick walked back to the B&B. On his way in, he passed two couples leaving for dinner. The four were old friends who now lived at opposite ends of the state, but met several times a year to explore new destinations. He doubted that they'd expected a murder investigation when they'd booked this trip. Rick bid them a good evening, then went directly to the kitchen.

When Alex saw him, she jumped up from her seat and rushed to give him a hug. "Daddy!"

Rick scooped her up in his arms and hugged her. She wrapped her arms around his neck and, at least momentarily, he forgot how exhausted he was. He put Alex down, gave Marquetta a quick kiss, then sat.

"I'm beat. And while I'd love to just relax tonight, I've got some research to do later." He filled them in on the day, being sure to leave out Vincent Pulley's name so that Alex didn't decide to do her own research.

By the time dinner was over, the banter between him, Marquetta, and Alex had recharged Rick and he was mentally prepared to dive into Vincent Pulley's background. Unfortunately, he knew that would have to wait until after they finished their evening chores—dishes, getting Alex started on her homework, and readying the B&B for the night. There was also the question of what to do about the wedding, which meant Rick didn't expect to get started on his research until after ten.

"Rick," Marquetta said. "You've got a lot to think about right now. Mom called me this afternoon, and she's coming over for a bit. I thought maybe we could start putting together some sort of wedding plan. If you want to go do your thing for Adam, Alex and I can handle the dishes and close up the B&B after we're done with Mom. What do you think?"

What did he think? Other than this being the best offer he'd had all day? "I think that would be incredibly helpful." He smiled at Marquetta, kissed her, and sighed. "If you're offering me a chance to get out of doing dishes, I'm taking it." He said goodnight to them both and headed upstairs to his office.

Upon entering the room, Rick flicked on the lights and eased the door shut behind him. Recessed lighting over the bookshelves illuminated old photos. On the far wall hung a handdrawn, topographic map of Seaside Cove, it's perfect calligraphy bringing back the few childhood memories he had of Captain Jack.

He let his eyes follow the intricate lines of the coast and its changing elevations. There was so much detail that whoever had drawn this must have been a master cartographer. Rick recalled how his grandfather had hidden letters behind the map. Those letters, which had contained Captain Jack's deepest secrets, hadn't been discovered until years after his death. Of one thing Rick was sure, Captain Jack wasn't the only one with secrets. What secrets was Vincent Pulley hiding?

Back at his desk, Rick cleared off the smattering of papers that cluttered the workspace and put his laptop squarely in front of him. He logged into his news search account and typed in Vincent Pulley's name. The list of more than 70,000 references included a 1901 news story about Honorable Mentions from a school in Virginia, a 'social mention' from Brooklyn in 1911, and a Lions Club committee appointment from 1961.

Pressing his lips together, Rick blew out a breath and made a sound that vaguely resembled someone burbling underwater. "Okay, that's not going to work. Let's get more specific." He narrowed the search to stories from the last decade.

This time he had a list of less than a hundred items. It was still a big task, but he didn't want to miss something important. Not wanting to filter out too much, he worked backwards chronologically and reviewed each piece. There were filings of estates, more social news, and a pair of notices about a Vincent Pulley in Belmont, California. Rick straightened up when he read the two pieces, one about Pulley having qualified as a Navy SEAL and the second about his being a party to a divorce decree.

Were the two Vincent Pulleys related? The same guy? Did it even matter? It didn't. Tuck Hall had been killed by someone skilled with a knife. A Navy SEAL would certainly have that kind of training. Rick read the full text of the article, saved a copy to print later, then refined his search to see if he could come up with additional information about this particular Vincent Pulley. A smile spread across his face when the search results came up. He'd hit the jackpot.

An article in the *LA Times* detailed the story of three men— Vincent Pulley, Theodore Hall, and a third man Rick had never heard of—who had served together in Iraq. Pulley was the alleged ringleader of the band and was investigated for the theft and smuggling of antiquities over the course of their assignment. Though none of the men had been formally charged or court-martialed, all three had received Other Than Honorable discharges.

Unfortunately, there was a lot that had been left out of the story, including what had actually been stolen. After jotting down the name of the reporter, Rick tried a search by the reporter's name. There were a few more articles, but it appeared the man's career at the *LA Times* had been short-lived.

At the sound of a knock on the door, Rick checked the clock to see how long he'd been working. Wow, he'd already been at this for an hour. He got up, went to the door, and opened it. "Hey," he said as he stepped aside. "How'd it go with your mother?"

"She's still downstairs, but we're getting somewhere. Mom's delighted we've set a date. She started out saying she'd like us to have a bigger venue, but once we talked about it, she understood the reasoning. Alex loves the idea of the gazebo. I gave them both a list of things to do. That should keep them busy. You having any luck?"

"Apparently, this was not Vincent Pulley's first foray into the world of antiquities theft. He was kicked out of the military because of his suspicious behavior. He was part of a little band that worked together in Iraq. The Navy couldn't pin anything on him, so they gave him an Other Than Honorable discharge."

Marquetta frowned and looked at Rick. "I've never heard of one of those."

"It's not good, but it's a lot better than a court-martial. One of the other men in that little smuggling band was Theodore Hall."

"The murder victim?"

"Maybe. Since Tuck is probably a nickname and Hall is a common last name, it's hard to say whether it's the same person or not. I'm going with that it is."

"Do you want to keep working, or would you mind coming down to talk to Mom? It really would be nice if you had a few minutes to spend with her tonight. We need to get Alex started on her homework, and I've got a glass of wine with your name on it."

Given the way this day was going, that was not an offer Rick wanted to refuse. He gave the notes on his desk a cursory look. The names were there, but nobody would be in this room. "It's getting late and it's been a long day. I'll send what I found to Adam. Tomorrow, he can see if any of these guys have records. I'll do more checking on them in the morning."

Marquetta kissed Rick on the cheek and grabbed his hand. "Okay, then come with me."

52

ALEX

"I WONDER WHAT HE FOUND?" I ask out loud.

Grandma Madeline looks at me and scrunches up her face. "Who, dear?"

"My dad. He's trying to find information about the man who forced his way onto Flynn's boat."

"Oh." She doesn't seem very interested. She picks at one of her nails and makes another face. "I really wish your father would not get involved in these murder investigations. It's dangerous."

"Daddy's always careful." I decide to leave off the part that I help him 'cause she doesn't look happy at all.

"Hmmpf. It's a job for the police," she says just as the butler door opens and my dad and Marquetta come in.

They're talking in low voices about a couple guests in the living room. What's the big deal with that? "What'd you find?"

My dad sits next to me. "Nothing earth shattering. It looks like the man Adam arrested was a smuggler who got started while he was stationed overseas. That's about all I know. I have a few more things to check, but Marquetta convinced me I should spend some time down here."

"Let's talk about the wedding," Grandma Madeline says.

"So what did he smuggle?"

This time, it's my dad who ignores me. "Good idea, Madeline. Alex has school in the morning, and I believe she has homework." He gives me the dad look. "Am I right?"

Oh, man, he knows I do. And Miss Redmond will be super unhappy with me if I don't finish. "Yes, Daddy."

"Okay, kiddo. Upstairs with you. I'll be up in about an hour to check on you."

"Can Marquetta do that?"

My dad looks at Marquetta. She smiles at me. "Of course. I'd be happy to."

I give everyone a big hug, then go out the butler door and through the dining room. When I get to the living room, Adela is sitting on the couch with Amy. Now I get why my dad and Marquetta were talking about the guests. It kinda sounds like Amy and Adela are talking about the murder. Seriously? I didn't even know they'd met.

Adela's like super persistent and is asking a lot of questions. I wonder what she'd do if she found out the stuff Flynn looked at wasn't valuable—but maybe the way to find out is to do the opposite.

Amy finger waves at me and smiles. "Hi, Alex. It's been quite the day, hasn't it?"

"It totally has." Do I tell them what Flynn said about the treasure? Or do I lie and set a trap?

Adela is just kinda glaring at me—and that helps me make up my mind. I'm totally gonna do it. It's kinda mean, but I'm gonna let her think the stuff from Dead Man's Cove is still here and that it's worth a lot of money. Besides, I don't trust her, so why not see what she'll do?

"Hey, Adela, You know that bag you saw this afternoon? Flynn checked it out and said it was super valuable."

"Good job, Alex," Amy says.

Adela's eyes are super big now, and she's facing me. "The old stuff you had on your kitchen counter?"

"For sure. It had a whole plate and some fragments. She says it's in awesome condition."

All of a sudden, Adela's smiling at me like we're besties. She's totally gone for the lie. Now I just have to make sure I don't overdo it.

"Did she say how much it was worth?"

"Nah. She said she has to take it to the lab, but she wasn't gonna be back there until tomorrow and asked us to keep it overnight. You know, for safe keeping." My heart is pounding. I take a breath. Let it out slow. Amy's looking at me like she suspects something's wrong.

"Where are you keeping it?" Adela asks.

Awesome. She's still in, all the way. "I'm not supposed to say, but since we discovered it 'cause of you, it's gonna be in a safe spot in our laundry room."

"The laundry room?" Adela makes a face and sneaks a peek back toward the kitchen. "Are you sure?"

"Totally. We've got a big cabinet in there. It's someplace nobody would think to look. Right?"

Adela stretches her arms out and fakes a yawn, then she stands. "Well, you were right, Amy, it's been a long day. I'm going to bed." She starts to walk away, but stops and gives me a fake sweet smile. "Thanks for sharing, Alex. Good work."

I can see her smirking until she disappears up the stairs.

"What was that all about?" Amy asks.

I walk over to the stairs and check to make sure Adela's not listening, then head back to Amy. I sit on the couch facing her with my legs crossed in front of me.

I whisper so nobody else can hear us. "She's here to steal the artifacts."

Amy does a double take, then rubs her neck. "So you were baiting her?"

"Totally."

"Your dad was right, you're a pretty good detective." She stretches out her hand and we do a fist bump. "Brilliant. So now that you've set this up, what's your next step?"

I scrunch up my face. "I dunno. I totally need to stake out the laundry room, but I have school tomorrow. Maybe I should talk to my dad. He'll be kinda mad at what I've done, but if it helps him find the killer, it's totally worth it."

"So you think Adela's the killer? I can't believe she'd be physically capable. There has to be someone else. Maybe she's working for someone."

It could be.

"Alex, think this through. If you stake out that laundry room and someone does show up, what are you going to do? Even if it's Adela, you're no match for her."

Oh, man. I'm totally gonna need help. And I'll probably get grounded if my dad finds out. "I didn't think about that. Do you have any ideas?"

"As a matter of fact, I do."

53

RICK

"RICK, YOU NEED TO FIND other outlets for that girl. She's too smart to be endangering herself with all of this murder falderal."

The tone in Madeline's voice reminded Rick of a parent scolding a child. Quite honestly, this entire conversation was making him bristle. His fingers tightened around the stem of his wine glass. While he didn't condone Alex's fascination with the subject of murder, he hadn't come down here to be lectured about his parenting style.

Madeline pulled her shoulders back and looked at Marquetta. "Don't you agree, dear?"

"Mom, Alex is a very precocious girl. I know you feel this is police business and that she should probably be playing with dolls or practicing piano..."

"God forbid," Rick snickered. "We'd drive all our guests away."

Marquetta shot Rick a mock sneer, and he immediately regretted his quip. "Sorry for the interruption. Go on."

"Anyway, you know that Seaside Cove is a small town. We have an understaffed police force and the *San Mañuel* has turned this town on its head in many ways. Rick and I keep a close watch on Alex and do our best to make sure she doesn't do anything dangerous. But, she is, after all, her own person and shouldn't be forced into some predefined mold."

Madeline's cheeks tightened, then she took a quick swallow of her wine. After a quick breath, she stood. "Well, I can see my opinions aren't welcome here."

The elation Rick had felt at having Marquetta come to his defense dimmed. He did not want her having to choose sides in a parental difference of opinion. "Madeline, Marquetta's not saying she doesn't respect your opinion. God knows I wish Alex had other interests—other than maybe the piano. I'm the first to admit that I'm probably the one most responsible for her interest in these investigations."

He went on to explain their years in New York and how he'd done his best to make Alex a part of his work so she wouldn't feel left out. "Over time, she developed this fascination with finding the truth. There are plenty of days when I want to kick myself, but what's done is done. And overall, I'd say she's turned out pretty well. Please, rather than have us try to stifle Alex's interests, why not help us in directing them?"

Rick counted the seconds as he waited for Madeline to say something. There was no way he wanted to come between Marquetta and her mother, but he also couldn't go along with an overprotective attempt to prevent his daughter from being who she wanted to be.

"I didn't realize all the background," Madeline said stiffly. "So, you're going to let her continue with this murder business?"

"We're going to try and let her investigate the safe parts. For instance, these artifacts Flynn came by to check out. That seems to be safe ground. Flynn likes Alex, which is why she agreed to take a look at the artifacts here, rather than in her lab. I'm hoping if we can keep Alex focused on the treasure it will keep her away from characters like the man Adam arrested today. His name was Vincent Pulley."

"Or someone like Tuck Hall," Marquetta added, then paused and frowned. "Rick, you checked the background of Vincent Pulley, and you discovered he was a smuggler at one point. Did you check to see if the connection with Tuck Hall continued after they were caught?"

"That's what I was about to do when you walked in."

"That's more important than sitting here drinking wine with us. Do you want to go back to it?"

"You're going to check on Alex for me?"

Marquetta placed her hand on his and gave him a reassuring smile. "Of course. I already made that promise to her."

"Then I'll get to work."

Rick bid Madeline goodnight, and Marquetta promised to stop by his office before she left. As he passed through the empty first floor, he stopped in the living room and turned off the fireplace, then straightened the cushions on both couches. He was surprised that Amy wasn't still sitting next to the fire and hoped that meant she was feeling more relaxed.

Up in his office, Rick picked up where he'd left off. After rereading the earlier article, he jotted down a few notes, then refined his search. Pulley had done time for minor offenses, but nothing significant. About a year prior to his appearance in Seaside Cove, the Crime and Public Safety section of the *Pasadena Star-News* reported on Pulley's DUI conviction. Rick added the word alcohol to his page on Pulley, underlined it, and added a question mark at the end. All in all, his search for information was feeling fruitless. He resolved to see if he could find another connection between Pulley and the murder victim.

He began with a search for Tuck Hall and came up with articles in different local LA papers about arrests for breaking-and-entering, burglary, and drug possession. One of the articles was also from the *Pasadena Star-News*. He jotted down a reminder to have Adam check on Hall's criminal record, then also noted the name and location of the three local papers with stories about Hall. Opening up a map of the LA area in his browser, he quickly discovered that all three of those local papers were within about thirty minutes of each other.

"So, this was your playground," Rick whispered. "Maybe for both you and your buddy Tuck."

Satisfied that he'd gotten everything he could from his news search, Rick switched to social media. It didn't take long to find Tuck Hall's profile. For an occupation, he listed 'diver.' It appeared that Tuck liked to post frequently on social media. He'd even posted a photo of a dive boat called the *Seven Seas*.

He had almost two-hundred friends, and Rick began combing through the names.

"I'll be darned," he said when he found Vincent Pulley listed. He bookmarked the profile, then clicked the link for Pulley's name.

Unlike Tuck Hall and his prolific postings, Pulley's last entry was almost a month old. The post was a photo of two men holding a long pole from which a dozen large orange fish hung by the mouth. Another five men stood behind the two holding the pole. Rick recognized Tuck Hall and Vincent Pulley in the group.

Pulley's only comment on the photo was 'good catch today.' Rick huffed and clicked back over to Hall's profile. He scrolled through the list of posts until he found the same photo. Unlike Pulley, who appeared to be a man of few words, Hall had done what he usually did and included plenty of information.

Caught a dozen Garibaldi today during our planning trip on the Seven Seas. Captain Ulster knows his stuff! The man's a genius, along with the big boss. We all struck fishing gold today, but we're all gonna have a real pot of gold by the end of summer! Might move to the South Seas.

A planning trip? The big boss? Hall was dead—it couldn't be him. Pulley was in jail and was most likely just a hired hand. Rick sat back and looked more closely at the photo. He checked the date of the post. It was from March 29, about two weeks prior to the article in the *San Ladron Times*. Could it be that this planning trip had been what kicked off the recent events taking place in Seaside Cove?

Unfortunately, Hall hadn't tagged the other men in the photo. "You could have made it easier for me, Tuck," Rick whispered as he saved the photo to his desktop. Not having names would make it harder to locate the others, but it was an effort he felt sure would pay off if he could identify the men who had been on the *Seven Seas*.

Rick returned to Vincent Pulley's friend list. After compiling a complete list, which was itself a tedious task even though Pulley only had a few dozen friends, he returned to Hall's profile and began comparing the two sets of names and faces. He ended up with five friends that the two men had in common.

The first name Rick checked was Fred Ulster. Rick recognized the name from Hall's post, and was able to confirm he was the owner and captain of the *Seven Seas*. The same photo had been posted to Ulster's profile, but this time the tone reminded Rick of an infomercial.

Today's trip with Tuck, Vincent, Paul, Roger, Eddie, Humph, and Larry was a huge success! Look at this catch! If you want a great dive or ocean fishing excursion, message me to rent out the Seven Seas.

* * *

Rick reviewed Ulster's friend list and found at least one match for each name. Even though it wasn't that late, his eyes felt like they were glazing over. Blinking a few times to clear his vision didn't help, so he got up and walked across the room to again inspect the map of the bay. The secret letters his grandfather had left behind the map had waited years before they'd been revealed. He didn't have years. This murder had to be resolved now—before a killer escaped.

Returning to his laptop, Rick took a closer look at the photo of the men on the boat, then across the room at the map. Secrets. That's what these men had in common. One big secret. Maybe there was a way to bring it out.

54

ALEX

AFTER MARQUETTA COMES UP TO say goodnight, I wait about ten minutes, then creep out of bed. I look both ways in the hallway, don't see anyone, and then go check on my dad's office. The light's still on. As long as he doesn't try to check on me after he's done working, it's all gonna be cool, so I go back to my room.

"Please don't check on me," I whisper a couple times as I write a note telling him I'm in the kitchen. If he comes in here and I'm not in bed, he'll freak out. And if he freaks out, he'll go through the whole B&B looking for me. It's better to tell him where I'm at and hope he doesn't worry or come to see what I'm doing.

After locking my door, I go downstairs. All the lights are turned down to the nighttime settings. It's bright enough for people to see where they're going, but the whole place isn't lit up. The only lamp on in the dining room is the one by the coffee and tea station. I go past that and push open the butler door.

The kitchen is almost totally dark. There's a little moonlight coming through the windows, but it's not much 'cause tonight the moon's only a small sliver. I go over to the kitchen sink and look out the window. With the silver clouds against the dark sky, it's pretty, but I don't have time to watch it. "Amy?" I whisper.

"Back here."

The voice is coming from near the back wall. There's a shadow against the window. My heart pounds in my chest. I'm not totally sure it's her. What if it's Adela and she figured out our trap?

I turn on my phone's flashlight and point it toward the laundry room. Amy holds up a hand in front of her eyes, so I turn it off. I whisper again, "Sorry."

"That's okay. It's better to be cautious. Come on."

I walk around the island, then along the wall to the laundry room entrance. The room's super cold. I forgot about that, it's freezing back here. "I should've brought a jacket."

Amy pulls a blanket out from the cabinet and wraps it around my shoulders. "There. That should help. Come on." She turns on her flashlight and lights up the cabinet. "So where exactly did you put the bag with the treasure?"

That's when it hits me. How did she know we kept blankets in the cabinet? I never told her that Flynn took the artifacts with her. And I never told her they weren't valuable. What if Adela's not the one who's after the treasure? My throat gets super dry. I'm all alone with someone I really don't know. She could be anybody.

55

RICK

IT WAS NEARLY MIDNIGHT WHEN Rick swung his legs over the side of the bed. He rubbed his hands up and down his arms at the chill in the air, then pulled on a pair of jeans, a long-sleeved tee, and a sweater. He'd hoped a good night's sleep would help him focus on the links between Vincent Pulley and Tuck Hall, but sleep, so far, had eluded him. He had to be up in five and a half hours and it was looking like he'd have nothing to show for his overactive mind except a bad case of exhaustion.

Hoping to answer a couple of the questions dogging him, he eased the door shut behind him and scanned the hallway. The security lighting kept the area lit, but it certainly didn't make things bright and cheery like they were during the day. As he passed Alex's room, he looked for light coming through the crack beneath the door. There was none and he didn't want to wake her if she was asleep so he padded quietly to his office.

As he settled into the old leather chair behind his desk and waited for his laptop to boot up, Rick rubbed his palms over his face. "I need sleep, not more of this," he muttered. Then again, if he couldn't sleep, why not answer those nagging questions?

He pulled out his notepad, flipped to a new page, and wrote Adela Barone's name at the top. Her relationship with Alex was one of the things that had kept him awake. He didn't see Adela as a murderer, but her appearance at the B&B and the way she'd intertwined herself with Alex had him concerned. And Alex's instincts were so often correct that he'd feel better if he checked out the mysterious Miss Barone.

Flipping the page one more time, he wrote another name at the top. It was the one person he'd considered above suspicion, but as he thought back to the previous day's events, he wasn't entirely sure. He wrote three bullet points under Amy Kama's name. *Was the one who found the body. Was seen near the Rusty Nail—was she looking for the treasure? Has kept herself involved in the case.*

He typed Adela's name into his browser. The first entry was for her Facebook profile. As he scanned the list of results, they all appeared to be unrelated—similar names, sites advertising background investigations, and more. He clicked on the link for the first entry.

Adela listed her occupation as a fashion diva and student. Rick had to reread the work description. How in the world did a fashion diva make a living? And better yet, why would she be so interested in a four-hundred-year-old treasure and the hard news of a murder? Her posts, at least until recently, were all about parties, fashion design, clothing, and accessorizing. Only since her arrival in Seaside Cove were there any entries concerning the town, her trip, or even the treasure.

Rick wondered how this all fit together as he summarized what he'd discovered in his notes. Somehow, it had to. Unfortunately, Adela had even more friends than Tuck Hall— nearly five-hundred altogether. That would take all night to sift through—but not if he was only looking for a couple of names. He began scrolling down the list, looking specifically for Tuck Hall or Vincent Pulley's names. At the end of the list, he made another note—*no connection to Hall or Pulley?*

Hall and Pulley were only two of the men who'd been on the *Seven Seas*, though. What about the other five? Looking at his list of the seven passengers onboard that day, Rick let out a tired sigh. He had five names to check against a list of five hundred.

"Needle in a haystack," he whispered to himself. He stopped to review the notes he'd made. There was really nothing to tie Adela to anything that had gone on in Seaside Cove other than her fascination with the *San Mañuel*. His eyes felt like they were starting to cross, so even if he found a match, he'd probably miss it.

He turned the page and grimaced. Amy Kama. He didn't want to believe she was involved, but if he were being thorough, he really needed to consider her a suspect, especially because she'd been asking more questions than Adela. With exhaustion slowly taking hold of his thoughts, Rick decided to look into Amy and leave Adela's friend list until the morning.

Following the same process he'd used to find Adela, he turned up Amy's name on social media and in the news. After reading two articles about the shooting at the courthouse, he was convinced that the version of the incident she'd given him had been truthful. He skipped over to social media and quickly realized Amy Kama was a cat person. She posted photos of her cat playing with yarn, hiding in a paper bag, and even lying on dinner plates in a kitchen cabinet.

Amy had about a hundred friends, plenty of whom had wished her well after the shooting incident. The support had continued when she'd announced her trip to Seaside Cove. She'd posted plenty of photos of the town, but hadn't said much about the treasure or the murder. Prudence? Or was she hiding something?

This was getting him nowhere. His best option would be to start fresh tomorrow and interview both women. Now that he knew more about them, he might be able to spot an inconsistency in their stories. He shut down his laptop, reclined in his chair, and wrapped his arms around him. He hadn't noticed the cold before, but now that he was done working, his fingers felt like icicles and he was chilled to the core. He rolled his neck and shoulders in circles, unable to shake the sense of unease brought on by all this focus on finding a killer.

It was time to get back to bed and warm up. He turned off the light and eased his office door closed, being sure to double check the lock when he was done. His bedroom was to the right, the stairs to the left. The rooms for Adela Barone and Amy Kama were beyond the stairs.

Sucking in a breath, Rick took one step to his left, stopped, and attempted to convince himself he shouldn't spy on his guests. Forget it. This was too important. And maybe if he saw that the lights were off in both rooms, he'd feel more confident that neither woman was a threat.

As he walked past the Jib Room, he checked for light coming from underneath the door. There was none. Good. Adela was asleep—or out. This was stupid. What could he tell from light under a door?

Rick grimaced and continued down the hall to the Mainsail Room. Again, no light, so it was the same story as Adela. He really had nothing.

As he retraced his steps, Rick did his best to walk silently. It was far too easy to disturb the guests in a hundred-year-old house like this one. When he got to the stairs, he stood on the landing and a slight shiver from the cold coursed through him. If he really wanted to settle his mind, he needed to check the downstairs, too. If there was nobody up, maybe then he could get some sleep.

He went down to the first floor. Everything looked normal. The front door was locked. There were no guests hanging about. He was passing through the dining room when he heard voices coming from the kitchen.

56

ALEX

I STEP BACK FROM AMY and turn on my phone's flashlight. She throws her hand up in front of her face and looks away.

"Turn off the light, Alex," she hisses. "Adela might see it."

"No."

"No? What's wrong?" A second later, her mouth opens and she smiles. "Oh, you think I'm the one who's after the artifacts."

"My dad's room is right above us. If I scream, he'll hear me and you'll get caught."

She's got both hands up in front of her and is squinting against the light. "I get it now. Clearly you no longer trust me. Alex, I'm not a treasure hunter. In fact, I've spoken to Chief Cunningham and would like to become one of your town deputies. I've decided to make Seaside Cove my home."

"How do I know that's true?"

"First off, the chief told me the mayor approved him hiring another deputy." She clears her throat, then adds, "He said she was very tightfisted with the pursestrings."

That totally sounds like the mayor. "How do I know you're not making that up?"

"Can I show you something on my phone?"

"Okay, but don't make any sudden moves." Like I could stop her if she did.

She pulls out her phone and opens a message from Chief Cunningham. It says exactly what she just told me.

"Sorry. I feel kinda stupid now."

"Don't. You didn't know my plans, so with the questions I was asking, I can see how you'd be suspicious. I'm glad you're cautious, but can we just turn off the light and wait now? Okay? We don't need to blow our stakeout because we gave ourselves away."

I turn off the flashlight, but the room is feeling super cold in the darkness even with the blanket wrapped around me. I can feel myself shiver, but don't want to say anything. Amy just has a jacket that she pulled over a tee shirt. She's gotta be freezing.

All of a sudden, the kitchen lights up and it feels like I'm being blinded. That's followed by my dad's voice—and he sounds super mad.

"Who's down here?"

I scrunch up my face. I am so dead.

April 21

Hey Journal,

I'm grounded. Again. When my dad found out what me and Amy were up to, he sent me straight up to my room. He said I should have told him what I was planning. Amy tried to tell him it was her idea, but he still thought I shouldn't have come down here with her alone. I get it. Even I was worried for a couple minutes. Now, I'm stuck up here while he's down there with her.

If Adela shows up, my dad's mad enough that he might kick her out of the B&B. I guess there's not much I can do now except lay in bed and try to make my brain stop spinning. Maybe tomorrow things will be better.

Xoxo,

Alex

PS I still think it was a good plan, even if it did get all messed up.

I close my journal, turn out the light, and snuggle down under the covers. This totally sucks. Just 'cause I'm only eleven, I can't do any of the good stuff that the grownups get to do. I shift around and try to get comfortable. At least it's warmer here than it was downstairs.

After a couple minutes, there's a knock on my door, then my dad pokes his head in. "Alex, can I come in?"

I huff. "I guess. How long am I grounded for?"

"Tonight only. And the reason for that is..."

"I know. I'm a kid. I shouldn't be doing anything without permission."

"What I was going to say was that, once again, you went rogue on me. You're my daughter and I'm responsible for your safety, but I also don't want to stifle your independence."

This totally sounds like it's gonna be another one of his speeches about how reckless I can be. "Daddy..."

"Let me finish. Amy's standing guard in the laundry room. I'll go down to relieve her in a couple of hours. I'd love to get some sleep tonight, but I don't think any of us are going to wind down enough. So, I want to show you a picture. Would you turn on the light?"

Whoa. This must be serious. I prop myself up in bed and turn on the lamp, then pull up the covers so I can stay warm. "What kind of picture?"

He opens his laptop and turns the screen so I can see it. My mouth drops open 'cause the photo is of a bunch of men on a boat holding up a pole that has a lot of orange fish hanging from it. "They killed all those fish?"

"Apparently, it was an ocean fishing trip."

"That's so totally wrong."

My dad clears his throat. "I know. Tuck Hall and Vincent Pulley are both in this photo. The third one from the left is Hall."

I look at my dad so I don't have to see all those poor fish. "The dead guy."

"Right. And this one is Vincent Pulley. He's the one who sabotaged the *Blue Phoenix*." He points at the man holding up the right side of the pole. "According to Hall's post, this was a planning trip and they were all going to be rich by summer. Given everything that's happened here in town over the past couple of weeks, I think they were planning to steal the *San Mañuel's* treasure."

"For real?"

"It's a theory, kiddo. Like one of yours."

I feel like I've got a big knot in my belly. "So I was wrong about Adela? She's not trying to steal the treasure?"

"That's not what I said. It was your suspicions about her that led me to my final theory. I think you're right about her. I do believe she's tied into this somehow. That's why Amy stayed down in the laundry room. Since you've been around Adela more than anyone, I want you to take a look at this photo and tell me if you've seen any of these other men."

Wow. This is like the first time my dad's ever asked me to help him solve a murder, but all I see when I look at that photo are those poor, dead fish.

57

RICK

RICK SAT ON THE EDGE of the bed, surprised by Alex's reaction to the photo from the *Seven Seas*. She'd screwed up her face in disgust, and now she couldn't seem to even look at his screen.

"What's wrong, kiddo?"

"The fish," Alex mumbled. "I can't look at them."

Rick turned the screen around, took another look at the photo, and wanted to kick himself. Of course. Though his daughter was fascinated by crime and murder, she had a soft spot for all the creatures of the world—except for spiders.

"Let's take care of that." Rick looked over at Alex's little white desk, found a notepad she used for school, and grabbed it. He positioned the pad over the bottom half of the photo and turned the laptop around so Alex could see it again. "How's that?"

Alex swiped at her cheeks with her fingers and nodded. "Way better." She craned her neck forward as she inspected the photo and pointed at the man standing next to Vincent Pulley. "I've seen him before."

"With Adela?"

"No. He was in Howie's Collectibles when I stopped in to see Grandma Madeline."

Rick reversed the laptop and read the caption. Were those names in the same order as the faces in the photo? "His name might be Eddie."

Alex's forehead puckered as she seemed to focus on the bedspread. "That wasn't it."

Rick read off the other names, but Alex shook her head at each one.

"Grandma Madeline told me the man's name, but he only used his initials." Alex bit her lower lip; the furrows in her brow deepened. "E.J.! That was it. His name was Mr. E.J. Bradbrook and he was an antique dealer from LA."

Rick reread the list. E.J.? Could that be Eddie?

"Adela's uncle's name is Ethan."

"There's no Ethan in this list, kiddo. There's an Eddie, but that's as close as we get."

"What if it's a nickname? Daddy, did you know that Sasha's real name is Alexandra?"

"Are you serious? You two have the same legal name?"

"Yeah, but Sasha's grandparents are Russian and they always called her Sasha. So it kinda stuck."

Rick wanted to smack himself on the forehead. "Why didn't I think of that? Brilliant, kiddo. Absolutely brilliant. I'm going to talk to Amy and let her know what we've found. You, try and get some sleep. Do not leave this room. If you do, you will be grounded for longer than just tonight."

"Seriously? Can't I go with you?"

"No," Rick said firmly. "You've done your part. Besides, you have school in the morning and if you fall asleep in the middle of class, Miss Redmond will have my hide."

Rick closed his laptop and turned out the light. As he padded along the hallway to the stairs, he wondered if Alex would leave her room or not. When he got to the first floor landing, he turned left toward the kitchen. Everything was still quiet in the living room and the dining room, but when he pushed open the butler door, he knew something was wrong.

At the opposite end of the kitchen, light from the laundry room spilled out like a garish blast of daylight. Rick rushed forward when two voices, both women, both sounding angry and defiant, blasted each other.

"Amy? Are you okay?"

"Sorry," Amy said as she entered the kitchen, her hand clutching the upper arm of Adela Barone. "Alex had her pegged. She came looking for the artifacts."

Rick's insides churned. This was a new situation. A guest, lured into a trap by his own daughter. That would have to go down in the annals of B&B lore as a bad move. "Miss Barone, why are you in my kitchen?"

When Adela didn't answer, Amy tightened her grip and Adela winced. "Alex told me about the treasure. I just wanted to see it for myself."

"So you got up in the middle of the night and snuck downstairs into our kitchen, which we've told you is against our policy, to what? Get a peek at some broken pottery?"

"I don't know," Adela stammered. "I thought..."

"No more lies, Miss Barone. Who are you working for?"

"I'm...I'm not working for anybody. I came here for a story about the *San Mañuel*. I told you that before. What are you gonna do to me?"

Rick flicked on the overhead lights and glowered at the girl, whose face was white as a sheet. Unless he was mistaken, she was petrified.

"I know what you told me. Now I want the truth. I don't think you're a dishonest person, Miss Barone, and I'd like to give you the opportunity to prove me correct." About the worst he could do would be to terminate her stay, but what good would that do? Maybe it was time for another bluff. "Miss Barone, I'll give you one last chance to tell me the truth. Would you like to sit down at the island and level with me, or should I call Chief Cunningham? I guarantee you he won't be happy if I wake him in the middle of the night."

"No police. Please," Adela croaked. "My parents would kill me."

Rick took her elbow and guided her to the kitchen island. He pulled out one of the stools for her and placed the laptop nearby. He sat in his usual place and indicated Amy should sit, too. Looking across the white granite at Adela she reminded him of a devastated child. She'd buried her face in her hands and was shaking her head.

"Could I get some water?"

"Sure." Rick filled a glass and handed it to her. "Now, why did you go looking for the treasure in my laundry room?"

"I really don't care about the stupid treasure," Adela grumbled, then stuck out her lower lip in a dramatic pout. "I want to be a fashion designer."

"You haven't answered my question, Miss Barone. Why were you in my laundry room in the middle of the night?"

The girl let out a dramatic huff and rolled her eyes. "My parents are cutting me off. My dad says I'm a professional student and I'll never amount to anything. The only way I was going to prove him wrong was to do something big. My uncle told me about this town and the treasure and we thought it would be a good way to show my dad he's wrong about me."

Rick looked across the island at Amy, who was shaking her head, a look of disbelief on her face.

"Treasure hunting is pretty far afield from fashion design. Why don't you connect the dots for me?" Rick said.

"My uncle said that if I could get a good story, he'd help me sell it. Don't you see? Once I was a published journalist, I'd be able to change my focus to fashion."

The look on the girl's face was so sincere that Rick felt sorry for her. "Miss Barone, I don't think you realize how competitive journalism is. Have you seen all the reporters here in this town? They all want the same story that you do." Rick stopped, bit back his next words, and decided to change direction. He wasn't her father or her guidance counselor. "You wanting a story doesn't explain why you were trying to steal those artifacts."

"I wasn't trying to steal them! I just...needed to borrow them. My uncle told me if I could get hold of them, he'd come up and do an evaluation. We were going to take pictures for the article and then I was going to bring them back." She shook her head indignantly. "They wouldn't have even been gone for a day."

Trying to reason with this girl was apparently a waste of time. She was as blind to the definition of criminal behavior as she was to her career options.

Amy reached out and touched Adela's arm. Her voice was soft and soothing. "So your uncle lives nearby?"

"Los Angeles."

Rick considered the coincidence. Tuck Hall. Vincent Pulley. The *Seven Seas*. They'd all been from Los Angeles. Could her uncle be one of the men in the photo? "Miss Barone, who's this uncle of yours?"

"Why do you want to know about my Uncle Ethan? He didn't do anything except try to help me."

"Do his friends call him Eddie? Is his last name Bradbrook?"

Adela looked both stunned and angry. She snapped, "How do you know his name?"

Rick opened the laptop, brought up the photo of the men on the *Seven Seas* and turned it around so Adela could see the screen. "Is your uncle in this photo?"

The girl's eyes widened as the last of the color drained from her face. With her complexion about as white as the granite countertop, Rick didn't need a verbal answer. The man Adela Barone called Uncle Ethan was in the photo. He had to be the orchestrator of everything that had happened recently.

And he was here in Seaside Cove.

58

ALEX

Hey Journal,

I'm like so not sleepy. I tried closing my eyes after my dad left, but I keep seeing that picture of those poor fish. All orange with big eyes. And dead. They just keep staring back at me.

Maybe tomorrow I can talk my dad into letting me help him on the case. If he hasn't solved it by then. I think I heard voices, but they were kinda faint. If Adela falls for my trap, my dad could be down there with her and Amy right now. This is so totally not fair. Me and Amy came up with the plan, and then Daddy grounded me.

The more I think about it, the madder I get. I'm totally gonna talk to him tomorrow. I mean, how can I believe in myself if every time I try to do it I get in trouble? In fact, maybe I'm not gonna wait. I should just go downstairs and tell him how I feel! I could totally do that right now! You know what? I'm gonna do it, Journal!

Alex

The first thing I do when I get out of bed is put on a pair of jeans, a long-sleeved tee, and my warmest sweatshirt. I totally love the purple and teal colors, but it's also super snuggly when it's cold. With this on, I can stay in the laundry room no matter how cold it gets.

Out in the hallway, everything's quiet. The lights are off in my dad's office and in his bedroom. He's either still in the kitchen with Amy or he's asleep. I'm gonna find out right now. I stay super quiet when I go down the stairs. I don't want anybody hearing me, and I especially don't wanna run into Adela before I get to the laundry room.

Even from across the dining room, it's easy to see the kitchen's all lit up. I hope my dad hasn't blown up the plan. I creep up next to the door and listen. I can hear voices, but I can't make out what they're all saying. I push the door open a crack and the voices get louder. Holy smokes. They caught Adela!

I pump my fist and say a silent, "Yes!" The plan worked! Kind of. Adela's not sounding very cooperative. In fact, all she's doing is defending her uncle. She's not gonna talk. Not to Daddy and Amy. But maybe she'll talk to me. I push open the door to peek inside.

Adela, Amy, and my dad are all at the kitchen island, and he's showing her his laptop screen. Adela is all dressed in black like she's on some kind of spy mission or something, but she looks freaked out. I think she's too afraid to talk. When she sees me, she points at me.

"This is all her fault! If she hadn't told me she knew how to get to that stupid bay, none of this would have happened."

"Alex? What are you doing down here?" Daddy's voice isn't nasty, but he's being super stern.

I walk toward Adela. "I get it, Adela. You're not a thief. You're totally into fashion. I kinda knew that when we went to Dead Man's Cove. You were wearing that pretty pink and gray dress and that cool hat."

"That dress is one of my favorites. I made it myself."

"It's awesome. I know you're totally mad at me right now. Right?"

She crosses her arms over her chest and sticks out her lip. "Yes."

"But it's not me you should be mad at. It's your uncle. He's the one who sent you here. Isn't he?"

Her eyes get all watery and her cheeks look hot. She swipes away a tear. "What if he did?"

My dad looks like he's gonna chew me out, but he stops when Amy shakes her head. His jaw is all tight and everything, but I think he realizes I can get through to Adela. "You didn't want to do this, did you?"

She ignores Daddy and Amy and looks straight at me. After a couple of sniffles and another swipe at her cheeks, she says, "No. I didn't. But I had to."

"Why?"

She uncrosses her arms and picks away a piece of lint on her sleeve. "I already told him." She gives my dad a nasty look, then ignores him. "I needed a story so I could prove myself."

I take a deep breath, then swallow. This is like so hard for me to admit, but I'm a lot like her. "You're doing the same exact thing I do with my dad sometimes."

"What's that?"

"Lying to yourself. Don't do it. It's so lame."

Her mouth opens and shuts a couple times, then her lip starts to tremble. A tear dribbles down her cheek and she hugs herself. "I don't know what to do," she mumbles.

"My dad and Marquetta are always telling me to just tell the truth. You know what? It's a lot easier. And I feel better after I do it." Okay, that last part isn't totally true, 'cause a lot of the time telling the truth only gets me in more trouble, but I'm gonna go with that for now.

She points at the laptop screen. "That's my Uncle Ethan. He's the one who paid for my trip."

"And his friends call him Eddie?"

"I think his old friends from the Navy do. He was a SEAL."

Daddy and Amy are looking at each other, but when my dad looks at me, he's got kind of a proud smile on his face.

"Why didn't he stay here, too?" I ask.

"He's in LA, Alex. Not here."

I shake my head. "No, Adela. He was in Howie's Collectibles two days ago. My Grandma Madeline pointed him out to me. She said he was an antique dealer from LA."

"What?" Adela's eyes get even more watery and a tear dribbles down her cheek. "He lied to me?"

Yeah. He totally lied to her.

59

RICK

ADELA BARONE MADE A GRAND entrance to the dining room the
following morning just before Rick was set to close the breakfast
service. It was so late that he'd begun to wonder if the girl had
pulled what Alex was now calling 'a Gibson' and skipped out in
the middle of the night. The good news was that she hadn't. He
picked up the day's menu, waved to her, and wended his way
through the mostly empty tables to where she stood.

"Miss Barone, I'm delighted to see you. I have a table for you
by the window."

She pulled back her shoulders and huffed, then followed as
Rick led her to the table where Adam Cunningham sat. When
Rick pulled back her chair, she stood, tall and rigid, an icy stare
trained on Adam. The early morning sun streamed through the
window, lending a cheery atmosphere to what was sure to be a
less-than-cheery discussion with the chief of police.

Adam stood and nodded curtly. "Miss Barone. I hope you
slept well."

"Actually, I didn't. The thought of this meeting and
betraying my uncle is enough to make me ill."

Rick started to hand her a menu, but the girl waved it away.
"I'm not hungry. Just a muffin."

It appeared the old Adela Barone was back—haughty,
spoiled, with manners leaving much to be desired. Obviously,

the shock of what her uncle had done must have worn off. Tempting as it was to remind her of the list of crimes she'd unwittingly helped facilitate, he simply asked if she wanted coffee.

"Yes. I need it this morning."

Rick filled her mug and topped off Adam's. "I'll get that muffin for you. You done there, Adam?"

"Tell Markie it was fabulous." He leaned back and let Rick take the plate.

When Rick returned with the muffin, most of Adela's attitude had vanished. He wondered what Adam had said to her during the short time they'd been alone. He placed the muffin in front of her, at which point she grimaced and muttered a reluctant thank you.

"You're welcome," Rick said as he sat. "Have you changed your mind, Miss Barone?"

"No. If my uncle really did kill that man, he should face justice." Her lower jaw puckered and she picked up her mug with both hands. She held it tightly, as though it were a lifeline of some sort, and took a steadying breath. "I thought..."

"You thought what, Miss Barone?" Adam asked.

"I thought I saw him when me and Alex went to Dead Man's Cove, but I'd convinced myself I was mistaken."

Adam pulled out his notepad, flipped it open, and said, "You weren't mistaken. He checked into the Seaside Cove Inn a few days ago. The boat from Dead Man's Cove was boarded this morning by the Coast Guard on its way to Los Angeles. They were going to pick up another diver. Tuck Hall's belongings were found onboard, and when the captain was informed that his diver was dead, he started talking. Apparently, Captain Ulster had worked with Hall before on some commercial dives. According to the captain, Hall was a good diver, but also had badmouthed your uncle. Hall claimed he'd shorted him on a previous job and wanted to get even."

"Was that Hall's motive for trying to steal the artifacts?" Rick asked.

"We may never know, but it's a distinct possibility. Miss Barone, your uncle has been a person of interest in cases ranging from art theft to drug smuggling. He's never been convicted because something always seems to happen to the witnesses. They either retract their testimony or disappear."

The coffee in Adela's mug rippled, giving away the quivering of her fingers. Her mug rattled when she lowered it onto the saucer. He hoped the girl now realized how dangerous her uncle was and that she had every reason to be scared to death.

"Are you worried he might come after you, Miss Barone?" Rick asked.

"Uncle Ethan? He would never..." She stopped, looked down at the table, and sighed. "I'm not sure. He's not the man I thought he was. He's always been so kind to me. And he paid for this trip."

"Remember why he did that," Adam said. "And also remember that you don't want to become an accessory."

She closed her eyes and pressed her fingertips against her eyelids. Her complexion turned splotchy as she fought back her emotions. After a grimace, she lowered her hands to her lap and looked at Adam. "I know. Yes, I'll make the phone call. What do you want me to say?"

The call, which Adela placed from the kitchen, went better than Rick expected. Bradbrook said he was at an antique show in San Ladron and could meet her at three at the Seaside Cove Lighthouse. She readily agreed to the meeting, despite Adam's attempt to get her to change the location.

Minutes dragged into hours, but at two o'clock Adam's 4x4 pulled up in front of the B&B. They all went to the kitchen, where Adam gave Rick a communications earpiece and went over the plan one more time. When he was finished, he said, "Let's go. It's a bit of a walk."

The three of them left the B&B using the decomposed granite trail that led out of the backyard and meandered toward the lighthouse. It wasn't until they were all positioned that Rick began to doubt the plan. "You think he'll suspect anything?"

"Not likely. Jackman and Kama have been here for more than an hour with the two sheriff's deputies. We've got the element of surprise on our side." Adam aimed his binoculars in the direction of the lighthouse. "I'm hoping Bradbrook won't do anything that might endanger his niece."

Rick snuck a peek at Adela through a small opening in the bushes. She stood near the entrance to the lighthouse. "I hope you're right. I feel sorry for her. Learning about her uncle like this."

Adela had worn a frilly dress in pastel colors and a wide-brimmed white hat with a pink ribbon that blew in the wind. When Rick had commented on how cold she might get, she'd told him she'd chosen the dress specifically because it was one of her uncle's favorites.

"That Adela has a lot more spunk than I gave her credit for," Adam said as he watched through his binoculars.

"I know. Once she discovered she'd been lied to and sent here as a spy, she really got her back up. For all the trouble she caused, I don't want to see anything happen to her." Rick stopped speaking when a voice came through his earpiece.

"Suspect has parked and is on his way. ETA, five minutes."

"Heads up," Adam said. "Jackman, you ready?"

"Roger."

"Kama? You in place?"

"Ready to roll, Chief."

Rick parted the bushes so he could get a better look at Amy Kama's position inside the lighthouse entrance. "I never thought the B&B would become a recruiting ground for new deputies."

"The mayor signed off this morning on hiring her on a temporary basis. LAPD gave her a solid recommendation. Their loss, my gain. Can't do much better than that. There's Bradbrook."

Ethan Bradbrook rounded the bend in the trail about a hundred feet to Rick's right. In his khakis and a light jacket, the man looked much as he had in the photo taken on the *Seven Seas*. He also looked considerably more relaxed than in the mug shot Adam had shown Adela during their morning discussion. When Bradbrook saw his niece, he stopped, waved, then approached, all the while scanning the area.

"Cautious to the end," Adam whispered.

Rick had seen the NYPD take down criminals periodically during his time as a reporter. The difference was that he'd never been this closely involved. Nor had he personally known any of the operation participants. This time, everything felt personal. From the shattering of Adela's naive view of the world to Alex's desperate pleas for him to protect Adela, everything seemed to matter more. Much, much more.

With each step Bradbrook took toward Adela, Rick's adrenaline level ratcheted up another notch. His pulse pounded in his ears, and Rick found himself mentally urging the girl to stay safe.

Adela waved and flashed her uncle a smile, then left her assigned position to walk toward him.

"You think she's going to warn him that it's a trap?" Rick whispered.

"Not waiting to find out." Adam said tersely, then punched the button on his radio. "Kama, stop her. Everyone else, close in."

Adam was the first to emerge from his position. Amy Kama was only a split second behind. Bradbrook dropped to a crouch. His hand moved behind his back as Amy stepped in front of Adela.

"Police!" Adam bellowed. "You're surrounded, Bradbrook. Put down the weapon."

With five officers pointing weapons in his direction, Ethan Bradbrook seemed to comprehend he'd been double-crossed and that there was no way out. He regarded his niece, who now stood behind Amy, and shook his head.

"Put down the weapon," Adam repeated.

"I'm unarmed," Bradbrook said as he raised his hands.

Adela sidestepped Amy Kama, but Rick rushed to the girl and wrapped his hands around her shoulders. He pulled her back before she could get between Amy and her uncle.

"Did you kill that man, Uncle Ethan?"

Bradbrook gave her a sinister smile and shook his head. "It was business, Adela. You wouldn't understand."

When the deputies patted down Bradbrook, they discovered he'd been lying about being unarmed. They secured him, then read him his rights.

Rick threw his coat around Adela's shoulders and guided her back to the B&B along the decomposed granite path. She didn't say a word until they'd made it to the edge of the B&B's property, at which point she stopped, shivered, and clutched Rick's coat around her shoulders.

"What will happen to him?"

"That will be up to the courts, Miss Barone."

She nodded absently, took a deep breath, and returned

Rick's coat to him. Pulling her shoulders back, she straightened
her posture and regarded him. "I'll be checking out in the
morning, Mr. Atwood. Right now, I feel a terrible headache
coming on. Thank you for your hospitality."

60

ALEX

APRIL 28

Hey Journal,

It's been kind of a boring week. Last week was awesome 'cause Chief Cunningham arrested Adela's Uncle Ethan. I totally wish I could've been there, but my dad never would have gone for it.

Me and Marquetta were super busy that day 'cause Daddy had to make sure Adela didn't change her mind on the deal. After the big bust, he was busy answering questions from all the guests who heard about it. They were all totally impressed that we helped the cops.

All the reporters are gone now. When they found out the stuff about Flynn was just a big lie to steal treasure, they all went on to other stories. Oh well, I guess nobody cares about four-hundred-year-old treasure unless there's some sort of big conspiracy going on. Amy's gone, too. She went back to LA to pack. She starts her permanent job as one of our deputies in a couple weeks, so I'm looking forward to seeing her again.

I know it's stupid, but I kinda miss Adela. Even though we got a new guest in right after she left, it's not the same without her. It's not like we were actual friends or anything, but most of the guests are a lot older and kinda stay to themselves. Even though she was just trying to get information from me, it felt

322

like we could've been friends if things were different.

I'm not gonna have a lot of time to think about her, anyway. Daddy and Marquetta have moved the wedding to June 14! Grandma Madeline's not very happy about it being on a Wednesday, but she's going along. The awesome thing is they moved it so it could be the week after school gets out. I'm gonna have lots of time to help get everything ready! Marquetta's gonna be my mom, Journal! Finally! I'm so happy I could just burst. She's gonna be up here in a couple minutes to say goodnight. She told me she's got a special role for me in the wedding and we're gonna talk about it when she comes up.

The wedding's gonna be small, but I think it's gonna be epic!

Bye for now,

Xoxo,

Alex

Made in the USA
Middletown, DE
20 July 2021